Four Hundred Bones

Stalin's Teeth in Academia

A Novel

ADA NICOLESCU

Order this book online at www.trafford.com
or email orders@trafford.com

Most Trafford titles are also available at major online book retailers.

Cover design by Patrick J. Neitz

Print information available on the last page.

ISBN: 978-1-4907-5291-4 (sc)
ISBN: 978-1-4907-5293-8 (hc)
ISBN: 978-1-4907-5292-1 (e)

Library of Congress Control Number: 2015900064

Because of the dynamic nature of the Internet, any web addresses or links contained in
this book may have changed since publication and may no longer be valid. The views
expressed in this work are solely those of the author and do not necessarily reflect the
views of the publisher, and the publisher hereby disclaims any responsibility for them.

Any people depicted in stock imagery provided by Thinkstock are models,
and such images are being used for illustrative purposes only.
Certain stock imagery © Thinkstock.

Trafford rev. 01/29/2015

 www.trafford.com
North America & international
toll-free: 1 888 232 4444 (USA & Canada)
fax: 812 355 4082

To my husband, LARRY LE SHAN, who has taught me that life is an endless chain of mysterious surprises.

Contents

ACKNOWLEDGMENTS

This book would have never come into being without the skilled guidance of my mentor, CAROL EMSHWILLER.- My friends and fellow writers, BARBARA FLECK-PALADINO, GAY PARTINGTON TERRY, MARGARET SWEENEY and MARIA TAMMICK have warmly and patiently contributed with precious advice and critical input. - I thank CAROLE PAUL for her inspired ability to clarify and smooth out complicated occurrences. – I have greatly benefitted from LINDA SULLIVAN's technical expertise and superior professionalism. –Like in the past, I am grateful to my husband, LAWRENCE L. LE SHAN for his wise understanding and loving support.

Introduction

This book is about the effect of the Communist dictatorship on the intellectual community in Bucharest, Romania.. The year is 1949.

This is a book of fiction, inspired by historical events. All characters are imaginary, and any resemblance with real people is coincidental.

Chapter 1

On a beautiful spring day, if you cross the bridge over the muddy Dîmbovița River in Bucharest, you will arrive at a wide boulevard shaded by old chestnut trees in bloom. Stately mansions, now in disrepair, border this boulevard. The plaster of their facades is peeling, and the fences around their gardens are rusty and broken. But young ivy climbs on walls and fences and hides these blemishes.

Beyond the chestnut trees a massive gray building dominates the street. Since it is flanked by monumental Doric columns, the building looks like a cross between a Greek temple and a mausoleum.

But there is something unusual about it: the columns and the facade are draped with red streamers, making you think of a huge chocolate box wrapped in red ribbons. This candy-box Greek temple-mausoleum is actually the oldest medical school in Romania. You enter it through the imposing front door which opens onto a large hall with a shining marble floor or you can sneak inside through a low and narrow door hidden on the side of the building. You enter this door and follow a dim corridor to a winding staircase which leads to the basement. Here you find yourself in the Department of Anatomy, with its white labs and dissection halls. You have entered another world, a world of hushed silence and stinging fumes of formaldehyde.

You hold your breath, open a door, walk through a big chamber and reach the room beyond the first dissection hall. Here Peter, the lab technician, a tall young man wearing an old hospital coat, sits perfectly still and listens. For this is no day of hushed silence. Outside in the corridor, on this spring day of 1949, men's voices resonate louder and louder. Heavy footsteps pound the floor and come closer. Doors are opened and slammed. Somebody barks orders in a shrill, angry voice.

Peter shakes his head. Such a commotion! And, for what? Just another Mayday parade?

He shrugs and resumes his work.

Perched on a high stool and leaning over a lab table covered with white tiles, he is stringing bones, human vertebrae, on a thin copper wire. One...two...three...four...equal sets of twelve vertebrae each, one set for each student. He handles them carefully, as if they were made of glass and could break in his hand.

After he finishes stringing several sets of bones which he places on a low shelf near the table, he feels hungry.

He lights the Bunsen burner on the workbench, pulls a red enamel pot of beans from under the table, slices a fresh onion which he mixes with the beans, adds some water from the faucet at the end of the room, and sets the pot to boil over the gas burner.

When the beans are ready, he walks back to the table, pushes a few loose bones out of his way, pours the beans into a deep dish, then sits on his chair and starts to eat.

But he has only swallowed a few spoonfuls when the door opens and a short man with black, bushy hair, wearing a dirty lab smock, bursts into the room.

"Just to remind you that tomorrow is the Mayday Parade and it starts at eight in the morning!" he shouts. "Everybody must be out in the courtyard at eight!"

Peter turns and is greeted by the icy blue eyes of the Secretary of the Party, Comrade Dumitru. He is frowning as he speaks.

"I hope you'll finish your soup by tomorrow!"

He laughs. His voice sounds hard and grating, and there is a strange, barking edge to his words. Here, at the medical school, every time Peter hears Comrade Dumitru's barking laugh, he thinks that he has heard it a long time ago, in another place. But he can't remember where and when.

Comrade Dumitru doesn't wait for Peter's reply. He turns around and storms out of the room, without shutting the door. From the corridor, the pounding and hammering sound is louder than before, as people are preparing posters and banners for tomorrow's parade.

Peter closes the door, hoping to find some relief inside the lab. This long and narrow room, which lies hidden between the dissection halls, is usually quiet and peaceful. It houses large crates full of long bones from legs and arms, crates full of collarbones and shoulder blades, and basins filled with small round bones of the hands and feet. The walls are lined with wooden shelves where rows upon rows of skulls are displayed. Near the far end of the room there is a tall glass cabinet which holds many transparent jars filled with human hearts and slices of brain, floating in clear formaldehyde.

The room has only one, tiny window near the ceiling, over the work table.

* * *

Ever since he was hired as an anatomy technician by the chief of the department, twelve years ago, Peter has worked in the dissection hall and in this lab. A few years ago the professor, Dr. Munteanu, allowed him to bring his folding cot, a few clothes and sparse belongings and move in for good. It happened quickly, one winter morning, after a freezing night when his next door neighbor was attacked by a pack of hungry wolves which were roaming the outskirts of the city. Peter was working late every night anyway, and nobody was waiting for him at home. He feels happy and safe in this quiet job where nobody bosses him around and where the work is always interesting.

Dr. Munteanu, a tall man with a hunched back, thick glasses and a rich mane of white hair, has taught him how to prepare the corpses for dissection and how to arrange the bones for the students.

"Never forget the students!" the professor told Peter. "Nothing is as important as the students! How much they learn shows who *you* are."

When he isn't teaching, Professor Munteanu spends his time holed up in his office, buried in research concerning genes and chromosomes. He has published articles about genetics in foreign magazines, and is well known abroad. He trained Peter for about two months, and then, one morning announced: "Okay, that's it, now you're on your own!" handing him a bunch of keys to the lab and to the dissection halls. From that day he never checked on Peter's routine work in the lab.

* * *

Peter's lunch is again interrupted by loud pounding and hammering outside his room. He gets up, goes to the back of the lab and picks a set of vertebrae from one of the crates. The bones are white, perfectly bleached, and look as if they were made of the finest, most precious porcelain.

When he returns to the work table he hears Comrade Dumitru scolding the people outside. His voice, once again reminds him of a forgotten meeting of long ago.

* * *

The next morning when he wakes up, the sun is shining, and the first demonstrators have arrived. Peter can hear them laughing and joking in the courtyard, while Comrade Dumitru shouts orders at them.

Peter gets up, washes and shaves at the sink beyond the crates of bones, watching his face in a chipped mirror that hangs from a wooden shelf. He gets dressed and gulps down a cup of ersatz coffee which he has boiled over the gas burner. He eats a thick slice of dark bread. Then he puts on his threadbare jacket, the only one he has. He notices that the sleeves are too short for his long arms. The cloth has become so frayed at the seam that he had to shorten the sleeves by one centimeter. When he finishes dressing he walks out of the room.

In the courtyard people are forming a long, noisy column, headed by Comrade Dumitru. He is carrying a red banner with a yellow hammer and sickle in a corner. Other people are also carrying red banners or large pictures of Lenin and Stalin. Behind them looms the wide facade of the building, entirely draped in long streamers from the roof to the ground.

* * *

Peter joins the last row of the column, just as it starts moving toward the gate. He hopes that standing at the end of the line of demonstrators will let him feel less cramped. He hates crowds, particularly noisy crowds.

It all goes back to the time he lived in an orphanage, until he was sixteen. He remembers the overcrowded hall where he slept with twenty other boys, the noisy dining room where they ate at long, wooden tables, and the communal showers without partitions. It was not possible to have a corner to himself!

When he turned sixteen, he ran away.

It was in the middle of the night in June. He slipped out through a back window, trembling with fear that the neighbors' dogs were going to start barking. But the dogs remained quiet, growling from time to time in their sleep. And in the moonless night Peter walked for several hours through the cornfields and small woods surrounding the orphanage, until he felt safe enough to step on the road to Bucharest.

Late the next afternoon he reached the outskirts of the city and wandered aimlessly through the dusty streets. Tired and hungry, he sat down near a fountain in front of a church wondering what would become of him. But the next morning an old beggar woman with a hairy wart on her nose—like a witch—and small, piercing eyes told him about the job as night watchman in the cemetery.

"Go to the gate of the cemetery down the road and tell them that you're looking for work. They'll hire you on the spot."

She nodded and laughed as she said these words, and the wart on her nose started to tremble and shake as if it had a life of its own. Peter thanked her and went on his way, following her instructions.

He was, indeed, hired as a night watchman at the cemetery.

From then on he was happy. He loved the dark, mysterious nights: the hooting of owls, the silent flights of the bats, and the distant croaking of frogs on the other bank of the lake, beyond the graves.

Sometimes a nightingale would sing in an old mulberry tree, right over his head. Those nights seemed particularly blissful to him.

* * *

At the medical school the demonstrators march out through the gate and for a while they walk briskly through the sleepy side streets bordered by blooming chestnut and acacia trees. They reach the wide boulevard where they are joined by other demonstrators with similar red banners and posters. Near the entrance to Piaţa Victoriei, the large plaza where the Party leaders are watching the parade from their official stand, the streets are so jammed that the columns can barely advance. Peter feels that he is drowning in a sea of burning crimson which is rising and waning, swelling and ebbing, making him very dizzy. In the next moment he finds himself pushed against a living wall of bayonet-carrying militiamen. They are pointing their weapons toward the marchers. Behind them are army tanks with their turrets and rifles also directed toward the demonstrators.

Suddenly the crowd bursts into shouts of "Long live the Socialist Revolution!" and "Glory to Stalin!" followed by the rhythmical applause of thousands of hands and the loud tune of "The Internationale." Then everything is drowned out by the deafening rumble of squadrons of heavy cannons and tanks pouring into the square.

* * *

Peter is caught in a whirlpool of droning machinery. His head is spinning; his throat is dry. He has to get out. He turns, steps out of his line and jumps on the sidewalk, past two militiamen standing at attention. He ducks behind a tank, where he's hidden from the soldiers. Then he turns a corner and runs away from the parade. He keeps racing, until he is out of breath. When he stops he realizes that he is standing on a narrow street which leads back to the medical school.

He looks around to make sure no militiaman is following or watching him. Then he breathes a deep sigh of relief, turns again to make sure he is safe, and checks his watch.

"Perfect! It's still early!" he tells himself. "As soon as I get back I'll stop in the library. I haven't been there for a while...Maybe they've got a new dissection manual or a new atlas of anatomy!"

Peter fancies himself browsing through a pile of thick, leather-bound volumes, embossed with gold letters. He loves looking at the illustrations, studying the colorful charts of muscles, vessels and nerves, and then trying to identify each of them, even the smallest, the most hidden ones, on the corpses which are dissected in the department.

* * *

He first saw an atlas of anatomy a long time ago when he was an embalmer's assistant at Mr. Bantu's funeral parlor, after he stopped working at the cemetery. It was Mr. Bantu, the embalmer, who had first let him look into his old, leather-bound anatomy books and taught him about the human body.

They had met one icy winter when Peter almost froze to death inside his wooden booth. Early in the morning Mr. Bantu found him lying stiff and motionless on the floor. He picked him up and dragged him through the snow to the small funeral parlor which stood at the far end of the cemetery.

Mr. Bantu had small feet and an unsteady gait, and they fell several times on the ice. When they reached the funeral parlor, the man was so out of breath that he kept huffing and puffing as he dragged Peter into the room.

It was dark inside and the air was stinging and choking, making his eyes teary and sore. It was only later that he learned about the formaldehyde fumes that filled the room.

Mr. Bantu made Peter lie down on a long and narrow table of gray stone. Then he took a lab smock which hung in the corner, rolled it up tightly, and pushed it under Peter's head as a pillow. The lab smock had the same biting, suffocating smell as the air in the room and it made him cough.

Mr. Bantu took off Peter's ice-covered boots, then his socks, and rubbed his frozen feet with an ill-smelling ointment which made his skin tingle and burn. When he finished, Peter fell into a deep sleep and woke up in the late afternoon, in the purple light of a setting sun.

When he opened his eyes he saw that he was flanked by two other tables, each covered with a curious bundle of rags. He recognized human figures partly hidden under pieces of cloth.

"Hail to the Seven Sleepers! Finished your siesta?"

Mr. Bantu put down the large syringe filled with formaldehyde with which he was injecting the bodies and walked out of the room. With small and quick steps he returned a few minutes later with a tall glass of tea in his hand. He added a jigger of rum and a large spoonful of honey before giving it to Peter.

"Feeling better?" he asked when Peter had emptied the glass and was sitting up on the table.

"Much better!"

Then Mr. Bantu tiptoed to the other room and brought two more glasses of tea with rum and honey. He was silent while he stirred the tea with his spoon.

"I tell you what," he finally said. "I have lots of work here. How about joining me in the funeral parlor? You can start as soon as you wish and I will teach you all there is to know!" He was staring at Peter, waiting for an immediate answer.

"All right," said Peter. "It's fine with me!"

And from that day on he stopped being a night watchman in the cemetery and became the embalmer's assistant.

* * *

Now, on this Mayday, as he walks toward the medical school Peter turns into a narrow street paved with cobblestones and bordered by small houses covered with vines. A stray puppy with large brown eyes is running after him.

But Peter barely notices the dog. He keeps thinking of Mr. Bantu, that short, quiet man who spoke very little and rarely smiled. A long scar ran down his forehead, looking like a permanent frown. It made him seem older than he actually was.

Mr. Bantu never worked Friday afternoons or Saturdays because he was half-Jewish and kept the holidays. Nobody seemed to care about this since there was no other embalmer around. He had learned the craft from his father, who had learned it from his father in turn. They had all worked in the same funeral parlor. One day when he felt more talkative Mr. Bantu told Peter that he had always dreamt of studying medicine. He called it the "Queen" of all the sciences. But he hadn't been able to do so because of political troubles at the University. In the fall of 1933, as he was starting his second year of medicine, he was attacked by a gang of students who hated Jews. They came at him with clubs and metal pipes and beat him on the stairs of the school building. The scar on his forehead was from that time. They had almost broken his skull. He suffered a serious concussion and, for a while, he could barely see and could not move his right hand.

Even though Mr. Bantu hadn't finished medical school, Peter thought that he knew all the secrets of the human body and loved to have somebody with whom he could share them.

"Remember, the dead are alive; they teach us all there is to know about the living!" he used to say.

Peter thinks of how they often worked side by side in the small room protected by thick walls covered with many layers of dark paint. It was as if they were in the depth of an ancient catacomb. Daylight was sparse. The only window was a long, narrow slit closed with a panel of stained glass so that nobody could look inside.

On the opposite wall, there were three large anatomical charts: one showing the exposed muscles, one the bones, and the third all the organs of the human body. Underneath was an old wooden bookstand which Mr. Bantu had filled with thick, leather-bound anatomy atlases with stained and greasy pages. Two handbooks about the art of embalming were on the bottom shelf.

* * *

In January about three years after Peter had started working there, Mr. Bantu decided to take his first vacation in ten years. In his quiet, almost secretive manner he told Peter about his plan only two days before leaving. He gave him the keys to the building and the basement, but he refused to tell him the destination of his trip.

"What does it matter where I go?" he said, shrugging his shoulders and acting as if he was just going across the street.

One month later he returned from his journey and brought with him a strange set of pictures which he hung on the walls of the room. They were large, colored prints from Egypt showing ancient Egyptian embalmers at work, the Royal Mummy of King Tutankhamen, the Pyramids of Gizah and the black jackal god Anubis, Guardian God of the Dead. He also placed a new, luxury edition of the Book of the Dead on the wooden bookstand.

"In Egypt, you know, everything is different from the rest of the world," he said to Peter. "In that country the dead are really alive. There you feel that the whole world is asleep and only the dead are fully awake!"

Peter noticed that since his trip Mr. Bantu had changed in a subtle way which was hard to describe. He had somehow become a different person. Not only was his pale face now deeply tanned, but he looked younger and much more serene.

As time went by Mr. Bantu told Peter all he knew about the secrets of the ancient Egyptians and their burial customs. Peter was so spellbound by the magical power of these tales and the might of these ancient heroes that while he worked he fancied himself as the Pharaoh's Chief Embalmer.

* * *

It is still early when Peter returns to the medical school. The building is empty and quiet and he feels at peace as he strolls through the silent corridors toward the library. He climbs the wide marble stairs to the second floor, crosses the hall under the gilt chandelier, and stops in front of the library door. He turns the polished brass knob and enters the room. He is planning to look at the illustrated anatomy atlases, as he needs to check the small branches of the facial nerve which are hidden under the parotid gland. It is always difficult to find these branches on the corpses and show them to the students since they look like white, narrow ribbons running deep under the yellow gland and resting on the shiny lining of the masseter muscle.

It is the pictures he needs to check. The text he can't understand, as it is always printed in French. Professor Munteanu had told him that there were no illustrated textbooks published in Romanian. All medical books are printed in foreign languages. But Peter loves and uses the books even though he can't make out the text.

He hurries up the narrow, winding stairway to the anatomy section, climbing the steps two at a time. But when he reaches the top landing he stops short and gasps. The anatomy stacks are hidden behind thick, crimson cloth. Peter looks around and realizes all the library stacks are concealed behind similar scarlet fabric. He tiptoes toward the shelves and pulls at the canvas—in vain. The cloth is nailed to the wood.

Peter doesn't know what to think. He wants to ask questions... talk to someone. But there is nobody in sight.

He is about to leave when an article on the bulletin board catches his attention. It is a clipping from the government newspaper which has been glued to the wall and framed with a gilded border.

Peter stops to examine it and finds himself reading the most recent decree issued by the "Great Communist Leader":

"All Western science is an expression of Imperialism and a mortal foe of Socialism." It continues, "Anybody who studies or practices any form of Western science is dangerous to the Communist society. He has to be annihilated without delay!"

Peter is reading the text over and over again, trying to understand what it means, when he hears loud voices and footsteps in the corridor in front of the library.

The door opens and Comrade Dumitru, followed by six other men, enter the room. They are carrying armloads of posters and banners. They are tired, sweaty and covered with dust.

Peter would like to disappear, to vanish into thin air, but it is too late. There is no place to hide.

"Here, you can leave the posters right here!" shouts Comrade Dumitru, wiping the sweat from his face. "The library is the best storage space for this stuff! The most perfect place, I'm telling you. It was never put to better use!" he adds, laughing at his own joke.

Toma, the fat secretary of the Communist Youth Organization, rolls his round eyes and gives a big sigh of relief as he drops five posters with the portraits of the Communist Founding Fathers on the floor.

"Finally home!" he mumbles. He pulls a small box of hard candy out of his pocket and slips one into his mouth. Behind him, Professor Munteanu's young research assistant, Dan, is struggling with an armload of red banners which keep getting unfurled in spite of his efforts to keep them rolled up.

When he finishes wiping his face and combing his hair, Comrade Dumitru turns and notices Peter.

"How come you're here before anyone else?" Comrade Dumitru asks. He gives Peter a quick, suspicious look. "It must be those long legs of yours! Making you fly!" he says with a grin. He takes a step forward and stops by the bulletin board. "Great article! Great piece of work! Should have been published a long time ago, don't you think?" He is staring at the text which is a direct quotation from Stalin.

Peter nods in silence. Then he turns and tiptoes out of the library. He crosses the hallway, passes the empty auditorium and goes down the stairs to the basement.

* * *

Dusk has already gathered in the corners and there is only a faint light coming from Professor Munteanu's study. Peter walks past it and finds himself in the dissection hall on the way to his room.

There are no students at work this afternoon, and the many rows of corpses lying on their tables of stone look like statues resting on pedestals. The bodies are soaked in formaldehyde and the air in the room makes one's eyes teary from the fumes. Peter is used to this and has learned to ignore it. His red eyes are tearing all the time, and he inhales the burning fumes as if they were fresh mountain air.

As he walks through the twenty tables of stone he looks at the bodies with tenderness, as if they were old friends. The room is silent except for the sound of his own footsteps on the cement floor, and he fancies himself the only worshipper in an ancient cathedral, surrounded by statues of saints. Or, better, he is the highest priest of Egypt, performing the sacred rites for the deceased Pharaoh deep inside the old pyramid of Gizah.

As he keeps walking a scared rat runs across his path and a pair of swallows that have flown in through the half open window stop nibbling the toes of an old woman and look at him with curious eyes. Peter doesn't mind these visitors. They remind him of the sacred animals of ancient Egypt who accompany the dead on his eternal journey. And they remind him of the belief that the soul of the deceased takes the shape of a bird.

He thinks of Mr. Bantu who taught him these things and the small funeral parlor in which they worked ten years ago. Suddenly, while standing in the middle of the dissection hall, a strong gust of wind opens one of the small windows completely and the two swallows fly out of the room.

* * *

Chapter 2

In the following weeks, as May rolls into June, Peter watches the students prepare for the final Anatomy exam. In the large basement hall, the corpses have their faces, necks and limbs completely dissected. On every table a body with its skin peeled off, its muscles, blood vessels and all its nerves laid bare, has become a strange figure covered with three-dimensional white tattoos or shrouded in a spider web of outlandish design.

At the same time Peter is also helping Professor Munteanu in his own lab. They are working feverishly, as the professor is trying to finish a piece of research before the end of the school year. For, in addition to teaching Anatomy and Embryology, he is also doing research in Genetics. He is spending most of his time in his office, plunged in the study of genes and chromosomes. He has perfected a new, simplified method of staining slides.

He moves from the tile-covered workbench with a large microscope and a stack of slides to his desk with the open notebook, green reading lamp and yellow begonia.

The galley-proof of an article for *La Presse Medicale* in Paris rests near his meerschaum pipe and two silver framed photographs of his children and grandchildren. In one picture the children are playing with a white rabbit and in the other they are holding their old dachshund.

The professor picks up his horn-rimmed glasses and gold fountain pen, and writes a note in the open book. Then he returns to the workbench to check the new slides which Peter has prepared for him. Peter has learned how to use the different chemicals to stain the slides for the microscope.

On other days when Professor Munteanu corrects the galley-proof for *La Presse Medicale*, Peter tiptoes carefully around him, trying not to disturb him. He hopes that his name will be added to the list of co-authors, as the professor has promised.

They are working around the clock. Professor Munteanu pays no attention to the changes in the library.

"We have a deadline to meet and that's all that matters," he says to Peter.

The Professor works many hours. In the evening, in the sharp light of the microscope lamp, Peter can see the huge shadow of his head with his wild mane of hair projected on the frosted glass panel of his office door. The gigantic head is bent over the equally large microscope and, when the two shadows merge into one, they seem to be growing beyond the walls of the room.

* * *

Outside in the University garden, the lilac, jasmine and hydrangea are in bloom filling the air with their color and fragrance.

It is during this time that upstairs in the main auditorium, the purges of the Communist Party Organization get underway. The first evening, as he walks past the door, Peter can hear Comrade Dumitru haranguing the crowd of Party members inside the hall.

The next morning Florica, the cleaning lady who attended the meeting and who is a loyal Party member, tells Peter everything that took place inside the auditorium. Her devotion to the Party doesn't stop her from having a special fondness for Peter, a fondness mixed with a trace of maternal tenderness.

Every spring Florica brings him cherries and apricots that she carries inside her mighty brassiere, hiding them, not to have to share them with others. And when she offers them to Peter, an aroma of garlic, fresh sweat and cheap cigarettes clings to the fruit, adding a spicy flavor to their natural sweetness.

After she finishes scrubbing the cement floor on her hands and knees, she tells Peter that the first Party member to be expelled was the Dean of the Medical School, Professor Albu. "He published an article in an American medical journal, a long time ago, before the war," says Florica, getting up from the floor. "And rumor has it that he has already been shot in the head inside his prison cell," she adds in a low voice. "People say that his American connection was too much to deal with, for the comrades!"

A few days later, after the second Party meeting, Florica walks into the dissection hall carrying her bucket with suds, in one hand, and a brush with hard bristles, in the other. She leaves the pail and the brush near the door and walks toward Peter. He has just finished placing a piece of cloth freshly soaked in formaldehyde over one of the dissected bodies. Florica stops by the table, unbuttons her stained lab smock and dipping her fist into her cleavage, she brings out a handful of small, very green, unripe pears.

"Here, that's for you, help yourself!"

She arranges all the pears on the dissection table and offers them to Peter. Then she tells him the latest news from the meeting.

* * *

"This time it was Doctor Ana Cordescu, Professor of Psychiatry, who was expelled from the Party and the University! I knew something was wrong!"

Florica is closing her smock, which is very tight. A button pops off as she pulls at the fabric. "I knew that something was going to happen! A few days ago when I went to clean her office at the clinic, a militiaman armed with a gun and bayonet barred my way. I looked around trying to understand what was going on. I noticed that the entrance door was locked with a large padlock, the windows were shut and all the blinds had been drawn. The militiaman refused to answer my questions and threatened to arrest me, or even shoot me, if I didn't leave right away. I got very scared. I almost wet my pants!"

Peter nods. He has stopped fussing with the cloth and the formaldehyde. He keeps listening to Florica.

"You know," she goes on, "the good doctor should have known better than to let her mind be controlled by the crazy ideas of some Jewish doctor from Vienna! A Doctor Freud? Or some other Jewish name like that. Everybody knows that the comrades hate these guys! What did she expect? People say that she has already been deported to a far off village and placed under house arrest. Nobody, not even her husband and children, can go to see her!"

Florica has found a safety pin and closes her smock. She goes on talking. "Women have no business in men's careers and professions. They get all mixed up from too much learning and thinking. They end up wrecking their own life and that of their families. But what can you do?"

She doesn't wait for Peter's reply. She picks up her brush and bucket and walks out of the room.

* * *

A week later the entire Department of Anatomy is ordered to attend an open meeting in the main auditorium. Peter follows the others into the high ceilinged room with wooden benches set in a half-circle like an ancient theatre.

He has been here in the past. He used to sneak in and sit quietly in the last row listening to Professor Munteanu's lectures and watching the blackboard. He imagined that he too was a medical student. He always chose a dark corner where he could not be seen. And he sat close to the door, so he could be the first to leave at the end of the class.

On the day of the meeting, Peter sits in his chosen place. At the front of the auditorium two large and colorful anatomical charts which flank the blackboard—the chart of the heart and blood vessels with arteries painted bright red and veins painted blue, and the chart of the digestive system, painted orange and brown—have been rolled up into a cylinder. Only the old, yellow skeleton suspended from its metal stand has been left in its place near the wall.

The large table on the dais is covered with a cheap scarlet fabric like the cloth in the library. Across the dusty blackboard a poster inscribed with the words "Death to Genetics!" has been hung.

Comrade Dumitru stands at the table and speaks to the crowd.

"Comrades, we know there are no such things as genes and chromosomes, no such thing as biologic heredity! These are poisonous inventions of the Western bourgeoisie, as Comrade Stalin has taught us. The Western biologists deny the theory of "Inheritance of Acquired Characteristics," or the inheritance of characteristics produced by the environment, the important discovery of the great Soviet scientist Lysenko! He and Comrade Stalin have taught us that Genetics are a diabolical Imperialist tool aimed against Communism and against our struggle for progress! All geneticists who follow in the footsteps of Mendel and Morgan are our enemies and must be annihilated!" he thunders. "We will not tolerate any geneticists in our midst, and they will be punished as they deserve!"

The crowd in the auditorium stands up and applauds with frenzy, then bursts into shouts, "Death to Genetics! Death to Geneticists! Glory to our Great Leader, Comrade Stalin!"

As the applause and shouts grow louder, Peter feels his heart sinking. His body is covered with cold sweat. He can barely wait to get out. He starts looking for Professor Munteanu in the audience. He scans the first rows where the Professor usually sits, then the middle rows, the right wing and the left, but he can't find him. Then he remembers that he hasn't seen the Professor in the last two or three days. They finished the article and sent it to France. The work was ended, and since then Peter has not seen the Professor. Where is he now? Where could he be?

Peter steps out of the auditorium and walks toward the dissection hall. He feels as if he carries a big load on his shoulders. He follows the corridor which leads to the Professor's office and stops when he arrives at his room. To his surprise the door is wide open and two students members of the Party organization are working inside.

From the doorway Peter sees that the office is mainly unchanged. On the wooden desk, the photos of the Professor's children and their pets still flank the meerschaum pipe and the yellow begonia. The green reading lamp still stands guard over the open notebook and the Professor's gold fountain pen. His horn-rimmed glasses rest on a half-written page.

On the lab table, the microscope has been left uncovered, with fresh glass slides ready to be examined next to it. The entire room looks as if Professor Munteanu has just stepped out and will be back any minute.

The two students are busy removing the leather-bound anatomy atlases from the shelves and are placing them in large cartons strewn all over the floor. Their backs are turned, but Peter recognizes Toma, the secretary of the students' organization, and Dan Brebu, the Professor's research assistant. Peter watches from the doorway and listens to their conversation.

"Did you hear the latest about the Professor?" asks Toma.

"No...Did they fire him?" says Dan.

"They sent him to a forced labor camp. One of the worst. I don't know if he can make it there. I heard that he has a bad heart!"

"Agh!" Dan gasps. But he doesn't reply. He tries to conceal his surprise in a yawn.

Peter, too, is shocked by the words. He tells himself that the students don't really know what is going on. Watching in silence he notices that one of the boxes which is piled with books sits near the door within his reach. Next to it on the floor is an Egyptian color print of Anubis, the Jackal-Headed God of the Dead, weighing a human heart. Peter has learned, from Mister Bantu, that this is the heart of the Royal Scribe Ani, being weighed on the Great Scales of the Righteous Truth. The picture shows the soul or conscience of the departed resting in the left pan of the scale. The right pan holds the Feather of Ma'at, which symbolizes all that is just, true, and righteous. In the middle, the Jackal-Headed God Anubis watches the scales.

In this scene, the soul of the deceased is lighter than the Feather of Ma'at; it proves that the dead man's conscience is pure and has no sins. As a consequence the God Anubis allows him to proceed and be born in the glory of Osiris, since he has no "dirt in his heart."

Peter looks up and sees that the students still have their backs turned. He bends down and grabs two books from the top of the carton with his left hand while he snatches the print with the right. He then hides his loot under his lab smock and hurries back to his room. He locks the door behind him, sits on his cot and examines his spoils carefully.

He finds the Professor's signature on the front page of the French anatomy atlas and smiles, as if he is seeing him waving in the distance. Then he places the books on a high shelf by the window, under a large skull.

But the Egyptian poster he pins to the wall facing his bed, so he can look at it every morning, as soon as he opens his eyes.

* * *

Chapter 3

On a warm August afternoon, Florica walks into Peter's room without knocking at the door. "I came to tell you that Comrade Dumitru wants to see you. He wants to talk to you right away!" she says, as she stops by his workbench.

"Where? Where is Comrade Dumitru?" asks Peter.

"In his new office, the office of the Dean, you know, the big room on the first floor."

Florica takes another step and stands so close that Peter feels the warmth of her body.

"Guess what I brought you?"

Without waiting for his reply she dips into her cleavage and from the depth of her brassiere brings to light two round, velvety peaches which she places on the table next to the bones.

"That's your dessert. I hope you ate lunch?" she asks with a trace of worry in her voice.

"Thanks!" Peter says.

She bends over the table. She isn't wearing her work smock anymore, but is dressed in a pink, short-sleeved cotton blouse with a print of red daisies and a deep cleavage. Her straight navy skirt is too tight on her hips. Her long hair is brushed back and held in place by a black silk ribbon tied at the back of her neck. A large brooch in the shape of a red star with a gold hammer and sickle in the center shines on her chest like a hero's decoration. Only her bare feet are tucked in the same dirty slippers.

"Come on, Peter, hurry up. You know Comrade Dumitru gets nervous when he's kept waiting!" She tilts her head to one side and flashes a bright smile, as if she were asking a personal favor.

Peter shakes his head but doesn't stop examining the bones that are lined up on his workbench.

"Why does he want to see me?"

"I don't know. He didn't say why. He only said that it is urgent and very important."

Peter nods. He stares at her blouse.

"Where is your smock?"

Florica shrugs. "I don't know. I'm not scrubbing floors anymore. I'm Comrade Dumitru's secretary now."

"I see! Well, congratulations." Peter keeps nodding. Then he gets up, shuffles to the sink and washes his hands and face which he dries with a faded blue towel. He combs his hair, watching himself in the chipped mirror. Why did Comrade Dumitru call him? What does he want from him? Peter doesn't look forward to a discussion with Comrade Dumitru. All he remembers is his barking laugh and crude remarks. But he can't say no. He can't get out of this meeting! He gets up and follows Florica to the dean's office.

It is very quiet and peaceful in the building on this August afternoon. The students have gone to summer practice at provincial hospitals in different parts of the country, and most of the teaching staff and lab technicians are on vacation. In the city, in the center of town, the streets are glaring white with heat and dust, but the basement and the hallways of the medical school are cool and slightly damp.

Peter keeps wondering why Comrade Dumitru has asked to see him. He feels anxious and ill at ease, wishing to turn around and escape somehow without Florica's notice. But it is too late now. They take a few more steps in the long corridor and stop in front of the Dean's office.

Florica opens the door and pushes Peter in. She leads him to a brown leather couch next to a coffee table decorated with ivory and mother of pearl. Then she walks out of the room.

A few minutes later Comrade Dumitru comes in and shakes hands with Peter. He sits down in a leather armchair that matches the couch.

"Welcome to my new office! I hope you like the furnishings and all the knickknacks!" he says with a grin which reveals two silver-capped teeth in the left corner of his mouth. He is in a good mood and offers Peter an expensive American cigarette out of a red lacquered box. Peter remembers the day, three years ago,when the Dean, Professor Albu, showed the box to him and Professor Munteanu, after Professor Albu had bought it in Vienna.

Comrade Dumitru lights Peter's cigarette and leans back. He isn't wearing his stained lab coat anymore but a light summer shirt with an open collar. His hair has been trimmed and his beard is carefully shaven. Only the nail of his little finger has remained as long as before, and he uses it to pick at the inside of his large ears.

"I'm glad you're here! I need to talk to you!" says Comrade Dumitru. He lights his own cigarette, then he waits for the match to go out and throws it over his shoulder.

"I hear you're a good worker, serious, reliable, competent...a man who knows what he is doing. And you don't talk too much, you don't gossip. That's what Comrade Toma and Dan Brebu told me. Is it true?" Comrade Dumitru stares at Peter with unblinking eyes.

Peter feels that he is blushing. He doesn't like to hear comments about himself. But before he can say anything, Florica walks into the room carrying a tray with two small cups and saucers and a *finjean* full of hot Turkish coffee. Comrade Dumitru waits until she pours the coffee and leaves the room.

"Where was I? You are a very serious person, and we need your help. I'm speaking about a project, a scientific project, which is just as important as it is secret. It involves corpses from the mortuary, fresh good corpses which have to be removed from there immediately after delivery and brought to the research labs of the Central Committee. They have to be sorted out *before* being injected with formaldehyde and before reaching the students in the dissection halls!"

Comrade Dumitru takes a sip of black coffee and goes on.

"This project is a secret. With very few exceptions neither the staff nor the students should know about it. But it is an important project; it is an order, *a mission*, which has to be carried out. And the corpses have to be selected by a trained and competent eye such as yours. Only the young, the healthy-looking bodies should be chosen, earmarked, and set aside, immediately after their arrival. And one more thing: since Professor Munteanu's departure only you have a key to the mortuary and you must always be there when the new corpses are brought.

Comrade Dumitru takes a long drag from his cigarette and exhales blue rings of smoke into the air. Peter squirms in his chair.

"You will be handsomely rewarded for your work. All the participants will receive a good cash award for their efforts."

The Comrade has finished his coffee and tilts the small cup in all directions, watching the slow movement of the black sediment.

"There is a slight hitch to this operation, one which can be easily overcome. You're not a Party member. But why not join us right now? You can fill out an application right here. I have some blanks which are already approved!"

Comrade Dumitru gets up, walks to the end of the room and starts rummaging through the top drawer of his large desk. Peter feels numb, as if all this is not really happening to him but to somebody else, or as if he is watching himself in a movie. With half-closed eyes he scans the room, taking in the soft blue carpet with its purple flowers and golden trees, the vaulted ceiling and crystal chandelier, the skillfully carved mahogany desk and the two matching bookcases. Professor Albu, the Dean, brought these pieces a long time ago from an old castle in the north of the country after it had been hit by lightning. Peter always loved the wood carvings on the furniture. He misses the Dean. He misses his lifelong devotion to the rescue of the old, beautiful things which he collected.

The room is still familiar. Nevertheless, he cannot miss the changes. There are large war photographs on the walls that were never here before. There are pictures of Soviet planes dropping bombs over German cities, pictures of Russian battleships firing at the enemy in the Black Sea, photos of antiaircraft guns shooting at planes, and pictures of night battles in the sky and on land, illuminated by tracer rockets which look like fantastic fireworks.

Pasted on the front of the old grandfather clock is a large photograph of a German tank exploding under the fire of the famous Katyusha rocket launchers. Photos of flame throwers, grenade launchers and submachine guns in action cover the life-size oil painting of the founder of the medical school. All that remains visible is the old man's forehead and half of his right eye.

As he looks at the pictures, it seems to Peter that he also hears the loud din of the war machine. He is ready to cover his ears with his hands, like he did at the Mayday parade. He can hear the roaring and howling of the raging war, the sharp whistling of artillery shells in the air, the loud whirring of bombs falling and the thunder of rocket explosions.

He is brought back to reality by the burning cigarette in his hand. He grabs a small ashtray from the table, and when he looks inside, he finds a few paper clips, and a small shell from a pistol. He picks the shell up and turns it around. It looks familiar. It has the same length and weight as the small shell he keeps in his lab, hidden at the bottom of a drawer. He examines it carefully and sees that, yes, even the lettering engraved on the base of the shell is the same as his own. It is the shell of a German pistol, the .38 Walther. What is it doing here? he wonders.

Just then Comrade Dumitru utters a triumphant bark.

"Damned! Damned! I found it at last!"

Bent over his desk at the other end of the room, he is waving a sheet of paper in the air like a flag of peace and is bursting into cascades of barks!

For a few seconds, Peter doesn't notice Comrade Dumitru pushing a pre-approved application toward him. He doesn't hear him opening the tall bookcase and fetching a bottle of *tsuică* (plum brandy) and two small glasses from behind the row of leather-bound volumes of the Collected Works of Lenin and Stalin in order to celebrate this special event.

* * *

Peter has slipped back in time to that spring morning of 1937. It was early April and he was rushing to work, walking toward Mr. Bantu's small funeral parlor. It was a sunny day and in the courtyards the apricot trees had burst into bloom, looking like pink feathers of light. The empty streets were still asleep, and Peter could hear mourning doves cooing under the eaves. He was walking briskly, inhaling the cool air, watching the sky, and enjoying the silence.

As he came near the funeral home, he heard a chorus of male voices and fragments of song. The sounds were brought by the wind and then blown away so that he couldn't link them together. They seemed familiar. He quickened his step. When he turned the corner and the funeral parlor came into view, he saw that the small building was entirely surrounded by a noisy crowd of young men dressed in brilliant emerald shirts and girded with black leather belts in which they carried pistols.

Peter recognized them as a group of Iron Guard militants, the Romanian Fascist Organization. They wore small bags of cloth filled with the "sacred soil of the land" hanging from their necks. Peter could now clearly distinguish the words of their songs and the anti-Semitic slogans they were shouting:

> "Wake up Romanian citizen
> From the deadly sleep
> Into which you were cast
> By the barbarous Jews..."

they sang. And "Down with the Jews!" "Death to the Jews!" they shouted. As he came closer, Peter saw that the walls of the building had been smeared with large, blood-red Jewish stars and the words "Dirty Jew—we'll kill you!"

Peter looked for Mr. Bantu but didn't see him anywhere. The Fascists had completely surrounded the funeral parlor and were closing in toward the entrance. One of the men was very loud and shouted orders to the others. He seemed to be the leader of the group.

"Get out of my way or I'll kill you with the dirty Jew!" he screamed at Peter who had advanced slowly, and was now standing near the door.

Peter stepped aside while the man took the pistol out of his belt and fired three shots through the narrow window. The colored glass panel shattered and fell to the pavement, gleaming in the sunlight. Then the man kicked in the door and stepped into the room, still brandishing the revolver and shouting.

The building was empty, and for a moment he looked disappointed. Then he took aim at the pictures on the wall and fired: one bullet through the mummy of King Tutankhamen, one through the body of the Jackal God Anubis, one through the Pyramids of Gizah, and one through the heart of an ancient Egyptian embalmer. The Fascists applauded as the man cursed loudly and started to laugh. He sounded like an angry dog.

* * *

"Here is the form. All you have to do is sign!" says Comrade Dumitru with a laugh.

That laugh...that barking laugh! Now Peter knows where he heard it. He suddenly also remembers the face. The same narrow forehead, the sharp, unblinking eyes, the dark, bushy hair.

* * *

After the Fascists left the funeral parlor, Peter took the pictures down and rolled them up into a cylinder. Before leaving the room, on his way to the door, he picked up one of the shells which had dropped to the ground. He remembers it all very clearly now.

* * *

He turns around in his chair and looks up. Comrade Dumitru is standing in front of him, the application in one hand, the two glasses full of shimmering plum brandy in the other.

"Well, sign this paper!" he orders.

He puts the form and the two glasses on the table and hands Peter a fountain pen. His face is set in a stern grimace, with clenched jaw and lips pressed together. Peter is watching him, but doesn't move.

"What now, what are you waiting for? Sign the application and let's drink to it!" says the Comrade.

Peter's mouth is sticky and dry. His tongue feels heavy. He gets up and takes a step toward the door.

"No....no. No, I can't sign now!"

Comrade Dumitru looks at him in surprise.

"You can't be serious!" he cries. Then he grabs Peter's arm and forces him to sit down again. He is pressing the white paper into his hand.

"Take it to your room and sign it there, stupid! Just bring it back to me by tomorrow. And now let's have a drink to celebrate your new venture!"

He raises one glass, clinks with Peter, and gulps it down all at once, for the sake of good luck.

* * *

When he returns to his lab, Peter sits at his table and tries to resume his work. But he cannot concentrate. His hands feel stiff and clumsy, as if made of wood and the bones keep slipping out of his grip. He is haunted by his meeting with Comrade Dumitru. Also, the three glasses of *tsuică* have made him drowsy. He lays down on his cot, closes his eyes and drifts off to sleep.

* * *

Chapter 4

It is late in the evening and the sun has set when he half opens his eyes. He feels a cool, soft hand caressing his forehead, his cheeks and his hair, and he recognizes Florica's voice whispering. Before he can say anything she is kissing him on the lips. Still sleepy, Peter tries to sit up and push her away but he is too drowsy and too weak to succeed. He falls back on the cot while Florica wraps her soft and warm body so tightly around him that he loses any trace of willpower and doesn't resist her embrace.

* * *

The next morning when he opens his eyes he is alone in the room. He vaguely remembers what happened and the more he thinks of it the more he believes it was a dream.

When he gets out of bed his head is swimming and his gait is wobbly. He drags himself to the sink, turns on the faucet and places his head underneath. The cold water wakes him up and after he dries his face and gets dressed he returns to the workbench to fix himself breakfast. Just as he is ready to light the Bunsen burner to boil some water for his daily cup of ersatz coffee he steps on a hard, pointed object. He picks it up and examines it. It is Florica's star-shaped pin with the shining hammer and sickle in the middle. He smiles, shakes his head and mumbles, "It was not a dream after all!" He turns the pin in his hand and looks at it from all sides. "Nothing but a cheap piece of tin! Doesn't make anyone better or smarter!" With a shrug he slips the brooch into the pocket of his smock.

After that he returns to his work table and finishes eating two slices of dark bread with apricot jam which Florica had brought him a few weeks before, and swallows his cup of watery coffee. Then he puts everything back where it belongs, in a big cardboard box under the table.

When he is ready for work, Peter decides to prepare the heart specimens for the students. This is his task every summer, in the middle of August, and this is what Professor Munteanu would expect him to do. There are 200 students, so 200 specimens have to be prepared.

Peter goes to the end of the room and opens a low and narrow door which leads to a small cubicle lined with shelves from floor to ceiling. From the shelf nearest to him Peter takes a full tray of glass jars, each of them holding a human heart floating in formaldehyde. He returns to the workbench and lines up the jars in orderly fashion. Then he puts on a pair of thick, red rubber gloves, opens the first jar, takes out a heart, and places it on a shiny aluminum tray. With a long surgical scalpel he cuts the heart lengthwise in four slices, leaving them attached to each other at one end so that they look like large tropical buds ready to blossom. The sharp edge of the blade makes a swishing sound as it slides through the rubbery mass. Then, before placing the heart back in the jar and changing the formaldehyde, he stops to examine the thick, fleshy walls, the inner lining, which the knife has laid bare and which shimmers like mother of pearl. He also looks at the large blood vessels that sprout from invisible depths, and resemble a cluster of hollow reeds cut near their roots. Everything is exposed to the eye now and can be studied with ease.

After he finishes the first batch of jars Peter takes them back to the small cubicle and starts another set. He thinks of the students who will each receive a jar with a freshly prepared heart that they can take home and examine at leisure. He feels happy that he can help them learn more about the secrets of the human body. He himself is always yearning to explore more of these mysteries, and he imagines Professor Munteanu watching him work and nodding with approval. He even remembers how, about eight years ago, the Professor let him participate in an experiment. They had taken the heart of a live chicken embryo out of a broken egg, cut it into very small pieces and placed them in a flat jar which they kept in an incubator. The small pieces of tissue were bathed in a clear, pink liquid. And they kept beating day in and day out, just like a living heart. For many years the little pieces have continued to beat in their flat glass dish, and they have even sprouted other fragments and cells that have gone on beating for a very long time. Peter looks at the heart he is holding. "Yes," he thinks, "if this heart were bathed in the same pink nurturing liquid as the chicken heart instead of being soaked in burning formaldehyde, it, too, might go on beating and throbbing for many, many years. And if the hearts can stay alive, the dead can stay alive forever and ever, and Mr. Bantu is proven right!"

Peter remembers the day in the funeral parlor when Mr. Bantu told him that for the ancient Egyptians nothing was as important as the heart, because only the heart was the real center of life.

They had finished a hard day's work, laboring on the body of a woman whose heart had been taken out at the hospital during the autopsy. Peter was washing the instruments at the sink and Mr. Bantu was standing nearby, brewing mint tea, to which he added lemon and rum.

"You know," said Mr. Bantu, "the ancient Egyptians never separated the heart from the corpse because without a heart the dead can never revive! Also they believed that all decisions, serious or light, were made by the heart, and that the rest of the body: the eyes, ears, legs, arms, even the brain and the tongue, the mind and speech, were only following the command of the heart. Even the Creation of the World started inside a heart, it was the desire born inside the heart of the Great God Ptah that commanded him to create the world."

Peter stares at the print he brought from Professor Munteanu's office and has pinned to the wall. It shows the weighing of the heart of the deceased by the Jackal-Headed God Anubis on the Great Scales.

The heart, resting on one scale, is as light as the feather that rests on the other. Only a very pure heart can be as light as a feather and thus assure the Truthful Dead of the Joys of the Afterlife. "The heart is a man's conscience, and it can testify against his own deeds," Mr. Bantu had warned more than once. Peter clutches the knife. He will never forget those words.

He doesn't hear the door open and close.

"I was admiring your skill at meat carving!" says Comrade Dumitru. Peter hadn't noticed him walking into the room.

"You could always get a job as a butcher—of course, if there is enough meat on the market to call for such a job," he adds and bursts into loud barks of laughter. "And speaking about work, did you sign yesterday's application? It's about time."

"No," says Peter. He places the heart on the aluminum tray and puts the knife on the table. "I was too busy preparing work for the students."

"The students...the students...always the students" I'm the one who needs your help! We have to start preparing for the transfer of the bodies out of the mortuary before the students arrive. I told you yesterday. Remember, it has to be done quietly, the teaching staff doesn't know about this. And if anyone leaks the secret he will pay dearly for it!"

Comrade Dumitru gives Peter a sharp, warning look. Peter stares at his feet.

"As you wish. It's up to you."

Comrade Dumitru scratches his left ear with his long fingernail. Then he turns around and stomps out of the room, slamming the door behind him.

Peter sighs with relief when he is gone. He picks up the knife, but then slams it back on the table. What a shame, a crying shame, to snatch the corpses away from the students! I don't want to be a part of it! He shakes his head and frowns. He picks up the scalpel again. But his hand is trembling and he has to steady it before cutting the heart lengthwise in four slices which he keeps attached to each other at one end. Then he places the preparation in a clean jar full of fresh formaldehyde.

"No, never, I will never be Comrade Dumitru's accomplice!" he mumbles.

He brings the hearts back to the small cubicle at the end of the lab and takes a new batch of jars from the wooden shelves.

* * *

Chapter 5

When Florica visits him in the evening, she brings a piece of feta cheese, three large eggs and a loaf of freshly baked bread, all wrapped in a red and white kitchen towel. From the depth of her cleavage she produces two ripe tomatoes and a smooth, green cucumber.

At first, Peter doesn't want to accept her gifts. He even hesitated to let her in. He doesn't love her. He doesn't even like her. He doesn't trust her devotion to Comrade Dumitru and to the Party. He wants to stop this closeness. The many gifts she lavishes on him make him feel guilty.

But when she stands in front of him with her chin trembling like a child ready to burst into tears he softens and can't say no.

"It was not easy to get these things," says Florica. "I bought them from Vasile, the Securitate guard. He smuggled them out of the Politburo restaurant. We almost got caught. As a matter of fact, they arrested Vasile a few hours later as he sold some milk and tomatoes to another fellow. Poor devil! They took him too. I hear that a stolen egg gets you now thirty years in prison instead of three months as it was until February!"

Florica has already started to slice the bread and cut the tomatoes. Peter clears the anatomical jars from the table and sets out plates.

"Now with Vasile gone I need a new source of milk and cheese. Don't you scientists say that without milk, cheese and eggs our bones will get soft, will crumble, and we'll get rickets...and then how will we build Socialism?" She shakes her head and starts to laugh. Peter smiles too.

With the feta cheese, thinly sliced tomatoes and three eggs, Florica cooks an omelette for two. They eat the cucumbers with fresh bread, salt and pepper, and an old, half-dried onion Peter found in his box, under the workbench. Even though they are hungry they eat slowly, trying to make the meal last as long as they can. After they finish, they sit on the cot, the empty plates in their laps.

"Yes," says Florica, "this nasty thing with Vasile! I have to find another source for milk and cheese. With crumbling bones, no construction of Socialism is possible!'

The mention of Socialism reminds Peter of the star-shaped pin she left in his room. He pulls it out of his pocket and gives it to her.

"Why don't you keep it?" she asks. "Please keep it. You may wear it someday."

"No, no," Peter raises his voice. "It doesn't do anything for me. Besides, I don't believe in these things."

"Too bad." Florica looks straight into his eyes. "I wish you would! It would be a lot better for you. But let's not talk about this." She gets up and puts the empty plates on the table. "Or let's not talk about anything at all!"

She turns off the light. She then comes back to the cot and sits next to him. Suddenly, almost by surprise, her face is very close to his and he can feel her warm breath like a caress on his cheek. Then her lips are kissing his neck, and her hands are unbuttoning his smock and his shirt, and gently, very gently, she is stroking his chest, his shoulders and the outline of his collarbone. And when he feels her large, warm bosom pressing against his bare skin he is again lost, swept away in her embrace. Florica's hair, which has gotten loose and is spreading out on the pillow, has the fragrance of freshly mown grass, and it makes Peter think of a soft meadow on a clear summer night.

* * *

Later that night he has a dream. He dreams that he walks through a meadow on a path that leads to the sea. At the end of the meadow is a beach and the water. He is not alone. He is holding hands with a young woman who has long, blonde hair and wears a sailor hat. He can't see who she is, her face is blurred. All he can see are her golden earrings with blue stones.

At the end of the path a sailboat is waiting for them. They climb on board and the breeze pushes them away from the shore, into the sunset. They sail all night and at dawn they reach a foreign shore with white mosques, tall minarets and seagulls circling above.

* * *

When Peter wakes up, it is morning. The sun is shining through the window, and Florica is gone. Only the red and white kitchen towel and dirty dishes are left. Peter sits up on his cot and thinks of his dream. He is puzzled. Who is the blonde woman walking with him? Even though he can't make out her face, he knows that she is a real person. He has met her before. The blonde hair, the earrings…and then the boat and the minarets. He has seen them before.

He buries his head in his hands and reflects. Suddenly he knows. It is Mariana, Professor Munteanu's research assistant. He is so startled, he jumps out of bed. And even though he is alone he feels himself blushing. He has never dreamt of Mariana before. But now he remembers: she had been to the lab just a few days ago. She opened the door, and when he turned around she was standing in the middle of the room, wearing a blue summer dress with a print of white sailboats, tall minarets and seagulls circling above.

Peter was surprised. He didn't expect her, knowing that she was away on summer practice with her colleague, Dan Brebu. She told him that she had come in for a few days to check on her grandmother who was old and sick.

Peter was glad to see her. He looked into her clear, blue eyes and she smiled at him. They spoke about work in the lab and about the students. Then she walked toward the door, ready to leave, but halfway out she turned. She had remembered something. Had Peter found a small, blue notebook, her diary? There was a letter inside she had received from abroad.

Peter shook his head. He hadn't seen any notebook or diary. Mariana became very quiet. She had looked everywhere. She had hoped to find it here.

Yes, Mariana had a habit of losing, forgetting or misplacing her things. She often lost her scarf, her gloves and her hat in the winter, or even her pocketbook or her wallet. Once, as a first year medical student, she forgot her bundle of long bones on the tramway. Getting them back turned into a complicated affair, which led to a criminal investigation. Where did those bones come from? To whom did they belong? Were they connected to a murder? The detectives wanted to know all the details. Luckily Professor Munteanu's brother's wife played pinochle with the wife of the Chief of Police and the investigation ended up in a friendly card game.

* * *

Peter kept thinking about Mariana. He knew her for many years, for a long time before she had become a medical student. The summer they first met she was a little girl with pink cheeks and blonde braids who spent her vacation at her grandmother's house, near the lake. And it was precisely her habit of carelessness which brought them together. At that time Peter was still at the orphanage.

The lake was not far from the orphanage. Mariana's grandparents' house stood between his home and the water. It was a stately mansion with old trees and a yellow fence. Mariana and her brother spent their summers there. Peter could see them sometimes at play in the garden.

In that year 1934 he had already won the running contest for his school and was training for the next step, the running contest of all schools in the city and surrounding communities. And that summer he was free to run alone whenever he wanted, as long as he wanted on the narrow path that bordered the lake, for the gym instructor was too busy romancing the post office clerk in the tall bushes behind the administrative building.

One evening after the rain, Peter ran along Mariana's grandmother's garden. As he came close to the dock he saw a little sailor hat in the grass. He bent to pick it up and as he did so he heard a child crying not far away. He looked around but did not see anybody. He kept searching left and right until finally, following the direction of the crying, he ran down a steep and narrow path which led below the dock, to the embankment.

There, beyond the gaping mouth of a dark tunnel half filled with water, he saw a little boy perched on top of a slippery rock. He was almost invisible in the dark. As Peter came closer, he saw that the boy was shaking and sliding, barely keeping his balance. It looked as if he could vanish under the waves any minute. Peter steadied his foothold, stretched out his arm and grabbed the child around the waist, pulling him out of the tunnel. He recognized little Sandu, Mariana's brother.

As he carried him to his home, he found both the garden gate and the entrance door to the house wide open. A girl's bicycle had been carelessly thrown on the grass and was drenched by the rain.

Peter rang the bell and knocked at the door but nobody came. He climbed the steps and entered the foyer. The sound of a piano came from the living room. He knocked again, and when nobody came, he stepped into the room. A girl of about eight with blonde braids was practicing at the piano. A slender woman with silver hair sat next to her. They were startled and jumped when he walked into the room.

"Oh, my God! Oh, my God! What happened? Look at him!" cried the old lady as she took the little boy in her arms. Then a door opened, and a nanny in a striped blue and white uniform with a starched white collar came running into the room.

"Take off his clothes! They're all muddy and wet!" ordered the grandmother. "Bring towels, rub him down with alcohol then put him to bed!" she added. "I'll go to the kitchen and make him some tea."

She turned toward Peter. "Where was he? How did you find him?" But she didn't wait for his response. "How can I thank you for finding him and bringing him home? Sit down. I'll bring you something, too!"

She led Peter to a green overstuffed couch and handed him a pink towel. Then she asked him his name and introduced him to Mariana, her granddaughter. "Nothing would have happened if *somebody* had not left all the doors open as usual!" she added, glancing at Mariana.

The girl's face turned purple and her eyes filled with tears as she ran out of the room.

Peter felt sorry for her. He would have liked to talk to her, listen to her play the piano. He sat on the green couch and looked around. On the piano stood a tall crystal vase with red roses and, behind it, hung a large painting of a beautiful young woman in a pink gown with a boy and a girl in white sailor suits. The woman had blonde, wavy hair and looked like the little girl. Peter guessed that it was Mariana's mother.

He turned around and saw a thick, open book which lay on the coffee table next to him. It was written in German, but it was full of large photographs. Peter looked at the ones in front of him, then started turning pages. He saw the picture of a thunderbolt which looked like a round fireball, a picture of the eye of a fly seen through a microscope, and a photograph of the Egyptian sphinx which he had never seen before. He was so engrossed in the book that he barely noticed the grandmother when she placed a cup of hot chocolate with whipped cream and a piece of raspberry cake in front of him. She asked him about school and about the orphanage. When he finished eating and drinking she gave him the big book.

He wrapped it into his sweater and waited until all the boys had gone to sleep. Then he sneaked up the stairs to the attic and hid the book inside an old wooden trunk where he had concealed a small flashlight and other books—those he had received as prizes at the end of the school year. He was a good student and loved these books—*The Iliad*, *The Odyssey*, and a collection of fairy tales he had received as honors in school. At night he loved to read with his flashlight after the other boys had gone to sleep and the evening staff was busy playing cards and drinking beer. He would stay in the attic until the bell in the church tower tolled midnight. Then he closed his book, put it in the trunk along with the flashlight and sneaked downstairs, back to his bed.

On moonlit summer nights, from the window in the attic he could see the shimmering lake beyond the trees, and the bright lights in Mariana's house. On some evenings, when the windows of the big house were open he could hear the piano. And sometimes it was accompanied by the sound of a violin. It was said that the great George Enescu visited sometimes and played the violin while the grandmother accompanied him at the piano.

Peter would close his eyes and sit motionless. He thought of the cool drawing room and the large painting with the young woman and the two children. A white candle was burning beneath the painting, just like under an icon. He had heard rumors that Mariana's mother had died and she and her brother were orphans like himself. The painting of the beautiful woman made him wonder about his own parents and grandparents. But since he didn't know anything about them and it made him sad to think about them, he tried not to dwell on them.

* * *

Peter sighs. That summer when he was free to run along the lake and read his books in the attic had been the best. But it came to an end too soon. In October the gym teacher was caught kissing the post office clerk in the bushes during working hours. A month later, the evening staff was discovered at their beer and card parties in the pantry. The gym teacher and the whole evening staff were dismissed and replaced. Afterwards, when the old principal was also dismissed, nobody was allowed out of the orphanage without strict supervision.

* * *

Chapter 6

Peter's visit to Mariana and her grandmother's house had taken place a long time ago. Now, with Florica always in the anatomy lab everything is different. Peter tries to stay away from her. He keeps his door shut and turns his head without speaking to her when they meet in the corridor. But she pays no attention to his attempts to avoid her. In the evening she marches into his room without knocking and places a bulging briefcase on the table. Inside is a large package wrapped in a greasy Party newspaper. She brings him all kinds of special gifts—a piece of cheese, eggs or freshly baked bread, fruit, tomatoes, green peppers or cucumbers—and he doesn't know how to stop her. Sometimes she surprises him with a treat, such as "*sarmale cu varză*" or "*sarmale în foi de viţă*," cabbage or vine leaves stuffed with chopped meat and rice. And sometimes she brings him "*mămăligă*," his favorite, Romanian corn mush. All these she boils or heats up in a pot over the Bunsen burner. And after they finish eating she often stays over and lies down on his cot.

"You know, we could get married some day!" she says one evening as she adds garlic to some spicy pork patties she is grilling over the flame.

She is very proud of these pork patties. It had taken her some cunning and palm-greasing to get them. She has quickly replaced Vasile, the guard from the Party restaurant, who was arrested, with Tudor, a truck driver from the slaughterhouse, who lives three doors away from her apartment. In addition to bringing her fresh meat and sausages, Tudor has set up a lucrative trade for his other smuggled wares—calf brains, tongue, liver, kidneys or pigs' feet, which he exchanges for milk, cheese and tomatoes that he gets from his customers who work at the nearby State Farm.

"We could get married," Florica goes on, "and, if we had enough space we could even raise a family. I see us living in a home with a real dining room, a large table of polished oak in the middle, surrounded by a dozen chairs upholstered with flowery chintz or cretonne." She stirs the patties inside the pan and lowers the flame. "And I hope we have a breakfront in which to display the china and the knickknacks we would receive as weddings gifts. And a sideboard with two brass candelabras on top."

"I don't know what you're talking about!" Peter says, shaking his head. "You are lost in a pipedream." He is pasting labels on the anatomical jars, trying to make them stick to the glass.

"It's no pipedream," Florica says firmly. "There are such dining rooms. I have seen them myself. The family for whom my mother worked as a maid had just such a fancy dining room, with a round table, elegant chairs, and two brass candelabras on the sideboard."

"Damned labels!" swears Peter." They curl, and they won't stick. Ever since this five-year plan, nothing works anymore. These labels are covered with dirt, not with glue!" He bends down to pick up the labels which had come unglued and fell on the floor.

Florica is watching him. Then she turns to the patties that are sizzling in the pan. "Whenever I went to visit my mother at work, Cocoana, the lady of the house, let me play with the family parrot. It was a gorgeous bird with shiny green feathers. When I spoke to the parrot it answered by singing arias from Italian operas. When it finished singing it shouted, 'Brave, bravo!' and flapped its wings."

"A rare bird, indeed!" Peter says. He is searching through a box of labels trying to find an old batch with enough glue on the back. At the bottom of the box he finds a few old labels that he pulls out and cuts in smaller pieces." Thank God for Professor Munteanu's thriftiness!" He says with a sigh of relief. He remembers the Professor saying that since he fought the epidemic of cholera and typhus on the Front during World War I "with bare hands" and with practically no medical supplies or equipment, he never throws out anything that could come in handy one day. Peter is smiling, while Florica goes on with her tale.

"The Cocoana also gave me honey cake and chocolate candies wrapped in silver foil and filled with sweet liqueur and told me to come back for more. Since then I have always dreamt of having a fancy dining room, just like hers."

Florica sprinkles a touch of black pepper over the meat patties. "Of course we never had such a dining room in my home when I was a child. There was never a chance for one then, and certainly not later, after my father drowned with his ship. She sank in the Black Sea, off the coast of the lepers' island. Remember? The Serpents' Island, where they send all the people infected with leprosy."

"Yes, yes," Peter nods. "Insula Serpilor...or Insula Leprosilor. I know very well."

He has started to push some of the anatomical jars toward the end of the table. He is hungry and wants to eat, while part of him thinks that he should go on working. He hesitates, until Florica hands him three meat patties on a plate, while she, herself, eats directly out of the pan. "Yes," she says, "There was no chance for a fancy house with rich furniture when I was growing up. But in spite of this I swore that one day I was going to have a real dining room, just like the one I saw when I was a child."

"Well," says Peter, who has already finished his first patty and started the second. "All this happened a long time ago, when there were many houses and plenty of space. But today people are lucky if they share their kitchen and bathroom with only two families instead of five. And even that is rare. Most people live like sardines in a can. So how can you speak of a grand dining room with a large table and a dozen chairs?"

"You can, if you really want it, "says Florica. "I swear you can get it if you want it badly enough, and if you are ready to work toward it."

"Work toward it? What do you mean?"

"Plan for it," says Florica with impatience. "Get ahead. Go along with Comrade Dumitru."

Peter looks at her and shrugs his shoulders. There is one meat patty left on his plate but he doesn't touch it.

"Come to think of it, "he says after a while, "I am quite happy with things as they are, and I can live very well without Comrade Dumitru's friendship, or anybody else's. As for marriage, I wasn't planning on it, certainly not for now."

Florica is silent. She isn't eating. She is rolling little pellets of bread between her thumb and her index finger.

As they sit together without saying a word, Peter remembers the star-shaped pin with the hammer and sickle in the center. He fishes it out of his pocket and offers it to Florica.

"No, no," she says, pushing his hand away. "Hold on to it. Who knows? Maybe one day you will change your mind!"

She is smiling now, a naughty little smile. "Eat your dinner! It's getting cold. It's not worth wasting a good meat patty on stupid discussions like these." She cuts small pieces of meat with her fork and chews them slowly, savoring them, then washes them down with short sips of beer.

Peter watches her in silence. He takes a cheap cigarette out of his pocket and lights it with the flame of the Bunsen burner. He has put his dish on the table and is smoking quietly.

A whole meat patty and a crust of bread are still lying on the greasy plate.

"Did you finish? Won't you have more?" asks Florica.

"No. Not tonight."

"Too bad. You'll be hungry later on...and sorry, too. Who knows when we'll get fresh meat for patties again. It wasn't easy this time. Tudor's truck was inspected, but he got away by giving the inspector a whole calf's brain, a good piece of porterhouse, and twenty eggs. The other driver, his neighbor, had only a sausage to give, and landed in jail."

Peter shakes his head and draws on his cigarette.

"Sure you won't finish your meat" Florica asks again.

"No. I won't."

"Then I'll eat it. It's a sin to throw food away, so my mother taught me. God sent us the food and we must respect Him and eat it, she used to say. And she was right, even though the Comrades say that there is no God anymore." Florica makes the sign of the cross. Then she takes Peter's plate and soaks a piece of bread in the fat, swallowing it with mouthfuls of beer.

When she is finished she takes the plates and the forks to the sink and washes them. Then she dries them with an old towel which smells of cooking oil and formaldehyde.

* * *

Watching her eating and drinking Peter thinks that all that matters to Florica are meat patties, beer, and having a formal dining room with a sideboard and many knickknacks. It is like a religious calling for her. These thoughts make him sad and lonely, as if he were alone in the world. He feels like being buried inside a coffin of glass, unable to touch the world beyond its lid and its transparent walls.

He has never felt so lonely, even when he was a night watchman at the cemetery where he could hear the hooting of owls, the croaking of frogs, and the song of the nightingales. And he had never felt alone in Mr. Bantu's funeral parlor when they were working in silence together or when he injected the corpses with formaldehyde, all by himself. And he never felt alone with the dead in the dissection hall or while stringing bones in his lab.

But the emptiness he feels now makes him shiver and he can't get warm, even though it is August and even though Florica lies down on the cot next to him and has wound her soft body tightly around him. This night he can't get lost in her embrace, it is as if the glass wall of the coffin has come between them and keeps them apart.

These feelings remind him of the days spent in the orphanage when he had to eat at the noisy tables in the communal dining room. There, in the midst of the crowded hall, Peter was so far from everybody else, as if he had been exiled to a different planet. He could not be by himself any more, since he was not allowed to run around the lake without supervision. The new gym teacher and the new principal kept everyone locked on the grounds of the orphanage.

But then, for a short while, there was a glimmer of hope that his life was going to change, and that this feeling of "loneliness" in the crowd was going to end.

This happened when he was fifteen years old and when he won the gold medal in the great running contest sponsored by the Principesa, the King's sister.

Now, lying on his cot in the basement with his eyes closed, Peter can watch himself the day of the contest, gliding swiftly on the smooth, well-sanded track of the open stadium on that sunny day in May. A mild breeze was cooling his body. As he was gathering speed, Peter felt himself getting lighter and lighter, almost weightless. It was as if gravity had ceased to exist, or as if miraculous wings were carrying him forward with the force of a whirlwind. He didn't notice the crowds standing up in their seats, applauding and cheering. He didn't notice the banners fluttering in the wind and the brass band playing the National Anthem. It was like a dream, and he only came back to reality when, perched on the high platform of the victors, he received the gold medal from the Principesa.

While she was placing the tricolor silk band with the winner's medal around his neck, Peter met her eyes, which were the color of lavender, and was immediately bewitched. Like a rabbit hypnotized by a mongoose. He had never seen eyes like hers—large, deep and misty, with strange amethyst fires suddenly flickering and then dying in a hidden abyss.

At first Peter thought that she was not real, a figment of his imagination. But then the Principesa took his hand and raised it above their heads, to greet the cheering spectators. Peter did not flinch at the noise, for he felt protected by her. When they climbed down from the platform, they were almost buried under the cascade of flowers that poured over them. There were huge bouquets of spring flowers matching the Romanian national colors—red poppies, yellow daisies and blue cornflowers, garlands and baskets of red roses, golden marigolds and blue forget-me-nots.

Meanwhile, fans of the Principesa were throwing armfuls of fresh lilac and blooming lavender which matched the color of her eyes.

At the foot of the platform they were greeted by Peter's gym teacher, a nervous young man with a long, pockmarked nose, and by the school principal, an older man whose shrewd eyes looked like two narrow slits in a round, oily face. Both men clicked their heels and bowed stiffly, kissing the Principesa's gloved fingertips.

The gym teacher was the first to speak. "You are the source of boundless charity! May God bless you and the entire Royal Family!" he cried. His voice seemed to rise from the hollows of his long nose.

"Without Your Majesty there would be no hope for the youngsters in our care!" the principal lamented, as he wiped an imaginary tear from his eyes.

The Principesa nodded and smiled at them. She was holding on to Peter's arm. "Come to tea at four o'clock at the palace, and bring this young man with you!" she said to the teachers. A minute later her bodyguards were easing her out of the stadium.

Peter barely had time to recover from all this. He too had been pushed out of the stadium and into a waiting car, which took off full speed toward the orphanage. He had been sitting in the back seat, flanked on the left by the principal and on the right by the gym teacher. They were both so excited that they were panting and sweating and dabbing at their flushed faces with big, white handkerchiefs. The principal was eyeing the gold medal during most of the trip.

"A great decoration you got there! Looks like real gold. Congratulations!" He bent toward Peter and took the medal in his hand. "Yes, a real piece of art. A small masterpiece, all made of gold. Better give it to me for safekeeping. I'll put it in the school's strong box and lock it up for you, for as long as you want!"

Peter remembered how the words of the principal had startled him. He shifted his body to the right, trying to slide out of his reach. But the hands of the principal were faster, moving with the swiftness of a pickpocket. Before Peter could count to three, the gold medal vanished inside the principal's breast pocket, leaving Peter dumbfounded and sad.

"Don't worry, you'll get it back!" The principal's eyes were blinking shrewdly in his oily face.

When they arrived at the orphanage, the two men started fretting about finding clean clothes for Peter. They screamed at the deaf housekeeper to convince her that he had to have a fresh outfit and needed a warm shower in which he would use a new cake of soap, all for himself.

When Peter looked in the speckled entrance mirror before leaving the house and saw his reflection all dressed up in a starched, white shirt and light summer pants, he barely recognized himself.

Downstairs, at the entrance, the Principesa's black, shiny limousine with Royal Crest affixed at the site of the license plates was waiting for them. Traffic had stopped in the narrow street and a hushed crowd of onlookers had gathered: nursing mothers hugging their naked babies, old men and women making the sign of the cross and mumbling prayers to God, and even the new butcher's apprentice. He was holding a freshly killed, still convulsing rooster in one hand and a sharp knife dripping with blood in the other.

When the three passengers arrived at the limousine, the tall chauffeur in his tight-fitting navy uniform with gold buttons and braiding, white cap and white gloves, bowed stiffly and opened the doors. When they were comfortably settled on the white leather seats, the car took off toward the Cotroceni Palace with a roar.

They sped through dusty streets startling a peasant family asleep on their hay-laden oxen cart and an organ grinder with a monkey picking its lice. As they drove along, they passed a funeral procession with a hearse drawn by six pairs of horses, all draped in black. They saw a small band of gypsy musicians, also dressed in black, playing a mournful tune.

All of a sudden, from nowhere a large cat clutching a dead bird in its jaws jumped in front of the car. The chauffeur slammed on the brakes. The cat stopped short in front of the wheels. It dropped its prey, and stared at them with fixed eyes. Its cheeks were smeared with blood and feathers. Then it picked up the bird and scampered away.

"*Mîncate-aş friptă, jigodia dracului!*" cursed the driver as he spat through the open window. "I almost killed it, but..."

"Dead cats on the road bring bad luck!" said the gym teacher, rubbing his head which he bumped against the ceiling when the car had come to a sudden halt.

"Bite your tongue!" snapped the principal, who was massaging his right knee. He fell silent, and nobody spoke as they rolled along the thick, foul-smelling Dîmboviţa River. Squeezed between the gym teacher and the principal, Peter barely dared to breathe for fear of creasing his beautiful clothes.

* * *

When they reached the north end of the city they crossed a bridge made of gleaming, white stones, then drove through the gilded gate of the park which surrounded the palace.

The Principesa greeted them on the great lawn where tea was to be served. The table was set under a large golden umbrella adorned with glittering tassels and rows of glass bells that chimed in the breeze. She wore tight riding breeches and leather boots, having just dismounted from Napoleon, her favorite horse. She walked toward them, keeping her tall, slim figure rather stiff, as befitted royalty. She held a leather whip in her left hand and carried a tiny lapdog which looked like a toy. Her large amethyst earrings flickered seductively in the light, adding a glow to her eyes. Drops of perspiration trembled on her upper lip.

The Principesa sat Peter next to her and then, prodding the butler in the white tuxedo with the end of her whip, made him fill Peter's plate with dark sturgeon caviar from the Danube Delta. Then she spread butter on his thin slices of bread, covered them with caviar, and squeezed fresh lemon on top. She paid attention only to him, ignoring the other two men.

"Your muscles are in great shape. You must keep them this way!" she said, as she touched Peter's left arm with her manicured fingertips. Then she dropped her hand under the table and gave his thigh a firm squeeze.

Peter's cheeks were burning, and he hid his face behind the glass of ice-cold champagne.

After they finished eating caviar and drinking champagne and after the used dishes and glasses were cleared away, the Principesa filled his dessert plate with a mountain of chocolate truffles, caramel puffs, glazed almond squares, and sugared hearts from a large silver tray. And, while pouring him strong tea from a samovar engraved with the royal arms, her face suddenly took on a serious expression.

"We must assure Peter's training for championship and his general education!" It was the first time she had spoken to the principal and gym teacher. "He needs supervised coaching in all aspects of his career. It will be your responsibility to watch over the project I am setting up for him," she added. Then she turned toward the butler.

"Grigore, call Ana, my secretary, and tell her to bring my wallet."

A few minutes later a mousy-looking young woman in a pinstriped suit appeared at the table carrying a fat wallet. She handed it to the Principesa who explained that she wanted to make sure that Peter had all he needed. She stuffed fistfuls of large banknotes and gold coins into the hands of the principal. His chubby fingers closed tightly around this unexpected treasure.

Seized with anguish, Peter wanted to stop the Principesa from giving her money away. He had a bad premonition, like a dark cloud floating on the horizon. He felt a strong urge to grab her hand, stop her in mid-air, and warn her to watch out.

Just then he caught sight of the principal winking at the gym teacher who was grinning. It made him feel even more anguished than before.

Meanwhile the Principesa kept talking: "In ten months when I come back from my trip to London and Paris, I will check what progress you've made and..." But she never finished her sentence. With a shriek, her face crimson with rage, she jumped to her feet, hurling the wincing Chihuahua to the ground. "Shame on you, you nasty bitch! Haven't I taught you how to behave?" she scolded the squealing creature, while furiously wiping a wet stain in her lap. Then, as she stormed into the palace, she struck the dog's back with the end of the whip. It gave a loud yelp.

The Principesa did not reappear. It was the end of the visit.

* * *

Peter remembered how he and the other two guests were escorted back to the waiting car by a silent bodyguard whose solemn face looked like a mask. But the principal and the gym teacher were cheerful and lively during the whole ride home.

"It will take a hundred years before she'll check up on us!" the principal whispered to the gym teacher. "Everybody knows that she never follows through with her projects and that she always jumps to new ones!"

These words plunged Peter into deep sadness. Could it be that the Principesa would abandon him? Could it be that it was meant only for show? He asked himself. The glimmer of hope still alive in his heart grew weaker and weaker.

As time went on he learned from the newspapers that the Principesa had prolonged her trip abroad by another six months. Upon her return, she never checked with the school or the orphanage. To make matters worse, just a few months after his visit to the palace, the principal and gym teacher bought themselves expensive foreign cars. Peter never saw a penny of the money the Principesa had intended for him.

A year later he decided to run away from the orphanage and managed to start work as a night watchman in the cemetery.

* * *

Chapter 7

From his basement Peter hears the sound of the old grandfather clock in the Dean's office striking one o'clock in the morning. He is alone now, since Florica left some time ago, very quietly, on tiptoe.

Peter is still feeling lonely and sad, but at the sound of the clock he gets up, steps out of the lab and walks down the long corridor, out of the building. He sits in the soft grass at the end of the park which surrounds the medical school. He is watching the dance of countless fireflies in the summer night. The warm fragrance of lilies and honeysuckle pervades the air. Then he lies down on his back and with half-closed eyes fancies himself turning into a firefly taking off toward heaven, higher and higher, until he reaches the Milky Way. There, he is changed into a star, peeping from above into the tiny windows of the dissection hall. When his flickering light touches the dead resting on their marble slabs it merges with their souls and guides them on their eternal journey, just like in the Egyptian Book of the Dead.

Peter stays in the garden for a long time. When he finally returns to his room he feels peaceful and tired and falls asleep right away.

* * *

It is in the beginning of September that Peter first meets Comrade Andronic, the new professor of anatomy. On that still warm and sunny morning he steps out of the dissection hall and follows the corridor which leads to the morgue of the medical school. He stops in front of the door and listens to the silence. Then he walks into the low-ceilinged room which has not been used during the entire summer. He wants to make sure the stone tables are clean, the sinks and faucets are working and draining well, and there is enough tubing and needles to inject formaldehyde into the new corpses. It is the start of the school year. In a few days the students will return, and fresh bodies have to be prepared.

It is Tuesday and he expects the truck with the transport of corpses. As he stands near the doorway he is overwhelmed by a whiff of hot, stale air mixed with pungent fumes of formaldehyde. Since the windows have been closed during the summer, the air is so suffocating that he has to step back into the corridor to catch his breath. He leaves the door open, and after a few minutes he walks in a second time and turns on the lights. Three naked bulbs hanging from the low ceiling shed a dim, yellow light over the gray stone tables and the two sinks. The workbench is hidden under piles of rubber gloves and tubing, dry cotton rags, and bottles of disinfectant solution and formaldehyde. At the far end of the room is a ramp leading to a metal door which opens onto a driveway in the back of the building where the bodies are unloaded.

With the tip of his shoe Peter pushes a dead mouse out of his way. Then he opens one of the small windows nestled under the ceiling. Soon afterwards he hears the approaching rumble of a car engine in the driveway. As he steps outside, he sees a dark van turning the corner, followed by a pack of barking dogs. The van stops near the entrance and two men jump out of the cab, waving their arms at Peter. The driver, who is the older of the two, picks up a rock and hurls it into the pack of barking dogs, cursing as loud as he can.

"Can't you poison the damned dogs? Every time I come here I have to fight them! Next time I'll bring some rat poison and feed it to them myself!" he says.

Meanwhile his assistant, who has wandered to one side of the road, is bending over a still blooming rose bush and breaks off a white blossom which he fixes behind his left ear.

"Well, you seem ready to charm the sleeping beauties!" says the driver, laughing at his own joke. He spits on the ground, rubbing the wet spot with the sole of his boot. Then they march to the back of the truck where they unlock the doors, pull out a wooden stretcher and start unloading the corpses packed on the bottom of the van, carrying them into the room.

There are eight bodies in this transport, and the men place the first three on top of three stone tables, leaving the others on the floor, near the wall.

They work quickly without saying a word, and when they are finished they wash their hands and their faces at the sink and invite Peter to join them for a drink at the *birt* down the road.

"Can't do this damned work without some booze!" grumbles the driver. "I don't know how you can stomach the fumes!"

"I'm used to it," Peter says with a shrug. He declines the invitation to join them for beer, but follows them to the truck and then watches them disappear in a thick cloud of dust. For a while he can still hear the dogs barking in the distance, and the sound of Communist marching songs played by the truck's radio.

* * *

When he goes back into the mortuary, he puts on a pair of red rubber gloves and takes a good look at the dead. Most of them are old and wrinkled, with gray hair, gray beards and hollow cheeks. There are also two very thin children whose knobby ribs are clearly visible under the skin of their sunken chests. Some of the dead are still wearing pajamas or nightgowns; others have on underwear or flowery shirts, or even their socks and their pants. Some are tightly wrapped in bedsheets, like a shroud.

Peter's attention is caught by the body of a young woman whose large belly is bulging under a thin nightgown of yellow silk. "Seven months pregnant!" he thinks as he stops at the table. For a minute he stares at the face that is tanned and at the freckles on the tip of her nose. Her arms and legs are also tanned, with lighter marks on the skin where the straps of a bathing suit had been.

What did she die of and why is she here? Peter wonders. Where did they bring her from?

Most of the corpses at the medical school come from the city morgue. Some come from the State Mental Hospital or from the TB sanatorium. A few come from the Emergency Hospital or other hospitals. They end up here if and when there isn't enough money for a burial, or if nobody claims them. But what about this young woman in her silk nightgown? Why has nobody claimed her? Where are her parents? Where is her husband? Is he still alive? Has he been arrested? And if so, is he in jail or was he deported to a forced labor camp like so many others?

The images of the Dean of the medical school, of Doctor Ana Cordescu, the Professor of Psychiatry, and of Professor Munteanu come to his mind. Nobody has heard from them since their arrest; nobody knows their whereabouts; nobody knows whether they are dead or alive. Will one of them also appear in the morgue one day?

With smooth, quick movements, almost mechanically, Peter removes the woman's nightgown and rubs her body with a disinfectant. Then he gives her a sponge bath with water and soap. But his mind is full of questions and puzzles.

The figure of Professor Munteanu haunts him, and Peter remembers him standing here in the room, hovering over the stone tables and shaking his mane of white hair. "Think of the students," he would say. "Don't waste your time poring over problems you can't solve. There is a better way: concentrate on the students. Think what a unique opportunity to examine so closely a pregnant woman and her fetus! Think that we can preserve the fetus for generation after generation of students, if we take it out of the womb and fixate it in formaldehyde! In this way the young people will be able to see all the marvelous details of its body!"

Peter remembers that only once did they succeed in obtaining a fresh fetus for their collection. The Professor himself had taken it out of the mother's womb and had opened it, so that all its organs could be seen—particularly the heart with the wall of its inner chamber not yet closed, so that the well-oxygenated blood from the mother could be pumped into all the blood vessels of the baby, allowing it to live in the womb without using its lungs.

The human fetus in the glass jar had been the pride of the department until the last year of the war, when the blast of an air raid explosion shattered it.

* * *

Bending over the woman's body Peter tries to remember the shape of the incision he needs to make in order to take out the womb with the fetus, but he isn't sure. Yes, he thinks, how easy it would be if he could ask the Professor or Mr. Bantu!

He recalls that once at the funeral parlor they had also worked on a pregnant woman who was ready to give birth, and that Mr. Bantu had wanted to show off his special skills by scooping the baby out of the womb, embalming it, and placing it next to the mother. It was a very little boy with a few soft ringlets on his head, and it made quite a commotion because he had to be christened and a priest had to be called to baptize the child before he was buried. But no priest wanted to come and baptize an unborn child at the funeral parlor. Only when they were ready to give up did they find a priest who was half drunk and willing to come to the funeral parlor and perform the baptism, on condition that the family would give him five bottles of aged *tsuică* on top of his fee!

The baby was placed in a tiny coffin padded with cushions of blue silk so that he looked like a doll in a crib.

Now in the morgue the woman's body has been washed and rinsed, and Peter is drying it with a soft cotton rag, thinking how important she is for the students. Just then Comrade Dumitru, followed by a tall young man with a small head, enters the room. The man wears thick glasses and his bulging, unblinking eyes are greenish yellow like those of a snake. His pink face is clean shaven and his small hands with clipped fingernails are red and coarse like those of a washerwoman. He wears a starched lab smock that looks stiff and new. A star-shaped medal with a golden hammer and sickle in the center—the badge of the Communist Party—is pinned to his lapel. He hobbles behind Comrade Dumitru, dragging his left foot.

"Peter, this is Comrade Andronic, the new Professor of Anatomy," says Comrade Dumitru when they stop at the table. "Comrade Andronic will replace Professor Munteanu, and you will work under his supervision. You must give him the keys to this room. We can dispense with your help here and you should feel relieved, since you didn't care to participate in our new projects anyway!" says Comrade Dumitru.

"From now on your work will be confined to the lab and the dissection halls, is that understood? And so, where are the keys?"

Comrade Dumitru has stretched out his right hand and is shaking it nervously under Peter's nose.

Peter bites his lip without saying a word. He plunges his hand in his pocket, digs out the keys and gives them to Comrade Dumitru. He then turns and walks slowly toward the door. Before leaving the room he hears Comrade Dumitru say that the body of the young pregnant woman would be the first to be transferred out, according to new Party directions.

"Let's face it. It's a rare windfall," he says. "It would be quite sinful to waste her on the students. We'll send her directly to the new lab of the Central Committee. They can use her body parts, particularly the fetus and the placenta for their special research. Then we will get our reward, as promised by the comrades! You can see for yourself, it would be a waste to keep these corpses here for the students!" Comrade Dumitru winks at Professor Andronic.

"The Party knows best," he replies. "All we must do is follow the rules."

Peter walks slowly back to his lab. His mind is drained of all thoughts and he feels faint. When he enters his room he looks around in a daze. As he catches sight of the Egyptian print of the weighing of the heart on the Grand Scale of Truth he sighs with relief. No, he says to himself, the old Jackal-Headed God Anubis would never stand by the new regulations!

* * *

One evening, sometime later, Peter sits in his lab smoking a cheap cigarette. The sharp, burning taste doesn't bother him, he likes it. He feels happy to sit quietly in the dusk and watch the blue clouds of smoke floating toward the ceiling.

The days are shorter now, but even though the sun has set beyond the trees and over the rooftops, there is still light in the basement.

Florica stands by the workbench, peeling potatoes with an old surgical scalpel. She has taken off her white blouse with red daisies and slipped on a worn smock with faded yellow polka dots she brought from home. She usually keeps it in Peter's lab, hanging from a hook near a glass cabinet filled with the collection of human hearts and brains.

While she throws the sliced potatoes into a large skillet, she is humming one of the Soviet revolutionary marches frequently played on loudspeakers all over town:

> "We will arise from the mud
> We will destroy the bourgeois enemy
> We will fight in towns and villages
> And in a triumphal march, all our barefoot heroes
> Will conquer the richest palaces..."

When she finishes with the potatoes, Florica turns to the skillet in which she has placed two thick pieces of beef, well rubbed with garlic on both sides. She got the meat from Tudor, the truck driver from the slaughterhouse, who lives close to her apartment. He sold her these parts for black market price, of course.

"These two pieces cost more than my salary for two weeks work!" She says as she greases the saucepan with the last bit of margarine scooped out of a small package of wax paper. Then she arranges everything on top of the tripod which stands over the Bunsen burner.

"I can't wait to eat beef! I've almost forgotten the taste, it's been such a long time," she adds, lighting the gas with a match and stirring the potatoes in the sizzling fat.

59

The aroma of good, frying meat mixes with the smell of Peter's cigarette and the fumes of formaldehyde. His mouth is watering. He closes his eyes and draws in the rich fragrance.

"I must say I have been lucky so far, very, very lucky indeed, because nothing has happened to me. Not like the Negreanus from across the street who have all disappeared, all five of them—two brothers, their wives, and even the ninety-year-old grandmother— after they bought some pork from Vasile, the security guard from the Politburo restaurant. An informer must have ratted on them and now they've been deported to God only knows what forced labor camp and God knows for how long!"

Florica wipes her hands on the smock with yellow polka dots and switches on the light. The naked bulb hanging from the ceiling is covered with thick, black wire to foil any attempt at thievery. Peter covers his eyes with his hand and quickly turns his head away. He always has trouble adjusting to sudden light.

"This damned meat cost me a lot of money," Florica goes on, "but I'm not worrying about the money. Comrade Dumitru and Professor Andronic have promised to raise my salary two months from now when they'll put me in charge of transcribing the minutes of all the organization's meetings. They're sending me to take a clerical course for Party members which will start next week. When I finish I'll make enough to enjoy good black market food more often, instead of being condemned to a starvation diet like all the other poor slobs!"

Peter is watching Florica grind some fresh black pepper and sprinkle a touch of red paprika over the meat. He has put down his cigarette, and the strong fragrance which now fills the room reminds him that he hasn't tasted any meat since the day Florica had brought him the "*mititei*" some time ago. It is true, he thinks, without her he would be confined to a daily diet of stale bread and cooked beans, like a prisoner locked in his cell.

"You're right," he says, "we are all condemned to a miserable fate." He has noticed a brown stain on the white surface of the work table, and tries to scratch it away with his fingernails.

"So, you see, it's not really the cost of the food I worry about," says Florica. "I'm pretty sure I can handle that. But it's the house, the damned house I'm living in, that drives me crazy! Can you imagine, sharing a kitchen and a bathroom with twelve other people? Last winter Comrade Popescu, who lives in the front room, slaughtered a pig in the bathtub after keeping it there for over a week. Can you see yourself using a bathroom with a pig staring at you from the tub and grunting loudly all day and all night, not to mention the stink and the dirt? For all we had to put up with, we expected Comrade Popescu to have at least the decency to give us some lard after he slaughtered the pig. But no! Not a chance! He sold every ounce of meat on the black market for a price you wouldn't dream anybody could pay!"

"A real bastard!" Peter is still trying to get rid of the brown stain on the table.

"And then three months later, Comrade Văleanu hid a white chicken in the bathroom. She kept it there with one foot tied to the toilet chain with a piece of string. I believe she even expected it to lay eggs on the cement floor! But one day the chicken jumped or fell into the toilet and drowned in the bowl. Maybe the string was too long or too loose, I don't know. Then old Comrade Fieraru who is a gypsy fortuneteller told her that this was a bad sign, a sign of danger. This made Comrade Văleanu too frightened to sell the bird on the black market! And since nobody in the house wanted to eat a chicken that had drowned in the toilet bowl, she had to throw it away, which was dangerous too, because of the Securitate informers who could enquire how you got a white chicken in the first place and where you got it from? So Comrade Văleanu had to wait for a moonless night and ended up burying the bird in the dead of night behind the house under a large mound of rubble and trash."

"Yes," Peter says, "poor Comrade Văleanu lost her chicken, but she was lucky not to be caught by the Securitate!" He feels like laughing at Florica's lamentations, but he makes a great effort to keep a straight face. He has finally removed the stain from the workbench and is now cleaning his fingernails with the tip of a scalpel.

Florica stares at him for a moment and shrugs. Then with the back of her hand she brushes a strand of hair from her forehead.

"Yes, you're right, but let me tell you about the kitchen. It's hell's kitchen, believe me! Whenever I walk in Comrade Maria Radin and her two daughters are there too! If I want to use the stove, they're using it already. If I go to the icebox, they are there too. They behave like those damned Western Imperialists, they occupy the whole kitchen as if it belonged only to them! They deprive me of my natural right."

Peter turns away from Florica. He can barely contain his desire to laugh. He feels sorry for her, but he finds her lengthy complaints peppered with philosophical wisdom very funny.

"You should fight for your rights! A Party member like you should never tolerate Imperialist attitudes!" he says.

Florica looks at him, feeling that he is making fun of her. She doesn't reply. She wipes the greasy knife with an old kitchen towel and starts chopping fresh parsley on an aluminum tray which lies on the table. With a fork she turns the brown slices of beef in the saucepan and tosses the finely minced leaves over them.

"But this is not all," she goes on. "There is the old fool, Comrade Dinescu's boyfriend, who always washes his dirty socks in my cooking pot! And not to forget Comrade Vlad's mother-in-law who is forever eating my food, the food I keep in the icebox or in the pantry. How the hell she always gets her hands on my provisions really beats me! Just this past Monday, only three days ago, I caught her munching a piece of fine black market salami from a package I put in the icebox to share here with you. But guess what? The old bitch had the nerve to tell me it wasn't my package at all! She said that it belonged to her, and that her sister had given it to her for her birthday! To tell you the truth, she doesn't even have a sister, and she never remembers her birthday! I don't think she even knows how old she is. But because she wanted to convince me that she was right and I was wrong, she swallowed the whole sausage, skin and all, and didn't leave a single bite for me. I wouldn't have been surprised if she had also swallowed the paper it was wrapped in! I swear to God that I wanted to strangle her with my own two hands, and I confess that every morning I feel like cutting my neighbors' throats with the kitchen knife. Or I would gladly push them down the stairs, all twelve of them, the whole caboodle, and have a good laugh watching them break their necks. I wish I knew how to get out of that crazy communal kitchen, out of that loony bin, and into an apartment of my own! I bet if we were married, Comrade Dumitru would help us find a decent apartment with a kitchen just for the two of us. I swear help comes much easier when you are married than when you are alone! But living with twelve other people is torture in hell!"

Florica turns to the shelves lining the walls and takes two large plates from under a skull. The plates don't match—one has a bright orange border while the other has small yellow and blue flowers painted on it. The first dish is larger and slightly cracked. She fills the plates with meat and potatoes and cuts several slices of dark bread with the surgical knife. Peter watches her dipping her fingers into a large jar and scooping out two cucumbers which she places near the meat. She hands him the dish with the orange border and keeps the other one for herself.

Peter has finished cleaning his fingernails and puts the scalpel on the table. Even though he is sitting next to Florica, his thoughts keep drifting away. The skillet, the meat, the potatoes, everything reminds him of the evening they feasted on *mititei*, and of the conversation they had at that time. He remembers Florica talking about a "formal" dining room with a large oak table and many chairs all around.

"What happened to your dream of a formal dining room with a sideboard and breakfront?" he asks. "That evening in the spring you talked so much about it and you were so eager to get it. What happened to that wish of yours? Did you forget about it? Did you give it up?"

Florica looks at him. She swallows her food and is ready to answer, but Peter goes on. "I mean...don't take me wrong, it's okay to cook here in the basement as long and as much as you want. But if you're still pining for that grand dining room you should probably ask Comrade Dumitru for help, or maybe Professor

Andronic. He could be helpful too, I should think, even though he's only a newcomer! But for a newcomer he is not doing badly at all. What I mean is...look at the way he always follows Comrade Dumitru around like a faithful shadow, trailing exactly two feet behind! The way he waits for him every morning in front of his office to give him the mail! It must really mean something to Comrade Dumitru to have a professor waiting on him hand and foot and following him everywhere, just like a puppy dog!"

As he is talking Peter feels anger mounting inside his chest. At the same time the image of Professor Andronic running after Comrade Dumitru like a puppy dog strikes him as so funny that he starts to laugh.

"Funny, very funny indeed!" says Florica, staring at him. "But why do you care so much about it?"

A large black fly lands on the meat in her plate, but she pays no attention to it. "Better let me tell you something, not so funny maybe, but something you should really care about. I didn't know how to tell you, but I did learn about what happened to you in the morgue. Last Friday when I made Turkish coffee for Comrade Dumitru and Professor Andronic I heard them talking about replacing you down there with somebody else. I intentionally pushed a stack of papers off the desk so that they fell on the rug and scattered so I had to pick them up and rearrange them. This allowed me to stay longer in the room and listen to them. I heard Comrade Dumitru say that you were very pigheaded and did not take his advice."

The big fly has finished its meal and is buzzing in the air loudly, circling around Florica's head. She finally notices it and chases it away with her fork.

"You see," she goes on, "this is all wrong. You must do something to change the situation. You must fight it!" She is stabbing the air with her fork. "Why don't you go to Comrade Dumitru and tell him that you have changed your mind, that you thought it over during the summer and you have now decided to join the Party? Tell him that you're ab-so-lu-te-ly ready to sign an application right now! After all, it's nothing more than a cheap piece of paper, so why make such a fuss? I bet that Comrade Dumitru will be delighted with your change of heart, and everything will be fine in the end!"

Florica puts another piece of meat in her mouth and looks at Peter, a broad smile on her face.

"By God," Peter thinks, staring at her with a feeling of dread. "My God, she really believes that all that's involved is nothing but a cheap sheet of paper! That is all she can understand outside of meat, potatoes and the black market!" He keeps looking at her, but his thoughts turn to his encounter with Comrade Dumitru, down in the morgue. He remembers standing in the middle of the room listening to the Comrade and Professor Andronic making plans for the transfer of the body of the young, pregnant woman away from the students, in return for a profitable reward. He can recall every word and can clearly see Comrade Dumitru grinning and rubbing his hands over this good deal.

Then Peter remembers Mr. Bantu's small funeral parlor surrounded by young men in green Fascist uniforms. He can hear the hard, rhythmic sound of their heavy boots on the pavement, and their songs of hate, promising death to Jews. He sees their young captain who he now recognizes by his bushy hair and ice-cold eyes, aiming his pistol at the Egyptian prints which hang on the wall, inside the embalming hall. He hears three shots reverberating in the empty space, followed by the loud noise of glass shattering. In the end, Comrade Dumitru's barking laugh. Peter sighs.

"No," he finally says, looking Florica straight in the eyes and shaking his head. "I couldn't join *them* even if I wanted to! I just cannot do that, no matter what. We have to leave it at that."

* * *

Chapter 8

Peter is hard at work in his lab on a rainy Sunday afternoon. He is surrounded by large crates and baskets filled with the long bones of the arm, the humerus, the radius, the ulna, and with collarbones and shoulder bones, all tied together in neat bundles. He has pulled all the large crates near the workbench in order to finish his work. He needs 200 bunches of bones because there are about 200 first-year students. After writing the names of the students on the labels he is busy pasting labels on the packages.

Three weeks ago he handed out the first bundles containing the long bones of the leg, the femur, the tibia and the peroneus, and even the short bones of the foot (the tarsus and the metatarsus) to the students. At that time he had marked down in his thick notebook with blue covers the names of all two hundred students. This year he had to go to the registration office himself and beg the clerk to give him the names of the new students. In the past, Professor Munteanu had always provided him with a list.

Now he is busy pasting labels on the packages and making sure that each bundle is complete and the bones are tied together. Later, if he finishes in time, he will need to check the picture of the branches of the facial nerve in the Professor's anatomy atlas. He is lucky to have the atlas since the stacks in the library are hidden behind heavy red cloth and the books are out of reach!

While he is working he hears the wind rattling the small window near the ceiling. When he raises his head he remembers that the glass is broken and sees that rainwater is trickling into the room. A small puddle has already formed on the cement floor at the foot of the table.

He has to do something. Moisture is a serious problem to be avoided at all costs! Wet bones can develop black or gray mold stains which spread to other bones. Once, a long time ago, when the faucet at the back of the room leaked, all the bones nearby turned green, as if covered with moss. None of these moldy bones could be used anymore, but getting rid of them became a big headache. Normally the bones were rotated among the students and there was no provision for the disposal of "skeletal parts." As usual, Professor Munteanu was very helpful and succeeded in having them incinerated at the city crematorium, even though no death certificate was available.

But Peter knows that he can't trust Professor Andronic or Comrade Dumitru with such a problem. He is afraid they will use even the damaged bones to their advantage, disposing of them through their connections, for the "Good of the Party," like they did with the corpse of the young pregnant woman in the morgue.

At the same time they didn't care about the rain flooding the basement. Peter had gone to Professor Andronic and complained about the crack in the window when he first noticed it a few weeks ago, but the Professor shrugged his shoulders and said it was too bad, he had no time, and there was no money available for such "luxuries" as replacing broken windows in the basement, since every penny had to be saved for the new Five Year Plan!

This is not what Professor Munteanu would have said. Peter knows for sure he would have changed the cracked glass right away. Maybe he would have even built the raised wooden platform for the crates and baskets of bones which Peter had suggested just before the Professor's arrest. It would have been the best way to protect the bones against flooding.

Peter sighs. Everything was different when the Professor was around. He pushes the bones he is working on out of his way, gets up, grabs an old rag and wipes the rainwater from the floor. It is already late and the semester is advancing rapidly, yet the students had not even finished studying the long bones of the leg! In past years when Professor Munteanu was still around they would have finished studying all the bones of the leg and the foot, as well as all the long bones of the arm, and would be getting ready to learn about the small bones of the hand. The students always had trouble with the round bones of the hand and the foot: there were so many different surfaces and they looked so complicated!

He shakes his head and chuckles when he remembers how hard it had always been for them to learn the eight bones of the hand: the scaphoid, the lunate, the triangular and the pisiform, the trapezium, the trapezoid, the capitate and the hamate. Each of them looks like a hard, bleached pebble molded by water and wind. Each has six different surfaces, some smooth and rounded, others rough and irregular, which serve to link them to other bones or to the muscles and tendons of the fingers and wrists. There was a lot to learn and remember and a lot to forget or mix up!

In the past, Professor Munteanu insisted that the students learn how to draw the bones before starting the actual dissection. This was a venerated tradition in the study of anatomy. Every day they had to sit for several hours around the gray stone tables and draw two different views of every bone from the bundle Peter had given them. The room was silent, and the Professor walked from table to table watching them draw, helping and correcting their work.

Every year he would bring an enlarged X-ray of a femur which was sectioned lengthwise. "Look at these thin layers of bone that crisscross each other like arches in a Gothic cathedral! No doubt, this femur is just like the finest cathedral ever built," the Professor said, and Peter clearly remembered the white, stony blades which met each other at perfect angles as if they were measured with compass and ruler.

In those days nothing mattered as much as drawing the skeleton. Nobody could pass the Osteology exam and go on to anatomical dissection without first completing this part of the work and having it checked and corrected by Professor Munteanu. Often some small details were either misunderstood or missed altogether, and then the drawings had to be repeated until they were perfect.

It was like an initiation into a mysterious religious order to which only a few select members were admitted!

A few years ago Peter, who thought of himself as a sort of medical student more knowledgeable and better prepared than the rest, made a set of drawings of all the bones and presented them to the Professor as an anonymous gift. He was too bashful to say they were his, but he could feel his face flushing when Professor Munteanu asked for the name of the author of this exceptional work. Peter often imagined himself as a real medical student, or even a full-blown physician or research scientist. If his school principal and gym teacher had been less greedy and more honest, and if the Principesa had been more reliable and true to her promises, he would have been able to finish his studies and become a physician or scientist!

This is ancient history now. This year everything is different. True—the students are still expected to make drawings from the bones they receive from Peter. During the anatomy classes in the dissection hall they are still seated around the stone tables with their pencils and notebooks on most afternoons. But Professor Andronic never comes to look at their work, to explain the peculiarities of this or that bone, or to correct their drawings. In his place he sends three junior assistants, medical students themselves, Dan, Mariana and Toma. Two of them, Mariana and Dan, had been Professor Munteanu's research assistants. But only Mariana takes her work with the students seriously. She had already started teaching under the Professor's supervision, and then continued to work as if he was still head of the department. Peter wishes that Mariana would take over all the seminars in the dissection hall. The days she comes in seem golden and sunny, even if the weather is stormy and the streets are drenched in rain!

He recognized Mariana's last name, Cosma, when she first came as a freshman medical student. Since then he never tired of looking at her clear blue eyes, her blonde hair, her slender figure, the dimples in her cheeks. She wore gold earrings with a small Egyptian lotus bud made of blue stone, the kind Mr. Bantu had shown him in his picture books. Also, he was struck by her resemblance to the portrait of the young woman he had seen about fourteen years earlier in the old mansion that stood at the edge of the lake. He got to know her better when, as a third-year student, she joined the small staff of the department as Professor Munteanu's junior research assistant.

After that, they all worked closely together. One day in the winter of 1948, while they were drinking tea in the Professor's office, Mariana told them that her old grandmother was forced to come and share her small student flat near the medical school, since the big house by the lake had been nationalized by the Communist government.

"Too big for a single person of *unhealthy* social descent," Mariana said. "It's okay, I am glad she is coming, but where will I put the piano? My grandmother would rather die than live without her grand piano!"

Peter remembered the discussion which followed and the decision they made to help Mariana move her bookcase and the armoire into the kitchen to make space for the grand piano in the living room.

"It was good timing," Mariana said later on, after Peter and Dan finished moving the furniture. "It was perfect timing, because *they* would have sent somebody, maybe a family with two or three kids to share my apartment, since two rooms are considered too much for a single person!"

Peter smiles as he remembers her words. He has finished about half of the labels but there are another hundred to go. Outside, the rain is pouring, much harder now than before. Driven by the wind, a few dead leaves come to rest on the windowpane. In the room, a new puddle is forming on the floor. Peter gets up and wipes it dry with an old rag, then pulls the crates of bones away from the window as far as he can.

As he sits down, he thinks of the anatomy course which is given in the auditorium. It is not the same anymore. How well he remembers Professor Munteanu's opening lecture, the first meeting between the new students and the faculty! What a celebrated event it has always been! In the round auditorium with high ceiling, the lights of the old chandelier were shining and sparkling like fireworks. The whole room was bursting with color, as the anatomical charts which hung from the walls, made one think of strange worlds waiting to be explored.

The auditorium was filled with first-year students, with the exception of the front row where the Professor's teaching and research assistants were seated. Sometimes other professors attended the opening lecture as well. Everybody wore starched, immaculate white coats which shimmered like snow.

After ten minutes of waiting Professor Munteanu walked into the room accompanied by the Dean, Professor Albu. There was a hushed silence when he climbed to the podium. His white mane of hair formed a halo of light around his large head, and even the skeleton which was hanging in front of the blackboard glowed, as if covered with silver.

Peter, who always attended Professor Munteanu's opening lecture, was sitting in his usual seat in the last row near the door. He remembered the Professor speaking freely, without notes, walking back and forth on the podium, his hands deep in the pockets of his white coat. He was describing the beginnings of scientific anatomy, more than two thousand years ago.

"It was in Egypt, in the city of Alexandria, near the Delta of the Nile, that the richest kings of the world, the Ptolemies, assembled the wisest, the most learned scholars and scientists of the time and put at their disposal everything they needed for anatomical research and dissection. Over the years the King came to build a large hall, the Museum, with special workrooms endowed with all the instruments they needed, and a rich library in which to study and write. The building was surrounded by vast gardens with shady sycamore trees and cool fountains where the wise men could wander quietly and meditate or discuss their findings with other scientists or their disciples. The King himself paid their salary in pure gold and didn't allow anybody to trouble them with trivial problems which would interfere with their work. They were to enjoy total freedom, like never before! The last hundred years before the end of the millennium were the best, most prosperous, and became known as the Golden Years of Scientific Anatomy.

"But if this period was so rich and thriving," Peter recalled the Professor saying, "we should never forget that Alexandria was part of Egypt, the land where for thousands of years, the dead were more awesome, more alive, than the living. And we should never forget that it was ancient Egypt where the great pharaohs entrusted their highest priests with the preparation of the dead for the afterlife. These high priests became the earliest embalmers and the earliest anatomists in the world!"

Peter was particularly fond of this part of the Professor's lecture. He could see himself as a young anatomist trying his hand at dissections in the Museum of Alexandria, in a quiet room with large, open windows. He was hard at work, uncovering and bringing to light new, unknown organs every day, organs which were unnamed and whose functions were shrouded in mystery. He could see himself at the end of the day, when his task was finished, strolling through the vast gardens with Professor Munteanu or Mr. Bantu and discussing the work. Would he have called the newly discovered organs by the names they were now bearing? Would he have chosen different names? And would the Professor and Mr. Bantu have agreed with his choice, or would they have thought otherwise?

Then his thoughts wandered to the high priests of the pharaohs and to their mysterious funeral rites. At this point he was tempted by the idea of offering the Professor the colored charts of ancient Egypt which he had brought from Mr. Bantu's funeral parlor so that Professor Munteanu could use them in his opening lecture. But what stopped him were the bullet holes which could not be concealed!

* * *

Chapter 9

Down in his lab Peter has almost finished pasting the labels on the bundles of bones, when he feels cold water seeping through the sole of his left shoe. "Damned window!" he grumbles, seeing that the rainwater is still pouring into the room. After he wipes the floor clean once again he pulls an empty basin from one of the shelves and jams it into the corner, under the window, hoping to collect the rainwater and prevent it from flooding the lab. He doesn't want the bones to get wet and moldy and he doesn't want to have anything to report to Professor Andronic. No, he certainly doesn't want to have a confrontation with Professor Andronic about the bones in the lab!

Peter returns to the workbench, and when it gets dark he switches the lights on. It keeps raining outside, and through the wet windowpanes he can see the dim glow of a distant street lamp.

Peter is pasting the last labels onto the bundles of bones with a quick, mechanical gesture. He thinks of the next day when Professor Andronic will be giving his first lecture. Even though it is the opening lecture of his course it is unusually late in the semester for such a beginning! Something is wrong; things have never been done this way in the past!

After he finishes preparing the bones he remembers that he hasn't eaten all day. He bends down and pulls the red cooking pot from under the table, goes to the faucet and adds fresh water to the boiled cabbage leaves which are floating near the bottom of the pot, and places it on the tripod over the Bunsen burner. He sprinkles some pepper and salt, stirs the soup with a wooden spoon, and lights the gas.

Since Florica's last visit some time ago, he hasn't tasted any meat. There is none in the stores and he has no black market connections. So he has been living on cooked beans, boiled cabbage and occasionally brussel sprouts for lunch and dinner, stale bread with pumpkin paste for breakfast.

The thought of Florica and the spicy *"mititei,"* fried potatoes and the juicy pieces of beef she used to cook for him make his mouth water and his stomach growl. For a minute he wishes she were here, with her basket of fresh bread and her big, warm bosom in which he could bury his face. But then he remembers how she insisted that he join Comrade Dumitru in his iniquitous corpse deals. "No, no," he mumbles, shaking his head, as he ladles the steaming cabbage soup into a bowl. "It isn't too bad after all!" He had enjoyed Florica's tidbits, but he can also do without.

Then he goes to bed and as he lies down and closes his eyes his mind drifts off to the Anatomy class and the lecture he will soon attend.

* * *

Next morning Peter is rushing to the auditorium early, making sure to get his usual seat. In the past, Professor Munteanu had allowed and even encouraged him to come to the lectures, particularly since he often needed his help with the anatomical demonstrations. Peter hopes that it will be the same with the new professor.

On his way to the class he keeps thinking how strange it will feel to listen to somebody else giving the lecture. He wishes that, through some miracle, Professor Munteanu would appear in the auditorium and deliver his speech.

But as soon as he opens the door to the lecture hall he realizes that he has been spinning a dream. The room is dimly lit because many lights have been removed from the chandelier in a new drive to save electricity. This campaign had been initiated by the Party authority. Now, the face and the eyes of the students, their lab coats, even the skeleton on the podium seem ghostly and colorless. The paint is peeling above the door and on the walls, near the ceiling. But what strikes Peter most of all is the bare look of the walls which have been stripped of all the colorful anatomical charts. The lecture hall looks like a deserted house after the tenants moved away, taking with them all their paintings, curtains, and rugs, leaving behind bare walls and empty floors. When he looks more closely he sees that the charts are still there. Some have been turned to the wall; others are rolled up tightly and hooked to the ceiling.

Why this strange arrangement? At first he thinks it's a mistake, and the assistants have forgotten to prepare the auditorium for the lecture. But then he remembers the library, all the foreign textbooks hidden behind a heavy red cloth in the stacks. He realizes that the anatomical charts share the same fate as the books, since they are "foreign," "capitalist" charts printed in France and imported from Paris by the Dean, Professor Albu.

His suspicion is confirmed when he arrives at his seat and looks in front of him. The blackboard is covered with a large banner inscribed with the words:

"Death to the foreign saboteurs!
Long live the Five Year Plan!"

Yes, he thinks, this is it: according to the Party line, foreign saboteurs lurk everywhere, hidden in the pages of old textbooks as well as in the drawings of anatomical charts. And what about the peeling paint on the walls, the poor lighting, the whole shabbiness of the auditorium? No one cares anymore; they all seem to have other things on their mind!

His thoughts are interrupted by Professor Andronic who walks into the room accompanied by Comrade Dumitru, Florica, and two strange men wearing gray coats and carrying leather briefcases. Peter has never seen them before. They don't belong to the teaching staff of the medical school, but since they speak with Comrade

Dumitru as if they know him well he thinks they must be Party officials who came to observe Professor Andronic's lecture. They sit in the front row of the auditorium at the foot of the stage, next to Florica and Comrade Dumitru, while the Professor climbs the few steps which lead to the podium.

This is Professor Andronic's first formal lecture. Peter is eager to hear him speak, since he learned from Florica that the Professor has taken a special fellowship at the University of Leningrad, an important achievement for a Romanian doctor.

Professor Andronic looks pale. The notes in his hands are trembling, and his left eyebrow twitches from time to time. He keeps looking at the two men with the leather briefcases. Then he looks at Florica, who is nodding, encouraging him to talk. He arranges his notes on the table, drinks a sip of water from a glass which has been placed before him, and starts to speak. In the beginning his voice is low, almost a whisper, the words difficult to hear.

He starts the lecture by reminding his audience of the "historical mission" which has been cast upon all of them, namely the mission of founding a new science of medicine, a science fit for the new Five Year Plan.

"But," says the Professor, "in addition to this historical mission, another heavy responsibility has also been placed on our shoulders. We have to be vigilant, always alert and on guard, because, in spite of our progress and our continuous successes the enemy is still watching, lurking in the dark, hiding in corners, like an invisible phantom of evil, ready to pounce, to stab us in the back. This shadowy enemy is like a pack of hungry hyenas prowling in the desert in the dead of the night."

Unlike Professor Munteanu, he doesn't walk back and forth on the podium while talking. He stands in one place, glued to the spot, reading his notes.

"As Comrade Stalin so brilliantly stated," the Professor goes on, by now his voice stronger and louder, "the further we move forward and the more successes we have, the grimmer and more embittered the survivors of the destroyed privileged classes become! And they will turn to extremes and use the most desperate means as the last resort of the doomed!"

The Professor puts his notes on the table and his pink hands whip the air, as if battling a fierce adversary. He warns the students and the comrades about the many faces of the enemy, well hidden under clever masks. "Particularly dangerous is the Western Imperialist medical science which is aimed to undermine and destroy our new Socialist science. It should be clear to everyone that those individuals who have any contact with Western science, Western publications, or with any foreigners, are embracing and helping the cause of the enemy."

The students are shifting uncomfortably in their seats. Fear and disbelief distort their features.

But when is the Professor going to start speaking about Anatomy? Peter wonders.

"It is our first duty to unmask these traitors hidden in our midst. Whoever shirks his responsibility to expose these venomous foes becomes an accomplice, guilty of treason, and will suffer the consequences of his criminal behavior!"

Professor Andronic's last words sound like a battle cry on the front.

After he finishes talking the whole auditorium remains silent for a few seconds. People move slightly away from each other in their seats, as if afraid of catching a dangerous illness. They look away from each other. Is everyone guarding a dark secret which cannot be shared?

There is a heavy silence. Then, all of a sudden, Comrade Dumitru bursts into loud, rhythmic applause, the kind Peter has heard at Communist meetings and demonstrations. The two men with leather briefcases and Florica join in, followed by the rest of the audience.

In his seat at the back of the room Peter feels angry and betrayed. He remembers the last meeting he attended in the spring, at the time of Professor Munteanu's arrest. Then too he had felt disheartened and deceived.

He gets up and walks to the door. From his corner he can slip out of the room without being seen. But before stepping out, he turns to take one last look at the podium. Professor Andronic hasn't moved from his spot. He is still staring at the two men in the front row and at Comrade Dumitru, as if waiting for a nod of approval!

* * *

Outside in the corridor, Peter takes a deep breath. Behind the closed door he can still hear the rhythmic applause in the auditorium, but he feels relieved to have escaped. He follows the long corridor toward the dissection halls. On his way he passes Professor Munteanu's former office which is now assigned to Professor Andronic. The door is not properly closed. He pushes it open and tiptoes inside.

Many things in the office have remained unchanged. The reading lamp with the green shade is still there, and so is the heavy desk, the old armchair, the bookcase and the chipped coffee mug. Even the familiar smell of Professor Munteanu's pipe is still in the air.

The silver picture frame is still near the reading lamp, but the family portrait with the white rabbit and the dachshund has been replaced by an official portrait of Lenin and Stalin wearing their Red Army uniforms. Hanging on the wall just a few inches above them is a large photograph of Pavlov with his faithful dog, Senka, on whom he had carried out his most successful experiments. Peter knows the picture well, since it is already displayed in many classrooms and labs.

While he is looking at the dog's intelligent eyes he remembers Professor Munteanu mumbling, "I can see us all turning into Pavlov's conditioned dogs controlled by buzzers and bells if we are forced to follow the Party line in thought and research!"

Peter has heard these words so clearly that he turns around, expecting to see the Professor hunched over the microscope, examining slides. But to his dismay he is alone in the room. Moreover, the old microscope has been pushed out of the way and relegated to a small table in the farthest corner of the office. Its honored place in the middle of the desk is now occupied by a life-size bust of *"Trofim Lysenko"*. His name is engraved with large letters on its chest.

What a cruel joke for Professor Munteanu to have Lysenko's bust installed smack in the middle of his desk! Wasn't he one of Lysenko's numerous geneticist-victims? How sad that it ended this way! Peter remembers that in the very beginning, soon after the war, when the Professor first learned about Lysenko, he was quite interested in his work. He read all he could find about him, and even studied Russian to be able to understand the original publications.

Lysenko's claim that he could prove the inheritance of acquired characteristics in plants and fruit trees filled the Professor with enthusiasm. "If his work is valid, we could indeed create better species of plants and fruit," the Professor had stated. And it was only after Lysenko's experiments could not be replicated by other scientists and his results proved to be fraudulent, that he lost respect for Lysenko's work.

He had long discussions which ran deep into the night with his young research assistants, Dan Brebu and Mariana, who were now being forced to "believe" in Lysenko rather than analyze his work.

"Science is simple and straightforward," said Professor Munteanu. "But if you want to be a scientist, you must use scientific methods, not political ones. Faith, mysticism belong in religion, never in science or medicine," he warned his assistants.

One day as they were having afternoon tea in the office as usual and discussing this subject, Mariana fully agreed with the Professor. Dan, however, was hesitating. He kept staring at the bottom of his tea cup and seemed very thoughtful.

Dan wanted to become a neurosurgeon. He loved surgery and neuroanatomy with a passion. He also played the piano— everybody knew that. His father, who was a priest, had been arrested last year for celebrating Christmas mass in church, though any observance of the holiday had been interdicted. His mother had taken ill after that, and there still were two younger sisters at home. How could Dan even think of going through the long, low-paying training for neurosurgery? Instead he'd have to take a position as a general practitioner when he finished medical school. And then would they allow him, the son of a political prisoner, to train for one of the very few and prestigious neurosurgical openings in the country? Peter understood Dan's painful silence.

He felt close to Mariana and Dan. They had worked together for several years and shared many memories.

Peter remembers the numerous studies and experiments they had done together in the lab, and the papers and articles in which the Professor always included their names. He thinks of the last article which was published in the United States about a year ago. Following the prodding of the Principesa who had a cousin suffering from haemophilia, the Professor got very involved with studying the genetics of the "Royal Disease," as it affected many members of European Royalty. Together with his collaborators, he was one of the first scientists who discovered that the "Royal Haemophilia" was caused by a different gene than the more common haemophilias.

The article, which bore the names of Professor Munteanu, as well as that of Mariana, Dan Brebu and Peter, was immediately published in the prestigious *American Proceedings of Genetics*, to great acclaim. The Professor was invited to make his presentation at the International Conference of Genetics in New York, where he was much acclaimed by other geneticists. The School of Medicine in Bucharest also received a lavish grant from the Rockefeller Foundation for further studies of his work.

After a week in New York, when Professor Munteanu came home, the Dean of the Medical School, Professor Albu, organized an official celebration in his honor. The Principesa was also invited, since the entire project had been started following her suggestion.

Peter, who took part at the feast, was again spellbound by the magic of her lavender eyes. In the ten years since he had last seen her, the color of her eyes had grown deeper and more mysterious. And her graceful figure had turned more elegant and youthful than he remembered. He admired her from a distance, since the

Principesa was seated on the dais, next to Professor Munteanu and to the Dean, while he, Mariana and Dan shared a table at the foot of the stage.

While the joy of this festivity was tainted by the sad memory of the Principesa having forgotten and abandoned him in the past, there was another celebration which he thoroughly relished.

This party took place at "The Golden Sturgeon," Mustafa's restaurant down the street from the school of medicine!

It was winter and very cold. The Crivăt, the icy north wind, was blowing, and it had started to snow. Mustafa, the owner, a fat Turkish man still wearing a red fez decorated with a silver crescent moon, had moved to the city from the coast of the Black Sea and opened a restaurant in this section of the town. On this evening he set a table for his guests in the low-ceilinged dining room, a hall with thick walls and small windows covered with frost.

A fire was burning in the fireplace, and storm lamps, the kind of gas lamps which are used by fishermen at sea, were fastened to the walls. Long shadows were gliding along the wooden floor and all about the room. A twelve-foot long fish, a huge sturgeon from the Black Sea, hung from the wall above the fireplace.

"It was over eight hundred years old when we caught it," Mustafa told Peter when he showed him the countless thin, black lines which covered the large fins. "These lines are believed to indicate the age of the fish," said Mustafa. "The sturgeon was caught off the coast of Balcic, right under the walls of the Royal Summer Palace." He was pointing to a picture of the Principesa sitting in the middle of a tropical garden overlooking the sea. In the background was the palace with its turrets and terraces.

But everything in the room, the tables, the chairs, the picture of the Royal Gardens and of the Principesa herself, were dwarfed by the gigantic body of the sturgeon. The fish had been glazed with varnish. Its smooth surface and round eyes made of glass beads reflected the flickering light of the gas lamps.

Near the opposite wall, the long dinner table was covered with a white, starched tablecloth. As they sat down to eat, Mustafa brought bowls of black caviar decorated with thin slices of lemon, baskets of freshly baked bread, plates of salty dried fish and several bottles of *tsuică*. To everybody's surprise, two gypsy *lăutari*, a fat one who was playing the violin and a tall, thin one playing the țambal appeared from nowhere. With their long black hair, brown skin and dark eyes, they seemed to have materialized out of the deep shadows lurking in the corners. And after settling under the large fish (as if they belonged to the same mysterious world), their backs turned toward the fireplace, they started playing their repertoire of alternating bittersweet and sad melodies. Suddenly, without warning, they burst into a fast and fiery rhythm. Everybody got up and started to dance, clapping their hands and stamping their feet. Even the two Turkish women, Mustafa's wife and her sister, who were still wearing veils and were not allowed to be seen in public, started turning and snapping their fingers in the kitchen. Their movements were revealed by the dancing shadows which appeared on the flimsy curtains that separated the dining room from the kitchen.

The dancing went on for a long time. Only when they got tired and out of breath and the musicians laid their instruments aside, did they return to their seats.

"A toast for Professor Munteanu!" shouted the Dean. "May you receive the Nobel Prize for your work, and may you take a trip around the world with your team of assistants!" He raised his glass and brought it to his lips. Everybody cheered, applauded and emptied their glasses as if on command.

How carefree and joyful they had been back then! It wasn't very long ago, maybe a little over one year, but to Peter it seems far in the past. Now, still in the office of Professor Munteanu, he turns and finds himself face to face with the bust of Lysenko. What a cruel joke, indeed!

* * *

Chapter 10

When he steps out into the corridor, Peter hears the crackling sound of the loudspeaker. He remembers that on this day many political rallies are held in the city. The sound of the loudspeaker jolts him back to the present. The voice on the radio says, "Workers from the factories Grivita Rosie and 23 August and students from the Polytechnic Institute, Law School and the School of Veterinary Medicine ask for the immediate punishment of all the enemies of the Five Year Plan. They have assembled for a large demonstration!" His words are covered by loud shouts of "Death to saboteurs! Death to the enemies of the Five Year Plan!"

Peter shudders and rushes down the corridor toward the dissection halls. A few minutes later, after a cascade of crackles, the radio stops just as suddenly as it had started.

Now he hears the shuffle of feet and muffled voices behind him. Two people are talking softly, almost whispering. He recognizes Mariana and Dan. They can't see him because they haven't reached the bend in the corridor; they have stopped just before the turn. Peter is listening to their conversation. They are speaking about Professor Andronic's lecture. Mariana is angry that he didn't say anything about anatomy.

"No reason to be disappointed," Dan is telling her. "This was a political lecture, a Marxist speech, not a scientific presentation. Professor Andronic wanted to show that he is a good Communist who follows the Party line!"

"I miss Professor Munteanu! He was such a fine lecturer!" Mariana complains.

"Shhhh!" whispers Dan, his voice barely audible. "Don't even mention his name! We're already in trouble and we don't need more aggravation. Don't you realize that? Not only have we been his close associates, but our names are on all the papers he published in the last several years, including those which appeared in American journals! I was thinking of that during the lecture, and I would do anything to have our names removed or to have those articles vanish."

Dan's voice sounds closer now, and Peter is guessing that they are walking in his direction. He is angry at Dan for not being loyal to Professor Munteanu, but at the same time he wants to see Mariana. He doesn't want to talk to Dan, but this would be a sign that he overheard their conversation. So, when they come around the corner, Peter walks toward them with his hand outstretched. To his surprise Dan backs away, frowning. He grabs Mariana's arm and drags her after him. Her cheeks turn red, but she follows him without a word, without a struggle. When she is at some distance she turns and nods at Peter.

For a minute he stands there, his hand still stretched out. It is very quiet.

Then the noise of many voices, stamping feet, and slamming doors fill the air. The lecture has ended. In the general clamor Peter can easily recognize Comrade Dumitru's laugh and Professor Andronic's high-pitched voice. The noise and footsteps are coming closer and before long Comrade Dumitru, Professor Andronic, Toma, the Secretary of the student organization, and the two Party officials appear from around the corner. They are talking about "the new medical science," about security and vigilance. When they catch up with Peter, Comrade Dumitru raises his voice and says: "The enemy is hiding among us, and we must always be on guard!" He stares at Peter with his small, suspicious eyes, then continues walking. The loudspeaker begins to crackle again.

"Death to the saboteurs! Long live the Victory over the enemy!"

Peter imagines that an enormous index finger is pointed at him. Is he the saboteur, the wrecker, the hidden enemy? Are the slogans of the workers' rally aimed at him? It is dangerous to remain here, in the corridor, a vulnerable, open target to his accusers. He wants to get back to his lab, away from the loudspeakers, away from the rallies, protected by silence and the everyday objects he knows so well: the crates of bones, the skulls on the shelves, the jars of formaldehyde. He wants to rush back to his unfinished work for the students, the bundles of bones which have to be labeled, the drawings of nerves in the anatomy atlas which have to be checked. There is still a lot to do, and he has to move quickly.

To avoid meeting with Comrade Dumitru and his group again, Peter walks down a narrow staircase and a short corridor. But half way through, the passage is closed, as the floor is being repaired.

He ignores the warning signs, leaps over the barricade and runs through the wet cement. His shoes leave ugly marks on the soft surface. The two men at work who are watching their job, are furious and curse him out. But he doesn't care. One more step and he opens the door to the dissection hall. He walks in, and sighs with relief.

The whitewashed walls, the gray stone tables, the stacks of carefully labeled bundles of bones, even the stinging fumes of formaldehyde welcome him, as if he is coming home from a long trip. Everything has a faint, friendly glow. Even the silence is music. It is peaceful and he feels safe in the basement. No waves of applause and no angry shouts from political rallies burst into the room. He cherishes these minutes of calm.

* * *

It is two o'clock when the students arrive. They all come at the same time, like a flock of noisy starlings. As usual they sit around the empty dissection tables, in front of them the bundle of bones Peter has selected for each. The students take their pencils and notebooks out of their briefcases, settle down and start to draw the bones which form the ankle articulation.

Even though neither Professor Andronic nor any of his assistants come to help or supervise them, they know what to draw. Most of them start with the big talus or the ankle bone, while a few have fallen behind and are still working on the lower extremity of the tibia and the fibula.

Peter wanders from table to table, making sure that everybody has a complete set of bones. At the last table he stops and bends down, helping a plump girl with freckled cheeks pick some of the short bones from the floor. They had rolled off her lap and now lay scattered under the chair.

"Don't drop them again!" he says, patting her on the shoulder and smiling as he puts them back on the table. Then he resumes his slow wandering through the room.

The afternoon is long and time seems to have stopped. He feels restless, impatient. The gray winter sky turns darker and darker until it reaches a deep indigo, and at four in the afternoon Peter switches on all the lights. One hour later he hears voices and footsteps outside, and when he looks through the basement window he sees Florica and Professor Andronic leaving the building. The Professor is following her with his waddling gait that makes him resemble an oversized duck. In the yellow light of the garden lamp Peter sees that they are both wearing big new, fur hats, the kind that can only be purchased at the special stores for Party officials.

Peter is glad to see them leave. He feels relieved without them. He is not envious of their new hats. He doesn't mind Florica's friendship with Professor Andronic. Only, he doesn't want to have anything to do with him.

At about seven o'clock in the evening the students get up, gather their notebooks and pencils and carefully tie their bundles of bones together. Then they wrap themselves in their threadbare coats that date from before the war. They hang around the empty dissection tables, laughing, joking, comparing their drawings, taking their time. They are in no hurry to leave.

When the last student is gone, Peter locks the door. Then he rushes to his lab, pulls a chair to the foot of the shelves, climbs on top of it, and reaches for the anatomy books he rescued from Professor Munteanu's office. He has waited all day for this moment and now he is finally able to take the books in his hands, open them and bury himself inside. He feels great satisfaction. The thought of the smooth and gleaming pages fills him with excitement, and even though he cannot understand the French words in the text, he knows that he will find the answers he seeks in the charts and the pictures. He also knows that, hidden inside the pages, he will find Professor Munteanu's knowledge and wisdom.

The two atlases are lying under a large skull that he placed there about six months ago. While he lifts the cranium, he feels it trembling and shaking as if it had a life of its own. He brings the quivering skull closer and looks inside, but in the dim light he doesn't see anything. He takes it closer to the lamp, and when he looks through the empty orbits he sees a white shadow sliding about. But only when he brings it right under the light, does he discover the little red, burning eyes staring at him. Only then does he realize that two white laboratory mice have made their nest inside the skull.

Peter is so dumbfounded by this discovery that for a moment he forgets about the anatomy books. All he can think about is an old legend Mr. Bantu told him long ago when he came back from Egypt. It is a legend about the wild white mice which live in the desert. These mice are said to gather in large numbers to dance in the moonlight! The ancient Egyptians worshipped these little creatures, Mr. Bantu told him. They made small, white earthen figures of them that they placed inside the coffins to accompany the dead in the afterlife. They were meant to bring the moonlit desert close to the dead. And those of the departed, who were lucky enough to possess the figure of a wild white mouse in their coffin, became princes in the eternally blooming desert of the afterlife.

Peter looks at the two mice that are staring at him from the bottom of the skull with their small, glowing eyes. He shakes his head and chuckles. How can he neglect these little creatures whose forebears were adored by the ancient Egyptians? He pulls the old breadbox out from under the workbench, opens the lid and takes out a stale crust of bread and a piece of cheese he was saving for breakfast. He breaks them into small crumbs by rubbing them between his thumb and index finger, then piles them in little heaps on a far corner of the table, behind the skull. He places the metal lid of a jar with a few drops of water right next to them.

After he finishes he climbs back on the stool and brings down from the shelf the two anatomy books hidden in a piece of blue velvet in which he had wrapped them.

It is quiet and peaceful in the lab. And when the old clock strikes midnight, Peter is still sitting at the table hunched over his books. In the farthest corner, near the wall, not far from the high window, the two mice have slipped out of the skull and are nibbling at their supper. Far above them, in the winter sky, the full moon peers into the room.

* * *

Chapter 11

A week before Christmas Comrade Dumitru and Professor Andronic walk into the dissection hall and stop in the middle of the room. Peter can hear them through the half open door of the lab. Comrade Dumitru has decided to have this anatomy hall decorated with posters and banners inscribed with slogans praising the victory of Communism. Also large portraits of the great leaders, Marx, Engels, Lenin and Stalin, will be part of the decoration. Comrade Dumitru and Professor Andronic are standing in the aisle between two rows of stone tables and are discussing this project.

A few days earlier a workman had been here and installed a loudspeaker in the corner of the room, right under the ceiling. When it was turned on, the room was flooded with voices and slogans. Peter turned it off as soon as the workman left.

On this Thursday morning Comrade Dumitru first turns on the loudspeaker at full blast to make sure that it works. Then, after listening for a few seconds he turns it off again so as to be able to speak. He and Professor Andronic are staring at the walls and trying to figure out how many posters, banners and pictures can fit in the hall and where to hang them. Comrade Dumitru points to various corners while Professor Andronic jots down notes.

"The Party has decided that the work should be done by the students and the whole staff of the Department on Christmas Eve and Christmas Day. I mean *everybody* will have to take part in preparing these posters and banners! All the students and the entire staff will have to cut and paste cardboard letters and photographs.

Also they'll have to hang the portraits of our great leaders on the spots we will select. This will insure that nobody has time to go to church and celebrate mass! Remember! Christmas... Religion... The opium of the masses! Well, we better concentrate on squeezing it out of the people's system!"

"Sure!" nods Professor Andronic. "If we get the students here to work on the holiday, it will help them get rid of their religious superstitions and other reactionary beliefs!"

"We can do all the work here in the dissection hall. There's plenty of room to prepare posters and banners for the entire building!"

Most of the stone tables stand empty. Only six of them are occupied by corpses, while the other fourteen are free. Peter is surprised that even this small number of bodies has reached the dissection hall despite the fact that there is no shortage of corpses in the mortuary. Even though he is not allowed to work there anymore, he knows what goes on in that room! He can hear the truck of the city morgue drive up the ramp to the back of the building and park right by the mortuary every day. He can't miss it because it is always followed by a large pack of howling dogs. The radio in the cab of the truck is usually blaring Communist marches. When the car finally stops at the gate, the three men who unload the bodies keep swearing and cursing at the top of their voices. And when they have finished, the truck drives away just as noisily as when it arrived.

After it leaves, the mortuary is gripped by a wave of frantic activity. Peter has often seen Dan Brebu, who is now working in his place in the mortuary, rushing down the corridor. If too many corpses have been delivered at once, he can hear Professor Andronic shouting nervously at him to get on with his work. "Make it snappy!" he yells after Dan. On those days Dan has a haggard look about him, his hair is disheveled, his face looks pale and is covered with perspiration, and there are bags under his eyes.

Dan always avoids Peter in the corridor and doesn't speak to him.

Then the frantic activity slows down. The next day following the arrival of the corpses, late in the evening, a large black van with shuttered windows and no headlights drives noiselessly up the narrow ramp and stops at the entrance of the mortuary. Peter has spotted a large zero on the license plate, a proof that the car belongs to the Central Committee.

Four men armed with stretchers descend silently from the van and enter the mortuary, only to return to the car and load it with corpses from the morgue. They move noiselessly, on rubber soles, like shadows of the night. Where are they taking the dead? Why are they doing this? Is the Central Committee really mixed up in this? Peter is perturbed by the mystery of this secret operation. He has observed one of the dark figures slipping money to Comrade Dumitru.

Sometimes he wonders whether it is wrong to keep watching the mortuary since he isn't allowed to work there anymore, and whether he should give up his night vigils. But he is possessed by the urge to watch, even though he cannot stop the black van from doing its work and he cannot return the stolen bodies to the students who need them!

* * *

Chapter 12

On this Thursday before Christmas, Peter is standing by the workbench checking the level of formaldehyde in a row of glass jars that are lined up in front of him, when he hears the door slam in the dissection hall. Comrade Dumitru and Professor Andronic have finished their talk and walk out of the room without saying a word to him. "They treat me like a leper!" he thinks. "Just like a leper of whom everybody is afraid, and from whom everyone is running away! Soon they'll throw rocks at me!" He sighs and buries his face in his hands. Then he returns to his work with the anatomical specimens.

In front of him are the tiniest human embryos floating in clear liquid. He examines them and marvels at the perfection of the transparent bodies which seem to be fashioned of small bits of pink, milky smoke. They look to him like thin strands of colored air trapped under glass.

He adds formaldehyde to the jars. Then he remembers that the students are coming at two. They have finished their work with the bones and are ready to start their dissection proper. But how can they do it if only a few corpses are available? He feels that it is his duty to come to their rescue and find a solution, but nothing comes to his mind.

Maybe Mariana will be here, he thinks with a glimmer of hope. She has indeed been down a couple of times to supervise the students in their work with the bones, and Peter overheard her telling them that she is going to do the dissections with them. On those days she did occasionally glance in his direction when she thought nobody was watching. But as soon as she saw him looking toward her she blushed and turned away. However, even if Mariana comes, without enough corpses for the students what can she do? The image of the empty stone tables keeps haunting him and he finds himself wondering what Professor Munteanu would do in his place?

He remembers the old anatomical pieces which had won first prize at the last International Show of Anatomy, long time ago, before the war. Peter knows that hidden away in the cellar are several perfectly dissected and preserved models of a human face, an arm, a hand, and a leg. Every muscle, every blood vessel, every nerve had been laid bare with so much skill and perfection, as if it were a piece of fine jewelry.

All the models had been dissected by Professor Munteanu, on real corpses when he was still very young. At that time, in addition to dissected pieces, anatomical models made of wax had also been imported from France and Germany. But since these pieces were too expensive for the University and so fragile that they often broke during shipment, the models dissected by the Professor were a real blessing for the department. They were, normally, displayed in tall glass cases in the corridor and every so often the formaldehyde had to be changed. But Peter hadn't seen them in a while.

Would Mariana be willing to use them with the students? Would she be interested if he found them and prepared them for her?

He gets up and, with a rusty key, he unlocks a low and narrow gate hidden in the wall behind the shelves. The door opens with a loud screech, and Peter steps into a musty alcove filled with cobwebs. There is no light here and he has to get a candle from his lab.

He feels his way carefully with the tip of his toes along the floor while he holds the candle in one hand and brushes the cobwebs out of his face with the other. It is drafty in this part of the basement. The flame of the candle flickers a few times and almost goes out.

Peter is not sure where the anatomical pieces are, but he figures since they haven't been used in some time, they must be hidden at the far end of the room. He advances, with small steps among heaps of rubbish on the floor that he can hardly distinguish in the dark. He stumbles against an old stool without a seat and bumps into a lab table with broken legs. He has to climb over a crate filled with broken bones. In the trembling light of the candle he recognizes old glass jars which still hold slices of dried organs. Then he hurts his knee against a hard surface. When he bends down to see what it is, he glimpses his own image reflected in a mirror lined with cracks. It is a ghostly sight and a bad omen!

Broken mirrors always bring bad luck! He remembers an old saying about flocks of demons that haunt these mirrors. They often choose to live in the cracks which allow them to pass into the underworld. Peter makes the sign of the cross and whispers the names of the Holy Trinity.

When he straightens up and lifts the candle he sees that he is standing in front of the glass cabinet containing the pieces he needs. He can clearly distinguish the round eye of porcelain staring at him from the dissected face. Its shiny surface reflects the flickering light, making the eye seem alive! Peter stares back and doesn't move. He hears the old grandfather clock strike twelve. He has to hurry, there is still so much to do before the students arrive!

He tries to open the cabinet, but it is locked and none of his keys fit. He goes on trying the keys but it is no use.

Time is running out. He has almost given up when he notices that one of the glass panels is partly broken and has a missing corner. This is the solution! He will break the whole front panel and lift the pieces out.

* * *

He hits and rattles the glass panel vigorously until it shatters. He pushes and pulls until the largest fragment swings free and slips in his hands. He catches it and feels a sharp pain in his palm, but he pays no attention to it and goes on with his work. Now he is finally able to reach inside the cabinet. He lifts the anatomical pieces off the shelves carefully and carries them to the lab. He has just finished lining them up on the workbench when the clock strikes one. It startles him. He will barely have time to wash them and wipe them dry. He then has to move them out to the dissection hall if they are to be seen by the students. Nobody will come to examine them here in the lab!

Peter is bending over the sink, holding a sponge under the faucet. He stares into the mirror and sees his face and hair covered with cobwebs. He looks like a ghost! He combs his hair with frantic movements and scrubs his face with a brush full of soap. When he is finished he returns to the workbench where he wipes and polishes the bell jars until they sparkle.

As he carries them out of the lab and lines them up on one of the stone tables, he imagines Mariana saying exactly what Professor Munteanu used to tell the students about the muscles of the face. She uses the same words Professor Munteanu used many years ago when both she and Dan were freshmen in this school and the Professor showed them the anatomical pieces.

"There are about twelve different muscles in the face. Most grow out of the bones and then attach themselves to the skin. Although they start out as separate muscles they don't stay that way. They end up blending together like rivers that flow into the sea. And they all work together to create the many expressions of the face; they are the muscles of expression. This one on the forehead, right under the eyebrow, is the muscle of frowning and suffering, the Corrugator. And this one at the corners of the mouth is the muscle of laughter and happiness, called the Risorius. Some of these muscles are short and narrow, but powerful indeed..."

Peter thinks that Mariana will feel excited to find the anatomical pieces lined up in the dissection hall. She will certainly feel inspired to give a fascinating lecture, a lecture that the students will never forget, just as he, Peter, had never forgotten Professor Munteanu's lecture!

He can barely wait for the students to arrive. He can't sit still and keeps rushing in and out of the lab. The time seems to pass slowly until 1:45 when they start trickling into the room. From the lab he watches the students pull their seats close to the tables and play with their dissection kits. They are like children with new Christmas toys, showing each other their sharp, gleaming scalpels. They are comparing the size and shape of their various forceps. But underneath all this activity the presence of the corpses pervades the hall with a feeling of awe.

* * *

At two o'clock sharp Peter hears footsteps in the corridor. He holds his breath, hoping to see Mariana enter the room. But to his dismay it is Comrade Dumitru, Professor Andronic and Dan who step through the door.

They walk like victors marching into a conquered land. The three men follow each other in goose step through the dissection hall, and when they reach the far end of the room they stop near the wall and turn to the students. Professor Andronic coughs a few times then steps forward.

"Comrade students," he says in a high-pitched, squeaky voice which startles everybody. "Comrades," he repeats in a lower voice. "Today as you start the anatomical dissection you will enter a new chapter in your life. A new beginning that will lead you to new accomplishments. But you should never forget that you don't stand alone in this endeavor, you must always remember that it is thanks to the struggle of thousands of workers that you are able to study medicine!"

Staring at the students with his bulging, unblinking eyes, Professor Andronic tells them that they have to be worthy of the sacrifice made by the workers and grateful for their opportunity to study medicine. He tells them that they are expected to show their thankfulness by fulfilling their duties in complete accordance with the new rules of the medical school.

Pulling at the tip of his collar with nervous fingers he tells them about the forthcoming "Christmas Meeting" and explains that it is going to be a "celebration devoted to work," and that attendance is mandatory. He gets so carried away by his words that he allows his voice to climb to a high pitch again. His excitement makes his small head look smaller than usual. When he stops talking he turns toward Comrade Dumitru for approval, just as he looked at Florica in the past.

"Yes," he goes on, "you must all be here next week, on the 24th and 25th of December. These are the iron rules of our organization and anyone who fails to obey shows contempt for the Victory of the Five Year Plan and is a saboteur!"

The students listen in silence, a blank look on their face. It feels as if everyone is drawing inward, trying to hide inside an invisible shell.

"We can begin the dissection as soon as you're all seated around the tables with cadavers, twelve students to each table. Two students can dissect the left side of the face, two students can work on the right side of the face, two students at the left arm, two students at the right arm, two students at the left leg, two at the right leg." He claps his hands several times. "Comrade Dan will teach and supervise you instead of Mariana, since she has been transferred out of the medical school. And one last thing before we get started, Comrade Dan, get rid of that junk!" he points with his chin in the direction of the anatomical pieces which Peter had lined up on their stands.

Dan steps forward to obey the Professor's orders, but Peter is faster. From the door of the lab he swoops down to the table with the anatomical pieces. He spreads his long arms out like giant wings to protect them.

"Don't touch these pieces! Don't dare touch them!"

Dan draws back in surprise, his mouth wide open, his arms hanging loose at his sides. It is very quiet in the big hall. They glare at each other. People have stopped breathing. Nobody blinks.

Finally Peter picks up one of the glass cases. "No need to worry about this, he mumbles, "I'll take care of this… junk!"

He carries the pieces back to the lab, one by one. It is only now that he feels how heavy they are, and for the first time his hands start to tremble under their weight.

* * *

When he has brought the glass cases back, he sits on his stool and buries his head in his hands. How can Professor Andronic and Dan do such a thing? How come they don't care about these wonderful models? And more than that, do they care about Mariana? Does anybody know where she is? Has she been transferred to another job? Is she still living in town? In order to remain in Bucharest one has to have a job in the city.

Or has she been arrested because somebody overheard her doubting the views of Lysenko, or saying good words about Professor Munteanu?

These days everybody has very long ears, and ears are sprouting everywhere, in the labs, in the classrooms and auditoriums, on stairs and corridors, ears glued to the walls, to the floors, to the ceiling...everybody is sporting these ears. It is either a new fashion or a sort of disease. Peter chuckles when he imagines Professor Andronic, Comrade Dumitru and Dan with long donkey ears. He remembers the story of King Midas, the legendary prince punished by Apollo by growing long donkey's ears which, out of shame, he had to hide under a cap. Only his barber knew this secret but he wasn't able to keep his mouth shut. Peter smiles as he imagines the three men trying to hide their long ears under a fool's cap. He turns around and when he sees the anatomical models lined up on the workbench he thinks again of Mariana and feels a twinge in his heart. Where is she? How can he find out about her? Whom can he ask, Comrade Dumitru? Professor Andronic? Dan? They will never answer his questions! They will hurry past him without a sign of recognition, turning their heads or giving him an icy look. But maybe Florica will answer his questions. He must approach her carefully, when nobody is around. Even so, she might laugh at him. She will guess how worried he is and make fun of him. Or she might point her finger and say, "I warned you! I told you so! Had you listened to me you could have gotten all the information you wanted and you wouldn't be in a pickle!" And then she would shrug her shoulders and walk away, without telling him anything about Mariana, as a revenge for the past!

Sitting alone in the lab he feels like the last reasonable man. On the floor above, the grandfather clock tolls four. He has to get on with his work. The anatomical pieces have to be carried back to their place. He gets up, takes hold of the cases, turns toward the back of the room, and, walking through the closet at the end of the lab he steps into the musty cellar. Searching through the dark, holding a candle in one hand and trying to avoid tripping over the rubbish on the floor. But his thoughts are with Mariana.

She has been keeping a secret diary; she mentioned it only a few weeks ago. Maybe one of the neighbors who shares her apartment found it and brought it to the Internal Police!

Peter can easily imagine the interrogation. He can see Mariana standing for hours in front of the grim officer, a naked bulb shining in her eyes while he screams at her. He is punishing her, just like Professor Munteanu had been punished before.

Peter can even see the investigator, a squat, heavyset man with round, greasy cheeks. Pounding the table with his enormous fists he is swearing at Mariana, making her eat the diary. She is choking, her mouth stuffed with paper and blackened with ink!

Had he known that Mariana was in danger, Peter would have tried to rescue her, no matter what. He would have even tried to help her escape from the city. Maybe this dark cellar beyond his lab has a hidden door or a secret opening in the wall connecting it with the maze of underground tunnels and passageways that crisscross the town and run through the country.

Mustafa, the owner of "The Golden Sturgeon" restaurant, had told him about the passageways that connect old buildings and ancient palaces within the city and all through the land. Since forgotten times people had used them to escape to the sea. One summer evening, sitting at a table in Mustafa's garden under the green vine, sipping *tsuică* and eating olives with salty dry fish, the old man told him about these dark galleries. He said they were dug many hundreds of years ago, in the time of Vlad the Impaler, as ways to escape the Turks. Secret tunnels connected his palace by the lake with an old fortress which stood on the grounds of the medical school. The passageways were dark and muddy, and some opened in hidden places onto the embankment of the lake, while others led to the park behind the fortress or under its basement. These galleries were connected to other tunnels which crisscrossed the country and ended at the sea. A friend once showed him a map of these galleries, Mustafa had said.

Peter remembers the dark tunnel by the lake, under the dock, where he found Mariana's little brother, a long time ago when he still lived at the orphanage. Surely it was the opening of one such secret passageway! He thinks of the ruins of a majestic staircase hidden under the shrubbery of the park that surrounds the medical school. Today it is only a heap of crumbling rocks overgrown with thistles and thorns. But once it was flanked by bushes of lilac and roses. Surely it must have led to the maze of underground galleries! The route through the tunnels was dangerous but if Mariana needed it, Peter was ready to try.

The first thing he had to do now, Peter thought as he finished placing the anatomical models back on their shelves, was to check the basement for a hidden trap door or a secret opening in the wall. Then he had to ask Mustafa for more details about this network of tunnels. He would certainly know how to travel in them and how to avoid getting lost. A wrong turn and just when you thought that you were well hidden under the dark crypt of an old church or inside an empty grave in the middle of a deserted cemetery you could fall into the hands of the Securitate. Peter thought that, with all these unpredictable dangers, this journey was not too different from that described in the Egyptian Book of the Dead, where the souls of the departed had to travel through the dark tunnels of the Land of Duat before being reborn into light. The long galleries of the Egyptian netherworld where fierce monsters were watching the souls of the dead and threatening to feast on their flesh, were just as dark and treacherous as the tunnels Peter was ready to cross. But in the Land of Duat, at the end of these deep gullies was the blissful rebirth into light, followed by the soul's eternal journey in the golden barque of the sun. It was not unlike climbing out of the ground at the edge of the sea. From here, he believed, a real boat could whisk them far, far away!

* * *

After a while, Peter's stomach growls. He is hungry. He feels a big hole inside. He could spend the rest of the evening dreaming about his escape with Mariana, except for the hunger! With all the events of the day, he has forgotten to eat, and now his stomach is writhing in pain. He looks under the workbench but to his dismay he finds that the breadbox is empty except for a hard crust of black bread. Only a few slices of potato are still floating at the bottom of the red cooking pot. Worse, he is totally out of cigarettes! A thorough search through the pockets of his pants and his lab smock yields nothing but a crumpled pack with loose shreds of tobacco inside. He will have to hurry to find a store still open tonight.

He slips into his winter coat, wraps his woolen scarf around his neck, puts his hat on, and counts his cash. His meager salary had been paid ten days ago and there isn't much left until the next payday. "Just enough to buy cheap Marasesti cigarettes!" he grumbles. He listens at the door before stepping out, to be sure that everybody has left. He walks quickly through the deserted corridors.

* * *

Outside it is dark and it has started to snow. A layer of ice coats the street, making it look like glass. It is very cold. Peter shivers and walks with small, careful steps, his mind still filled with plans of escape. If they could only reach the sea and find a boat, even a very small fishing boat, maybe they could set sail on the Black Sea and land in faraway Turkey! Even this is not without danger, since the sea is always patrolled by the Coast Guard.

There is no doubt, Peter will have to consult with Mustafa, not only to learn more about the tunnels and subterranean passages, but also to find more information about boats. Mustafa certainly has the right connections and information since he had boasted of helping others escape by sea. Peter will have to meet with him as soon as possible.

* * *

Walking as fast as he can Peter has just stepped off the curb when he is forced to jump back. A large black car has appeared out of nowhere. It moves very slowly, its dark windows covered with curtains. Its headlights are turned off, it looks like the black van that picks up bodies at night from the medical school mortuary. Peter shudders. He imagines the corpses lying inside, stacked up in the dark.

But where is he? Where is he going? For a moment, he feels lost. He doesn't recognize anything. Then he sees the church tower in the distance. He has walked toward Mariana's house. He is standing only one block away from her home. Lost in thought, he has forgotten to turn left at the first corner to go to the store but has instead walked straight toward her block.

What should he do now? He could still turn around, go to the store and buy bread and cigarettes. But he continues walking. In a short time he has reached Mariana's street.

It is a quiet, residential block with few lights. They are so dim as to make the street as dark as in the blackout nights during the war. An icy wind has started to blow, and Peter wraps his muffler tighter around his neck. The wind cuts through his overcoat. In the deserted street he can only hear the loud whistling of the blizzard. From time to time an icicle breaks off from a tree and falls with the sound of shattering glass.

Peter stops in front of an empty lot close to Mariana's house. A frozen snowman, leaning to one side, is standing right by the fence. The snowman wears a red "pioneer" bandana tied around its neck. Behind it the vacant yard is filled with rubble and the ruins of what had once been an elegant mansion, destroyed in an air raid during the war.

The ruins in the yard are covered with garbage and serve as shelter to packs of stray dogs. When they see Peter, they crawl out of their lair and gather around him, growling, baring their teeth, sniffing his coat, wagging their tails. They circle around him several times. But when they don't get any food, they march off, relieving themselves on the snowman, all in the same spot, making him tilt even more.

Peter stops in front of Mariana's house and asks himself what he should do? Should he ring the doorbell? He looks up at the windows and sees a dim light shining through the curtains on the third floor. Is there a shadow moving behind the draperies? He is not sure which is Mariana's window: this one, or the one above? The fourth floor is totally dark and looks deserted.

A narrow courtyard separates the house from the street. Peter stops at the gate and his attention is caught by a large, dark object propped against the fence. It looks like some prehistoric monster flanked by a broken sink and a cracked toilet bowl. He takes another step, and it is only when he comes so close as to distinguish the black and white keyboard that he recognizes Mariana's piano, more precisely her grandmother's concert piano!

It is the same piano he first saw fifteen years ago when he pulled Mariana's little brother Sandu from under the dock by the lake. The same grand piano he and Dan carried upstairs into her apartment when the grandmother's large house was nationalized by the Communist government and she was forced to move in with Mariana. Now one of the beautifully carved legs is broken, but the shiny surface of the piano still looks as smooth and polished as silk.

Why is it here? Who has thrown it out? And what about Mariana and her grandmother, where are they? Are they okay? Peter remembers the grandmother well. It is only one year since they last celebrated Christmas at Mariana's! Everybody was there, even Professor Munteanu. They had feasted on *sarmale* in *foi de vită* and *mămăligă* with *mititei*. While they were finishing their Christmas cake, the grandmother went to the piano, sat on the velvet-covered stool and started to play.

Peter admired her long fingers and graceful hands. Under their touch, the strings of the piano sounded at times light and cheerful like crystal bells, other times grave and melancholy like organ music.

Stille Nacht... Heilige Nacht... He can still hear the song in his mind. And he can smell the hot scent of melting Christmas candles blending with the fragrance of the tree. It made him think of an old pine forest.

* * *

Now, on the street, he steps forward to open the gate. He hears a noise behind him. When he turns, he stands face to face with a Securitate officer. A gun with a bayonet is pointed at him.

"Identification papers!" The officer has a commanding voice. He is a large man with broad shoulders. A big fur hat covers most of his face.

"Your papers! Hurry up!"

Peter searches frantically through his pockets.

"I don't have them!"

The officer steps closer. He looms over Peter, almost crushing him. He reeks of garlic and cheap wine.

Behind him is a black car. It has stopped at the curb. The man prods Peter toward the car with his bayonet. He slowly opens the door. All Peter can see is darkness. His knees turn to jelly. He holds onto the fence and closes his eyes.

But the sudden, high pitched squeal of a dog startles him. He opens his eyes and sees the officer kicking a small dog in the mouth.

"Damned bitch! Pissing on my new boots! I'll wring your neck with my own hands!" he screams. The dog runs away, limping and squealing.

The officer wipes the blood and piss from his boot with a white handkerchief, the gun still pointed at Peter. When he is finished, he folds the handkerchief very carefully and slips it back in his pocket. Then he turns to Peter.

"Next time you'll come with me in the van! That will teach you to run around without your papers. Now give me your name and address," he adds as he pulls a pad and pencil out of his pocket.

"Why are you here in the first place? Don't you know that this block has special restrictions?" The officer turns his head in the direction of a tall building on the other side of the street. "Only the residents of this block are allowed here, and they must carry their ID cards to prove that they live here."

While the officer writes down his notes Peter sees that the tall building is dark and its windows are protected by black curtains and metal bars. Near the entrance stands a soldier's garret, while a large banner with hammer and sickle covers the front of the house. Peter remembers that until a few months ago this was the music school where Mariana's grandmother used to give piano lessons. Now it has become one of those Party headquarters shrouded in silence and mystery.

* * *

When the officer is finished, Peter hurries away. Slipping on ice and holding onto fences and walls, he walks to the nearest corner and turns left. He soon reaches a broad avenue bordered by old chestnut trees. Their black branches are covered with snow. The street is empty, except for an occasional streetcar that trundles by with a loud clatter and screech.

He is very hungry now, and his need for a cigarette is torturing him. He reaches the tramway station and the small wooden kiosk nearby. The door is locked and the windows covered with ice. Peter has to knock several times with his bare knuckles on the glass before the man inside opens a small window just enough to take his change and give him a pack of cigarettes. Through the frozen glass he can barely make out the man's dark mustache and his woolen hat.

Peter slips the cigarettes into his coat pocket and hurries toward the far end of the block where a crowd of people are standing in line in front of a bakery. They have been waiting for some time. Snow covers their heads and shoulders. From somewhere above the crowd a loudspeaker is blaring Communist marches.

Peter finds himself standing in line behind an old man who is coughing incessantly and muttering to himself, and a young woman who is cradling a baby in her arms. The baby cries in a shrill, piercing voice. This makes people angry. They start pushing and shoving, but nobody steps out of line. They are all mesmerized by the lights inside the bakery, because as long as the lights are on, it means bread is still available and there is still hope.

Peter stands in line for about half an hour. Then, all of a sudden, the entire crowd is seized by a violent convulsion. It seems as if high voltage current has been shot into them. The lights have gone out inside the store and the heavy metal shutters are being pulled over the windows and door. The crowd is tense and ready to explode. At the head of the line, angry men shake their fists at the windows. An icicle zips through the air, whistling by Peter's car, and lands on the roof of the store with a bang. People are cursing loudly. But when several militia men armed with machine guns topped with bayonets appear from nowhere, they quickly scatter to nearby streets.

Peter walks straight ahead, unsure what direction to take. He remembers another, older bakery, only two blocks away. He continues walking and soon he sees the sign of the store.

The lights are still on but there is no line. What does this mean? Are they open? Are they still selling bread? He doesn't know what to think but his hunger pushes him ahead. Last year this bakery belonged to Nicu Brutaru, a plump, balding man with hands as big as shovels and bow-legs. Nicu used to keep the ovens burning all night baking bread, cakes and pies so that at dawn the entire neighborhood was bathed in a warm, delicious aroma. But Nicu isn't there any longer, the ovens are not used anymore, and cold loaves of bread are delivered late in the morning by trucks from the factory.

Peter learned from Florica some time ago that when the State took over the bakery they made Nicu move out from the two rooms behind the store where he lived with his wife and three daughters. They didn't even give him time to pack his belongings. Nicu became so despondent that he tried to kill himself by swallowing a bottle of rat poison. But since it was the first batch of "Socialist rat poison" and they did not know how to prepare it, it was not strong enough. In the end Nicu didn't die but only lost all his front teeth and his fingernails.

Peter tries to open the door of the store but it is locked and the woman inside waves him away. He pays no attention to her. He knocks at the window and returns to the door. He is so hungry, that he refuses to leave.

In the end, however, he must give up. He crosses the street and sits on a bench under a tree. He lights a cigarette and when he turns around and looks at the store, he sees the tall Securitate man walking in through the door. A few minutes later he steps out, a loaf of bread wrapped in a newspaper under his arm.

Peter rubs his eyes. Was this a dream? Did he fall asleep on the bench? He keeps staring across the street. No, it was not a dream! He can still see the militia man with his loaf of bread turning the corner at the end of the block.

When the officer is out of sight, Peter gets up and walks toward the tree-lined boulevard to the small kiosk by the tramway station. It is very late and the snow-covered street is deserted. But to his delight, the kiosk is still open. Behind the frozen windows, the old man has fallen asleep. He wakes up with a start when Peter knocks on the glass. But the pretzels are gone as are the popcorn and sunflower seeds. All he can still buy are dried squash seeds which he now has to eat for supper and breakfast.

* * *

Chapter 13

For days after this walk Peter is haunted by the image of the piano leaning against the fence. Sometimes, while he is labeling bundles of bones in the lab, he imagines himself again in the dark street, the Securitate officer pushing him against the wall. He hears the squealing dog and the muffled purring of the black van. He tries to chase these memories away, but when he succeeds, he finds himself worrying about Mariana and her whereabouts.

The city is full of rumors about the fate of the people who have been arrested and have disappeared. He tries to distract himself from these thoughts by concentrating on his work. Nevertheless the bad rumors and the mystery about Mariana's fate keep haunting him.

He imagines her at the end of her first interrogation. The fat investigator orders the guards to take her to a cell in the basement. It is hot and stuffy in this windowless box which is so long and narrow that she has no place to stand but must lie down on the dirty cot. As soon as the door is locked, a million bedbugs drop from the ceiling and come crawling out of the cracks in the wall, attacking her face, her eyes and her body. She is kept in this cell for days with nothing to eat but a small bowl of watery soup every morning. Finally, they take her out for another interrogation. Now they keep her standing for many hours in front of the officer's desk. When she faints they bring her back to consciousness by pouring ice water over her face. Peter has heard rumors about these kinds of torture. They fill him with horror.

It is also said that women prisoners are forced to stand naked for a long time while the prison guards walk by, insulting them, calling them names like "slut," "dirty bitch," or "rotten whore." Sometimes officers make the women kneel on the floor and then spit or urinate in their faces. Peter knows that they are not allowed to rape or fondle the prisoners. Any Securitate agent would be shot on the spot for such lewdness! But he can torture and humiliate the women and their families as much as he pleases. Such things could be happening to Mariana!

At night similar thoughts keep him awake. He once learned about a device, a sort of metal box in which the arrested person has to put his hand. This trap is lined with sharp iron claws which dig into each fingertip. Peter is haunted by the fear of Mariana having her hand locked inside this box while the pointed hooks pull her fingernails out slowly, methodically, one by one. After that she would never play the piano again.

She will have to sign a "confession." And if she keeps refusing to sign the declaration which the investigator has typed out for her, or if she is unwilling to give him the names of other "accomplices," he will go further, torturing her with other devices. One popular instrument is a metal ring which is screwed so tightly around her head that she will black out from the pain.

"These are old techniques and devices from the years of Fascism, just as many of the guards and investigators are left in place from the Fascist era," Mustafa told him. "They are good at what they do, 'experts' who know their jobs well. They need no further training." Mustafa knows what he is talking about. Some of these men had been patrons at his restaurant.

So, one sleepless night, after tossing and turning, when he couldn't stand it any longer, Peter gets up. Staring at the dim street light across the road, he decides to go to Mustafa and ask him for help. Maybe Mariana has not been arrested after all; maybe she has only been transferred out of the city and had no time to take the piano with her! Mustafa should be able to give him some information or advice. He has never let him down in the past. Peter gets dressed quickly and runs out into the night.

It is very late. An icy wind is blowing in his face and it is still snowing, but he feels relieved. It is good to get out and take action. Peter can barely wait to speak to Mustafa.

While walking through the snow-covered streets he thinks of the many evenings he has spent at the restaurant with Professor Munteanu, Mariana and Dan. They always sat at the same table, facing the wall on which Mustafa's sturgeon was displayed like a trophy! It was twelve feet long, 800 years old, and it was caught by Mustafa's great-grandfather, off the coast of Balcic, in the Black Sea. But to his real friends, Mustafa confided in secret that the fish had been caught in the Danube Delta, not in the sea.

"Because it was so big and so old everybody thought it was the ghost or the soul of the Danube River itself. It must have been charmed and endowed with great magic power since it brought abundant riches to my great-grandfather when he was a young man. The Sultan appointed him to an important position at his palace in Istanbul." Mustafa lowered his voice, "The sturgeon is charmed; it has secret powers. It can bring good luck or bad! It is my priceless treasure, my greatest possession! We can't make it angry; we must treat it with great veneration!" Mustafa looked at the fish with fear and awe. "We must always strive to keep it content!"

Peter had seen Mustafa making a libation of wine and offerings of mussels and small fish to the sturgeon at the time of the new moon.

* * *

Peter hurries through the cobbled streets covered with snow that run among grand old houses, their broken windows replaced with cardboard and plywood. He hurries along sleepy gardens with old trees which were once part of the park where the medical school now stands. He passes Mustafa's outdoor restaurant with its wooden fence interlaced with a snow-covered vine. He stops at the main entrance door under the glittering sign of the Golden Sturgeon.

He expected to find the door to the restaurant wide open, the dining room lit by many gleaming oil lamps, the entire place filled with laughter and music. But the house is shrouded in silence and darkness, the front door locked with a padlock. He walks around the building to the back of the house and sees a dim light through the kitchen window. He has to knock several times at the narrow back door until a veiled woman, Mustafa's wife, opens it slightly. When she sees him, she throws up her hands, bursts into loud wailing and flees inside the house. Peter follows her into the kitchen. He stares at the empty shelves lining the walls and at the pots and pans gathered on the floor and tied into three large bundles. As he stands in the middle of the room, Ali, Mustafa's eighteen-year-old son comes to meet him. He looks pale and drawn, with dark circles under his eyes.

Ali takes Peter into the dining room where the familiar smell of stale wine, smoked fish, sour pickles and cheap cigarettes hits him. The room is in shambles, with upturned chairs, broken ashtrays. Pieces of glass from a broken mirror and shattered storm lamps are strewn over the floor.

On the wall where the sturgeon used to be, only the large tail and the end of the spine, still covered with varnished skin, can be seen. The pieces are dangling from the iron chain which had supported the fish. Everything else lies scattered on the floor, the giant sea monster now reduced to three dozen large, snow white vertebrae, several ribs, and long strips of skin studded with flat, bony plates. Everything is mixed up with sand, wood shavings and tow which had been packed inside the belly of the fish.

"All this is from two days ago when they came and took my father away... He hasn't come back and we don't know where he is!" Ali raises his voice over his mother's wailing.

"How...how did this happen?"

"They came late, at about two or three in the morning. I don't remember how many there were. We were asleep. There was a pounding at the door and when my father opened it, they rushed in and demanded his gold coins and foreign currency. My father told them that he didn't have any, that he had given all his gold coins to the Central Bank at the time of the money reform in 1947. He didn't have anything left. But they didn't believe him. They threatened to search the whole house and destroy everything in their way. One of them, a tall fellow with square shoulders, big nose and a red scar on his cheek started smashing the crockery on the shelves and the tables and the kerosene lamps on the window sill. Two others opened the closet, the chests of drawers and threw everything on the floor.

They pushed my father in a corner. He kept quiet, but when they started poking the sturgeon, asking what was hidden inside, he threw himself in front of them and yelled, "Kill me, beat me, but don't touch the fish!" This made them so angry that they started jabbing and hitting the sturgeon madly with the butts of their guns...They hacked it to pieces with their bayonets, as if it were the devil himself. They were particularly hard on its head, screaming that surely there was something hidden inside! They kept hitting and poking it until they shattered the skull and gouged out the eyes!"

Ali's words are interrupted by loud weeping and sobbing which comes from the kitchen.

While staring at the remains of the sturgeon, Peter sees a few red stains on the wall near the tail.

"What is this? Did they hit your father?"

"I don't know...there was such a commotion. My mother kept screaming and crying hysterically, and that's when they herded us inside the kitchen and closed the door. I couldn't see anything but I could still hear the awful noise of things being broken and smashed. Later they grabbed my father and pushed him, and I could hear the sound of his head being knocked against the wall. He must have gotten cut by the hooks that supported the sturgeon!"

"My God!" says Peter. "How terrible! What then?"

He keeps staring at the red stains on the wall near the tail of the fish.

"Later, I managed to sneak into the pantry and peep through the window. They had blindfolded my father, tied his hands behind his back, and they were pushing him toward the van. Near the curb he slipped on the ice and fell. In the morning there was blood on the pavement. It's hidden now under the snow."

For a while nobody speaks. The silence of the room is broken only by the howling of the north wind in the hollow chimney and by the weeping of Ali's mother in the kitchen. Ali bends down and picks up the sturgeon's glass eyes and a spool-shaped vertebra.

"My father loved this fish." He smoothes the pieces with his fingers. "He believed that it was protecting him and bringing him luck. He called it his priceless treasure. Maybe people thought that a real treasure was hidden inside when they heard him speaking like this."

A whiff of cold air blows through the chimney, the oil lamp flickers and sends trembling shadows over the walls and ceiling. Suddenly the door flies open as if pushed by an invisible hand, and then slams shut with a bang. Peter shudders. He turns toward Ali who is still stroking the pieces in his hand.

"My mother and I must leave the house in two days since it is being sealed by the Securitate," said Ali. He stops and looks at the glass eye. Then he gives it to Peter.

"Here, take this with you. A small token from my father's treasure. Maybe it will protect you and bring you luck!"

Peter buries his fists in his pockets, shakes his head and is ready to say no. But when he meets Ali's mournful eyes, he swallows his words. Instead he takes the glass eye. Then he says goodbye and leaves the house without looking back.

* * *

It is dark and still very cold outside. Peter looks up into the black, whirling sky with its heavy clouds, ready to engulf everything. There is no trace of the moon, and the stars seem to have disappeared forever into the dark whirlpool. Peter sighs. As he wades through the snow, he thinks of the fish with its broken body and crushed skull. It feels like having witnessed an execution. He worries about Mariana and Mustafa. They have both vanished in the deep gullies of a bureaucratic maze which is more frightening than the darkest passageway in the Land of the Dead.

He too feels lost and powerless in this strange world. He doesn't know how to find Mariana and rescue her. With the tip of his finger he touches the glass eye in his pocket. It makes him think of Mustafa's love for the sturgeon. "My priceless, my precious treasure!" He tightens his grip around the glass piece as if trying to squeeze magic power out of it.

* * *

When he finally reaches home he is so exhausted that he falls into a deep sleep. The next day his worries about Mariana return and torment him as before. Sometimes he stares at the sturgeon's glass eye as if waiting for help. He is obsessed with the need to ask somebody about her. But who? The only person he can think of is Dan. He must know what happened to her or where she is.

On the day he decides to talk to Dan, Peter watches him from the moment he walks through the door in the morning and takes off his hat. As the hours go by he worries that Dan, who has a bad cold, will leave before the end of the day. He wants to wait until everybody has left, for he knows that Dan won't talk about Mariana when other people are around. And he is relieved to see Dan still sitting on his stool half an hour after the others have left. His back is turned toward the door and he is cleaning his dissection instruments. From time to time he is shaken by a violent cough.

Peter walks toward Dan slowly, afraid to make any noise. When he reaches the table he stops for a moment. He is so close to Dan, he can hear the wheezing inside his chest.

"Working hard?" he says, leaning over the chair.

Dan doesn't answer. He goes on cleaning and polishing his instruments. Peter can't stop himself any more. He asks Dan about Mariana, her fate and whereabouts.

"You must know where she is and what's happened to her. Is she free? Is she okay?"

Dan still doesn't answer. He goes on with his work without raising his eyes. After a while he puts down the scalpels and the forceps, gathers them in their case and says, without looking at Peter, "I don't know whom you're talking about. I have never heard this name in my life." He gets up, slips his instrument case into his bag and walks out without looking back.

Peter is left standing there. He stares at the door. He finds himself listening to the silence and holding his breath as if waiting for a miracle.

* * *

Chapter 14

A few days later he wakes up very early. It is dark outside and the street lamps are still burning. It is snowing and Peter can see the large snowflakes being blown into the windowpane and melting as they touch the glass.

The blizzard hasn't stopped in more than a week, and the city is buried under a thick blanket of snow. It is just like ten years ago when Professor Munteanu offered him a cot in the lab. Then too everything was covered with snow, and there were rumors about hungry wolves roaming the streets at the edge of the city. One night a neighbor was attacked by a pack of wolves, and it was after that incident that Professor Munteanu allowed Peter to move into the lab.

Now there are other rumors. People in line at the bakery were saying that a pack of wolves had attacked a funeral procession on the way to the cemetery, right in front of Mr. Bantu's mortuary. Everybody ran away, they said, leaving only the dead in the hearse, prey to the wolves. But others claimed that several relatives had been trampled in the commotion and were left lying there in the snow. Nobody knows for sure what really happened.

The man in the cigarette kiosk tells Peter that in another part of the city hungry wolves had broken into a gypsy hut and eaten a little girl. "Nothing but a pair of red slippers and a few small bones were left," he said, shaking his head and making the sign of the cross.

At night the people in that neighborhood are building fires out of wooden fences and broken furniture, hoping to scare the marauders away. But the fires don't frighten them and the wolves still roam the streets and howl under their windows!

Peter knows how scared the people must feel. He is glad that he can sleep in a warm, safe place and doesn't have to worry about wolves. He thinks about Professor Munteanu and thanks him for giving him a bed in the lab.

He closes his eyes and, as soon as he drifts back to sleep, Mariana's image comes to his mind. He sees himself sitting at the table in her apartment, next to the Christmas tree, while her grandmother plays the piano under the flickering lights.

It dawns on him that it is Christmas Eve right now. Half asleep he tries to listen for the church bells which always chime on holidays. But all he can hear is the grandfather clock sounding seven, followed by the crackling noises of the loudspeaker in the dissection hall. It reminds him that everything is different now. There is no more Christmas celebration and no more tolling of bells! As a matter of fact, many churches are closed and many large bells have been taken down from the towers and have been melted, to be turned into machines for the new factories of the Five Year Plan.

High above the clouds the empty bell towers have become nesting nooks for eagles and hawks, whose shrieks he can hear in the night. One moonlit night he had even seen a large bird swooping down from a church tower, landing in a nearby courtyard and flying back to the bell tower with a chicken in its claws.

Peter pulls the covers over his head. He knows it is time to get up and get dressed but he wants to stay in bed and sleep, as one does on holidays. Memories of Christmas past haunt him, and he starts humming a Christmas carol he learned as a schoolboy. It is an old song about the three Magi and the Star of the East:

> "The Star rises in the sky
> Like a great mystery
> The Star glitters and shines and makes known to the world
> That today the pure
> And Immaculate Virgin
> Has given birth to the Messiah..."

He had sung this song when he was caroling with other children. Three of them were dressed like the Kings of the East in shiny red, blue and green paper costumes with silver paper crowns on their heads. The fourth was carrying a large golden star fastened to the end of a wooden stick.

They went caroling from door to door on icy winter nights, and people gave them nuts, apples, candies and sometimes a few pennies. In the last years Peter always gave the children a few pennies or nuts. But this year he hasn't seen any children around. At the breadline he heard rumors that it was forbidden to sing Christmas songs and that only a few days ago the Securitate officers had caught some young carolers and had driven them away in their van. But first they broke the golden star and ripped their costumes. Yes, Peter sighed, it seems to be the end of all the Christmas songs.

* * *

The loudspeaker is turned on in the dissection hall, and Peter can clearly hear the words of a Communist marching song:

> "We will arise from the mud
> We will destroy the bourgeois enemy
> We will fight in towns and villages..."

The voice of Comrade Dumitru covers the singing. "Move this junk out of the way! Have you finished yet?"

Peter remembers him saying that this Christmas had to be celebrated with "special work" here at the medical school. The entire dissection hall was to be decorated with banners, portraits and slogans in praise of the Five Year Plan!

Slowly and grudgingly Peter crawls out of bed and goes to the sink where he washes his face and brushes his teeth. Then he boils water over the Bunsen burner for his ersatz tea, and after he gets dressed, he slips his lab coat over his sweater and pants. Then, while he washes down a slice of bread with the hot, sweet liquid, he slips his left hand into the pocket of his smock and pulls out the two sleepy mice. They sometimes slide out of their nest in the skull, and snuggle inside the pocket of his smock. He puts them on the table and gives them a few crumbs of bread and cheese from his plate. They eat quickly, standing on their hind legs and holding the crumbs in their forepaws.

Peter watches them. They are his closest friends and will never betray him. He remembers Mr. Bantu saying that their ancestors, who lived in the ancient Egyptian desert, knew many secrets about the world of the dead!

He gives them a few more crumbs and, when they finish eating, he slides them back inside the skull which rests on the table. Then he locks the bread and cheese back in the tin box under the workbench.

While he is cleaning up, the two mice climb out of the skull and run back to him, pulling themselves up and clinging to the folds of his smock.

"No, no! You stay here!" he says, gently detaching their sharp claws which are hooked in his coat. "You have no business running around and getting in trouble!" He cradles them in the palm of his hand and then puts them back in the skull. At first they try to climb out again, but in the end they hunker down and stay in their home.

* * *

When Peter finally steps into the dissection hall, Comrade Dumitru and Dan are standing at opposite ends of a stone table. The partly dissected body of a tall woman with a large belly and enormous breasts rests on the table. Her skin has been cut open and peeled away from her face, throat, arms and legs, laying bare the red flesh of her muscles speckled with fat.

The two men are trying to lift her off the table by pulling and pushing her around. It makes the flaps of her loose skin swing about like bits of old rags.

"Come on, help us lift this sack of potatoes!" orders Comrade Dumitru. "She's as heavy as if she were full of rocks! Come quickly, we need all the tables for work!"

Peter grabs the woman's feet, Dan supports her head and shoulders, and when they have caught hold of her firmly, Comrade Dumitru makes them carry her to the far end of the room. As they lift her, Peter notices that the tendons of her left hand had been partly cut at the wrist, and that her hand is now dangling in mid-air and swinging to and fro with every move.

They are going to place the woman's body on top of a few other corpses which are lying there in a disorderly pile, discarded from their stone tables. Their dissected arms and legs are sticking out from the pile and their loose flaps of skin spread on the floor.

As they drag the woman through the room they knock her left hand against a table. It comes loose at the wrist and falls. Comrade Dumitru bends down, picks it up and tosses it onto the heap.

After they finish with the woman they lift a few more bodies and carry them to the pile, until all the tables are free. The mound of corpses on the floor is growing taller and the bodies are starting to slip. The last one, a young woman with a thick braid of dark hair, rolls off the top of the mound and comes to rest on the floor.

"Damn!" swears Comrade Dumitru as he grabs her by the hair, lifts her slightly and kicks her out of the way. The dull sound of a cracking skull accompanies his movement. "Damned bitch!" he swears again, making sure with his shoe that the body is stable enough so as not to slide down again. "Now go clean the tables, and quickly!" He grabs Peter by the shoulders and pushes him toward the middle of the room.

Peter takes a few steps and stops at the nearest table. He washes it first with a sponge, then wipes it dry with a flannel rag. He goes to the next table and polishes it until it sparkles. But he keeps turning back to glance at the corpses. He shakes his head. He thinks that Comrade Dumitru's heart would never pass the ancient Egyptian test of the feather: his heart is probably no lighter than the heart of the tomb robbers who plundered the old graves of the pharaohs. And when he stares at the pile of corpses which look like a heap of skinned animals covered with rags, he wishes to rearrange them in a more respectful manner.

But he can't even get close to the corpses. Comrade Dumitru is chasing him from table to table.

"Hurry up! Damn it! Don't dawdle!"

* * *

He is still busy wiping the tables in the dissection hall when the students arrive. Even though they have left their snow covered coats and boots in the corridor, they bring with them a whiff of cold air. They are blowing into their red hands and stamping their frozen feet.

"We will turn into Siberia and spring will never come!" says a boy with curly hair and a very red nose.

"Last night the pipes froze and then burst in the kitchen. It drowned all the roaches!" says a freckled girl who sits next to him.

"So you're safe now. A good way to get rid of vermin!"

The students snicker as they settle around the tables.

* * *

Florica and Professor Andronic are next to arrive, both wearing their new fur hats from the special store for Party officials. Florica walks in first with stiff little steps and looks away from Peter. Professor Andronic follows, dragging his foot. He also turns his head when he sees Peter.

On a table nearby, two students have built a tiny snowman out of snowballs. It has small black eyes, made from the tips of two matches. But Professor Andronic leans on the table and flattens the snowman with the palm of his hand.

"Damn!" says one of the students under his breath. The Professor stares at him with his yellow snake eyes, but doesn't say anything.

More students and staff come into the room, shivering, blowing into their hands. After a while it grows warm and steamy. Peter's eyes start to tear and itch from the fumes of formaldehyde. He rubs his eyelids with an old handkerchief, and when he opens his eyes he is startled, thinking for a moment that Mariana is standing next to him. His heart is beating fast and the blood rushes to his face. But when the girl turns around he sees that he is mistaken. Only her blonde hair and brown sweater resemble Mariana's.

People are gathering inside the dissection hall, milling around the stone tables and whispering in hushed tones, as if in church. The wooden stools screech as they are pushed and pulled over the wet floor. Everybody is trying to settle down.

When the room is filled with students and staff, Comrade Dumitru orders Dan to lock the doors. Then he walks quickly to the front of the dissection hall. His boots pound the floor with military authority. The party medals fastened to his smock knock into each other with a metallic click. Each medal displays the portrait of a Communist leader—Lenin, Stalin, Marx and Engels—and the colorful ribbons with which they are attached make them look like military decorations.

Comrade Dumitru stops at the front of the room and passes around three lists of names which everybody has to sign as proof of attendance. Then, standing straight and holding his chin high, he looks over the crowd with the air of a victorious general.

He is flanked on each side by a large slab of black marble cemented onto the wall. Both plaques are engraved with gold letters but their content is different. The slab on the right lists the names of all the doctors who died while caring for their patients, during the epidemics of cholera, typhus, and poliomyelitis. It is a tribute to the recent generation of physicians and to their predecessors who taught them the art of healing. Peter knows that the names of Mariana's grandfather and Professor Munteanu's oldest brother are listed there.

The slab on the left is taller and wider than the first, and the letters are larger and bolder. It displays several passages from the Hippocratic Oath.

Comrade Dumitru is scratching his ear with his long fingernail and steps forward, blocking Peter's view of the marble plaques. Then he coughs a few times and claps his hands.

"Comrades!" he says. The room is silent. "Comrades, we are here today to celebrate the end of the old, bourgeois holidays and the dawn of a new era. The old holidays are dead for good and the new, revolutionary days—our new holidays—have arrived. Now we must devote all our efforts to the success of the Five Year Plan and to the liquidation of our Imperialist enemies. It is our first duty to show our commitment to the Socialist victory by decorating this room with revolutionary posters and banners, and by covering the walls with the portraits of our great leaders." He makes a sweeping gesture as if inviting the cherished leaders into the room.

He stops, wipes his face with his sleeve, and unbuttons his collar "We also have the privilege of preparing decorations for two other enterprises, the factory 'The Red Tractor' and the State Bakery 'The New Dawn'. But before we start working we have to organize several work teams which will compete with each other in a Socialist race, just like the comrades are now competing in our factories. Winning this contest will be proof of your commitment to the victory of the Five Year Plan and of your vigilance against saboteurs. The names of the winners will be displayed on our Honor Panel." He points to a large piece of cardboard which is propped against a wooden ladder. "Their names will also be passed onto our leadership who will honor them as Heroes of Labor, a great distinction in our new society. The winning team will be entrusted with a very special task, which will be announced later. Those who sabotage and interfere with our work will be punished and treated like foes of the plan." He shakes his fist at an invisible traitor.

For a moment nobody speaks. Comrade Dumitru stares in front of him with his cold, piercing eyes. Then he pulls a bunch of papers out of his pocket and starts reading the list of work teams in a monotonous drone. He stamps his foot every time he pronounces a new name.

Peter watches his boot hitting the floor and notices a small object lying nearby. It looks like a piece of wood, a stick or a pen, but soon he sees that it is a short finger with pale skin and a black fingernail. It is still wearing a thin silver ring, probably a new Communist wedding band, since the use of gold has been prohibited. It may have belonged to the fat woman whose hand had fallen off when they moved her away from the table. Peter wants to step forward, pick up the finger, wrap it in soft gauze or at least in a clean handkerchief, take it to the end of the room and place it on the heap where the corpses are resting. He steps out of line to reach for the finger when the voice of Comrade Dumitru brings him back to attention.

"Ana Marinescu...George Nicolau...Comrade Vasile Ionescu..." There is no end to it. As he goes on reading Comrade Dumitru slowly turns around and, without being aware of it, kicks the ring finger under the table. Then he stops moving, propping himself in front of the left marble plaque.

Peter stares beyond him at the large black slab inscribed with the Hippocratic Oath and, in his mind, the voice of Comrade Dumitru fades away and is replaced by the voice of Professor Munteanu reading the oath. He always read the oath to the freshmen students at the start of the year, making sure that they understood this testimony which, since ancient times, had bound all physicians into a covenant of honesty and devotion to both their patients and their disciples.

"I swear to Apollo the Physician, to Aesculapius, to Hygeia and to all the Gods and Goddesses that I shall fulfill, to the best of my ability and judgment, this Oath and Covenant. I will hold my teachers in as great respect as my parents, and I will be deeply devoted to my patients and students..."

When he comes to these words, Peter wonders what kind of physicians will these young people be, trained as they are to give more respect to empty rituals and phony Party directions than to the study of anatomy? How will they learn to cure future epidemics and commit themselves to their patients and students? He shakes his head, and goes on reading the oath.

"In accordance with my power and judgment, I promise to use my medical knowledge for the benefit of those that suffer—as judged by myself to be fair—and I swear to avoid doing them any harm or injustice...

"I promise to keep my life and art pure and immaculate, but if I ever transgress and commit perjury, I swear that I will take the punishment which I deserve."

Peter remembers that Professor Munteanu loved to tell stories about Hippocrates of Kos, the Father of Modern Medicine. He was the first to separate medicine from religion and to state that diseases were not punishments inflicted by the gods, but conditions which developed due to natural, not supernatural or divine causes. His methods of diagnosis and treatment were based on careful observation of the symptoms of the patient, not on religious superstitions or magic. But while he had many followers among students and fellow physicians, the authorities in power, who still cultivated the old religious beliefs, persecuted him and gave him a twenty-year prison sentence. There are also stories, true or false— nobody can tell—that he was banned from the island for some time.

Nevertheless, one of the most important monuments of Kos is the Tree of Hippocrates, a gigantic plane tree with a crown diameter of 12 meters, which is said to be more than 2000 years old, and under which the wise physician used to sit and lecture his students.

About twenty years ago, when Professor Munteanu and the Dean of the Medical School, Professor Albu visited the Island of Kos, they brought back a small cutting from the tree. They planted it in the garden of the Medical School, by the entrance. The cutting took root and grew into a tall and beautiful plane tree. Over the years, a nightingale built a nest in its branches. On many summer nights Peter sat under the tree and listened to its wonderful songs.

But not long ago, after the arrest of the Dean, the tree was cut down by order of the Party and a statue of Lysenko was erected in its place. In his mind, Peter can hear Professor Munteanu saying: "We're going back to the old superstitions instead of pursuing scientific advancement! Medicine is turning into a cult dominated by a mortal and fraudulent God!"

* * *

Suddenly loud applause shakes the dissection hall. Comrade Dumitru has finished reading the list of the work teams and is folding the papers he holds in his hands.

Now everybody in the room is moving around. People are getting up and joining their work teams. Peter stands motionless while students bump into him. Who is his team leader? To what group does he belong? Who should he ask? He takes a step toward Florica, hesitates, then turns and walks slowly toward Lucia, the blonde student he had mistaken for Mariana. But he changes his mind again and stops before reaching her.

He feels a tap on his shoulder.

"Hey, come with me! Don't just stand there and do nothing! I need you quickly. You're on my team and we have no time to waste!"

Peter turns around and finds himself face to face with Toma, the Secretary of the Communist Youth Organization. He is looking at him with large, round eyes. Everything about him is round, his eyes, his face, his belly, and he is always chewing something, popcorn or a piece of pretzel, a gluey "*covrig*," or sucking on a hard candy.

Toma became a Junior Anatomy Assistant after Professor Andronic joined the department. But he rarely comes to the dissection hall. Peter remembers him better from the day he and Dan were packing Professor Munteanu's books in his office after the Professor's arrest. He also remembers Toma walking into the library with Comrade Dumitru after Mayday parade, loaded with posters portraits, and slogans.

"Come on. We have to get going!"

"Where to?"

Toma grabs Peter's arm and pulls him toward the far end of the dissection hall, where his team of twelve students and technicians have gathered. Lucia, the blonde student who resembles Mariana, is on the same team.

They are crowding around two stone tables piled with sheets of white cardboard and scissors.

Toma divides his team into four groups of three, assigning a leader to each of them. He distributes the cardboard and scissors among them, telling them to start work immediately.

"Begin by drawing the letters on the cardboard, then cut them out, and we will paste them on the red canvas I'll bring you," he says. He pulls a crumpled piece of paper out of his pocket and unfolds it on the table.

"Here are the slogans we have to make. I will read them and give you the measurements. All group leaders please write down the words:

> Long live the Victory of the Five Year Plan!
> Death to saboteurs!
> Long live the heroes of labor!
> Long live the workers from the factory, The Red Tractor!
> Long live the workers from the State Bakery, The New Dawn!
> Glory to our Great Leaders!
> Victory in the struggle against Imperialism!
> Victory in the struggle for higher productivity!
> Long live the Romanian-Soviet friendship!
> Glory to Comrade Stalin!

When he has finished reading, Toma folds the paper and slips it back into his pocket.

"Two more things," he adds, clearing his voice. "Each of you has a special assignment. The group of Comrade Bălan will draw and cut letters from A to F, the group of Comrade Popa the letters from G to L, the group of Comrade Radian the letters from M to R, and the group of Comrade Valente the letters from S to Z. As you finish cutting the letters, Peter and Lucia will assemble them for pasting on the canvas I'll bring you. In addition we have to make three banners of each kind, one for us, one for the factory 'The Red Tractor' and one for the State Bakery, 'The New Dawn', as Comrade Dumitru has mentioned. Now go to work. I will make sure that you have everything you need in due time."

Toma rubs his chubby hands as if he had closed a good deal. Then he turns toward Peter and, pushing him slightly from behind, he says "Let's go, we have to get the stuff!"

They walk quickly through the deserted corridors. Peter follows Toma as they climb two floors and continue in silence toward the library. Suddenly above their heads a loudspeaker booms, announcing a meeting from the factory 'The Red Flame', and Peter feels that the shouts of "Long live our Great Leaders" and "Death to the Enemies of the Five Year Plan" will deafen him forever. He would like to cover his ears with his hands, to shut out the din, but with Toma so close to him he doesn't dare. Besides, Toma is running so fast on his short legs that Peter can barely keep up.

They stop in front of the library and Toma unlocks the door. It screeches on rusty hinges. As they enter, the stale, dank air of the room hits them in the face. It smells like a basement which is always locked. Toma tries to switch on the light, but the gilt chandelier remains dark. Peter can hear water dripping on the floor. Touching another light switch, Toma turns on a small lamp on the library desk.

It seems to Peter that nothing has changed in here since Mayday when he had last been in the library. The bulletin board still displays Stalin's decree in which he branded all geneticists as "Enemies of the People" who must be liquidated. The bookshelves are still hidden behind layers of crimson canvas, which is now dusty and faded. The rug too looks threadbare and stained, and there are burnt matches and cigarette butts strewn all around.

Looking at the floor Peter remembers the old librarian, Isolde, who made sure that the parquet was regularly polished and waxed. He can still smell the strong odor of fresh floor polish mixed with the scent of new books in the library. Isolde moved noiselessly around in her slippers of green felt and drank linden tea from a French china cup. She kept this cup at the bottom of a display case in which some of Professor Munteanu's ancient Egyptian medical papyri were on view. The display case used to stand in the middle of the floor, but now it isn't there. Peter walks through the room looking for it.

"Where are you going?" asks Toma when he sees Peter wandering about. "We have to pick up things from here, hammers, pliers, rolls of canvas, boxes of nails. There is no time for fooling around! Let's get to work. What we need is right here on the floor to the left of the library desk!"

Toma, crunching hard candy in his mouth, disappears on the other side of the bureau, while Peter, following the munching sound, discovers the old display case hidden behind the wooden desk. He stops, full of excitement, hoping to get a look at the ancient treasures, but the showcase is empty. He wonders what happened to the Professor's collection of papyri when Toma calls him again.

"Come on, let's get going!"

Walking toward him and nearing the canvas-covered bookcases, Peter stumbles over the old banners and portraits from Mayday Parade. Underneath are the boxes of nails and tools they need, and next to them the rolls of canvas and the jars of paste. A regular storage room! he says to himself as he bends down to help Toma pull out a hammer and two boxes of tools from under the pile of lumber and cardboard. They work for a while in silence lining everything up on the floor, and then Toma helps him pick up the hammer and the two boxes of tools. But as he stands up and turns toward the door, one of the boxes slips out of his grasp and its whole contents—pliers, screwdrivers, pieces of wire and nails—spill on the floor. Peter bends to collect them, and as he crawls between the bookcases to pick them up, he discovers a stack of magazines tied together with a piece of string. To his surprise he sees that they are American medical journals addressed to Professor Munteanu. He recognizes recent issues of the *Proceedings of the Society for Experimental Biology*, a July issue of *Genetics*, an issue of *Science*, and a fall copy of the *Journal of Experimental Medicine*.

Why are they here? Who is paying for them? He remembers that shortly before his arrest the Professor had taken out a four-year subscription so the journals were paid for four years. But why were they here?

"What are these and why are they here?" With the tip of his shoe he points toward the pile of journals.

Toma shifts the roll of canvas he has lugged on his shoulder and bends down to have a better look at the publications.

"Oh! These are for the doctors who do research at the special lab of the Central Committee. They're waiting to be shipped there at night, with the van."

"The van that carries the corpses?" Peter doesn't let Toma finish his sentence. He immediately feels sorry for talking so fast, without thinking.

"Yeah! You know about the van?" Toma gives him a suspicious look. "My father works there and I hope I will too one day soon... Sometimes Comrade Dumitru lets me ride in the van when he has a good stack of journals to ship out. It's a little spooky to ride in the middle of the night with the corpses, you know, but great fun all the same!" He closes one eye, and winks at Peter like he's told a good joke.

"You must come too! I want you to!" He is serious now. "I know the driver well. I'll talk to him and it'll be okay. I could introduce you to my father and then you could work there someday too." Toma is so excited that he lets the roll of canvas slide from his shoulder and gives Peter a slap on the back.

But he doesn't share Toma's excitement.

"All these corpses are taken away from the students, they're actually stolen! It's not right! I'd rather stay out of this!" He is frowning and biting his lower lip.

"Stolen, you said? You make me laugh. Let me ask you, who took Professor Munteanu's anatomy atlases out of his office the day we were packing his books? Do you remember that morning? I watched you in the mirror and I saw you sneaking into the room, looking around, then grabbing the atlases and the Egyptian print. You hid everything under your smock and then tiptoed out of the office. And, mind you, what did you do with them afterwards? Did you sell them on the black market for a good price? I was always curious to know. Just don't talk about stealing to me!"

Peter swallows a few times. He can feel his chin trembling. He is trapped. He doesn't know what to say. Toma leans against a bookcase, his arms crossed over his chest, watching him.

"Look here, old fellow," he takes a step forward and puts a firm hand on Peter's arm. "I haven't said a word about this to anybody. It's our secret. But now I need you just as much as you need me. I have to win this damned competition. It's important for my career! Contests like these are more important than earning good grades! I must win, and you will help me, whether you like it or not! If you want to know, it was me who asked Comrade Dumitru to put you on my team because I know your work." Toma stops. He scoops a handful of popcorn out of a bag in his pocket and tosses the popcorn into his mouth. When he has finished chewing he goes on, with a tone of urgency. "I have plans for the future. I don't want to be sent to a godforsaken village and rot there for the rest of my life. I want to do research when I finish my studies, and my father told me that, in that case, I must be on good terms with Comrade Dumitru. I will need Comrade Dumitru's support."

Toma bends down, grabs the roll of canvas and lifts it back on his shoulder. "To tell you the truth, I don't really care whose dead bodies I work on. It can be God's fairest angel or the Devil himself; it's all the same to me. All that matters is that I should be allowed to do research!"

* * *

Back in the dissection hall they unload the rolls of canvas and tools on an empty table. The room is still filled with the sounds of the loudspeaker blaring out speeches from the factory meetings. At the stone tables people are busy drawing letters on sheets of white cardboard and cutting them out. Nobody speaks and only the metallic click of scissors accompanies the noise of the speaker.

"How is my shock-brigade?" asks Toma after he finishes arranging everything on the table. "Remember, we have to win this race to prove our commitment to the Victory of the Plan! We have to show them that we deserve the title of Heroes of Labor! And remember, we're in competition with all the other teams in the room!" He walks from table to table watching his group closely, teaching them, giving them courage, praising them.

"Great work! You'll be a winner!" he says, giving a young student a pat on the back. "Keep in mind, we're at war with the others!" he adds jokingly, pointing toward Florica who is standing a few steps away.

Peter is sitting at a table which Toma had chosen for him. It is now covered with white cardboard letters the students prepared while he was in the library. As he assembles them he thinks about what is going on. He frowns. He wants to get out of here, to walk away and stop all this make-believe, this silly game! But they will brand him an "Enemy of the Plan, a saboteur, an Enemy of the People!" And he will be punished; there is no way out. He has no choice but to keep assembling letters into words and pasting them on canvas.

If Professor Munteanu would see what they're doing, he would be dismayed. Peter tries not to think about him. Become a mindless contraption, a work-machine, an automaton, he says to himself as he turns out banner after banner.

Next to him Lucia, the blonde student, helps arrange and assemble the letters. She works quickly and quietly, with skillful hands.

"I will be known as Doctor Cardboard or Doctor Paste-up," she whispers to Peter.

"You may not be called Doctor at all if Comrade Dumitru doesn't like your paste-ups!" says Toma who is passing by.

Next to them, Florica's table is so crammed with large sheets of cardboard and canvas that there is no room for the finished letters. Florica takes a handful of cutouts and shoves them inside her blouse. As Peter watches she takes one out, but it is so moist and wrinkled, it won't stick to the canvas.

"We'll lose this race because of your crazy work method!" Professor Andronic explodes. "Keeping white cardboard inside your blouse!"

"Then show me a better technique! We'll lose because of your lack of a system! There is no place where to keep the letters!" she says as she slides a few other pieces inside her cleavage. Professor Andronic, who is the head of Florica's team, shrugs but has no other suggestion.

* * *

At noon Peter gets up to stretch his legs and his stiff back. Others stand up too and move around. Peter sees Toma hiding between the tables, a long, wooden pointer in his hand, pretending to be taking aim at people from other teams. He's trying to entice them back to work, Peter thinks.

"Don't forget, we're at war! Let's get the others!" Toma jokes. "Attention! Get ready, shoot!" The students snicker. "Let's get Florica!" he shouts, aiming the pointer toward her as everybody laughs.

"Cut it out. You disturb the whole room!" Florica shouts. Anger shines in her eyes. She jumps up and all the banners, the slogans, and the pieces of cardboard piled on her table fall to the ground.

"Monkey! Gorilla! You belong in a zoo!" she shouts.

"I hope you'll join me there," says Toma. "We'll start the first revolutionary menagerie. You'll be a prized, unique specimen. You can depend on that!" Everybody laughs.

"What's going on? What's this pandemonium?"

The noise has brought Professor Andronic to their table. He is dragging his foot more than usual and his face turns pale with envy when he sees the heap of finished posters piled near Peter's table.

Toma shrugs and looks straight at the Professor. "Excuse me, Professor, but Comrade Florica wishes to join our team. She says she's tired of competing and afraid of losing the race. She wants our two brigades to unite into one brotherly team" Toma is standing at attention facing Professor Andronic and holding his pointer as though it were a rifle.

"Nonsense! Cut it out!" shouts Florica.

Comrade Dumitru appears in their midst. "Why aren't you working?" he barks, turning off the loudspeaker. "What is this, a counterrevolutionary conspiracy? Organized sabotage? I'll have you all arrested if you don't stop!"

Everybody freezes. At last Toma steps forward.

"We were celebrating our forthcoming victory in the race." He smiles unctuously at Comrade Dumitru. "I hope, with all my heart, that you'll be pleased!"

"If you're so keen on victory why aren't you working?" snaps Comrade Dumitru. "Everybody back to work!" He pounds on the table. "Enough dawdling! This is not a coffeehouse where people waste their time in idle gossip. Back to work everyone!"

"We'll go, we'll go!" grumbles Professor Andronic, looking at Peter and Toma with anger. "He who laughs last, laughs best," he mutters as he walks away.

Comrade Dumitru watches everybody go back to their place, then turns to the door. Toma follows. When they pass the last table he scoops out of his pocket a handful of expensive chocolates which he offers to Comrade Dumitru. "From my father," he says, "only the best for the heroes of the Five Year Plan!"

"Thank you!" Comrade Dumitru smiles coldly. With a quick gesture he slides the chocolates into his pocket, then opens the door.

Two men with leather briefcases have just arrived.

* * *

Peter recognizes the Party officials he had seen at Professor Andronic's opening lecture. As they step in, silence spreads through the room. Comrade Dumitru helps the men out of their snow-covered coats and hats and then wipes their briefcases dry with a rag which smells of formaldehyde.

While he lays down their clothes on an empty table, the two men stamp their frozen feet and blow on their hands. There is a forbidding, unfriendly look on their face.

Slowly they start to walk through the dissection hall, carrying their bulging briefcases like trophies of war. When they stop near Florica and Professor Andronic's table the latter jumps up. "Hello, Comrades!" the Professor greets them, and stretches out his hand. He steps in front of his table and tries to shield it with his body. It is covered with a banner which, when finished, will read, "Long live the Brotherhood of all Communist People!" But the work is only partly done, and the table is strewn with stained and wrinkled letters of cardboard which Florica has kept inside her blouse.

The men stare in silence. They ignore Professor Andronic and walk toward Dan and his team. His table is covered with a large wall poster with the words "Healthy Workers for the Five Year Plan!"

"Good work! Comrade Stalin himself would be proud of these banners!" says Comrade Dumitru who has joined them. Then, followed by the two men with the briefcases, he walks toward the loudspeaker and turns it on full blast.

The meeting at the factory 'The Red Dawn' is ending with the song of the Internationale, and the entire room is suddenly flooded with the sounds of the anthem:

"Arise ye prisoners of starvation
Arise ye wretched of the earth..."

Standing with both arms raised as if directing an invisible band, Comrade Dumitru urges everybody to join in the song:

"For justice thunders condemnation
A better world's in birth..."

explode the voices in the dissection hall. They are soaring and powerful, and the awe with which everybody sings has something contagious and inspiring. Even though the words of the song call for rebellion and war the tune reminds Peter of the religious hymns he had heard in church in his childhood. He forces himself not to fall under the spell of the song, but he remembers the voices flowing together in the chant of *Kyrie Eleison*. It was always sung at Easter on the night of the Resurrection. He sees himself inside the church, breathing the fragrance of incense, surrounded by a sea of candles reflected by the gold of the icons.

He never joined the choir in church. He was too shy to sing out loud. He liked to sit in the back with his eyes half closed listening to the chants and to the sound of the organ. At those times it seemed to him that the whole world was turning into a serene and peaceful place!

Now just like then he has closed his eyes and is listening to the song, when he hears Toma whisper, "Sing! Sing! Don't just stand there! Sing, for God's sake, open your mouth! They're staring at you!" Peter looks up and sees that Comrade Dumitru and the two men with briefcases are watching him. "Sing!" Toma whispers again, kicking him under the table.

Peter looks at the three men and begins mouthing the words of the Internationale without making a sound, just as he did with the hymns in church as a child.

> "No more the victors' chains should bind you
> Arise ye slaves no more in thrall
> The earth shall rise on new foundations
> We have been naught; we shall be all."

When the song ends, Comrade Dumitru and the two party officials break into loud applause and are joined by everybody in the dissection hall. Then Comrade Dumitru orders them back to work.

* * *

After some time, he decides to call a sudden end to the race. "Everybody stop working right this minute!" he shouts from the front of the room, waving his arms and clapping his hands. "Put down your scissors and pencils! We'll walk from table to table and look at what each of you has accomplished. It'll tell us exactly how committed you are to the Five Year Plan! And we'll also find out who is the winner."

Panic sweeps through the room, and there are cries of "No, no, not yet! Too soon!" Florica's voice is among the loudest, while Professor Andronic throws up his hands and shakes his head with a defeated expression. Comrade Dumitru watches the commotion, grinning and flashing his silver teeth.

"You can't bargain with me!" he cries. "This is a medical school, not a Turkish bazaar! We have to find out where everybody stands and how much they have done. Those who have not yet finished will stay on until later." He rubs his hands.

Peter, Lucia and Toma have just pasted the last letters on their banners when Comrade Dumitru and the two Party officials stop at their table. One of the men is short and fat with an almost baldhead and small, hairy hands. The other is tall and thin. A smell of stale sweat comes from his suit.

"Line up your posters along the wall!" orders Comrade Dumitru.

Toma and Peter prop the posters carefully against the wall while the two men open their briefcases and pull out pencils and sheets of paper. First the baldheaded man wipes his shiny face with a green handkerchief. The tall, skinny one puts on his horn-rimmed glasses. Then they both bend down, examine the posters, scribble something on their papers and without saying a word count the banners on the table.

"All done!" says Comrade Dumitru when they have finished and walk toward the nearest group. Their next stop is the table of Florica and Professor Andronic.

"Line up your posters!" orders Comrade Dumitru. Florica, the Professor and their two students hurry to do so. But many of their posters are still covered with wrinkled and stained letters of cardboard.

"What's this?" Comrade Dumitru stares at them with a frosty glare. The Professor doesn't answer immediately. He grabs the edge of the stone table and holds on to it.

"Poor quality materials," he says. "What can we do? We sweat to do the best we can with our bourgeois heritage!" He throws an angry look toward Florica.

"Yes, yes, always this damned bourgeois heritage!" Comrade Dumitru imitates the Professor's tone and looks at Florica with irritation.

Meanwhile, the two Party officials go on counting posters and banners, examining them and scribbling notes on their pads. When they finish they move to Dan's table where they do the same, and then continue throughout the room. In the end they sit down at an empty table at the front of the dissection hall with Comrade Dumitru. He passes around a pack of cheap cigarettes and, hidden behind a curtain of smoke, they pore over their notes. Only muffled voices and an occasional cough can be heard from their table. Meanwhile in the big room everybody is still rushing to finish their work.

After a while, Comrade Dumitru gets up, smoothes his smock and his hair, and turns toward the crowd.

"Comrades!" he says, throwing his head back so as to look more official. "Comrades, our championship for the Victory of the Five Year Plan has ended. The first prize has been won by our first 'shock-brigade,' the team of Comrade Toma. He and his colleagues have finished all their posters and banners in less than required time. Comrades, let's applaud their victory!" He starts clapping as loud as he can.

The two men next to him close their briefcases and join in the applause. Then everybody in the room starts clapping. After a few minutes Comrade Dumitru stops the applause and goes on with his speech.

"The second prize has been won by Dan and his team. They have finished almost all their posters in the required time. Let's applaud for the second prize winners!"

The third prize is shared by two different teams who also receive applause and ovations. However, none of those who follow and who have been distinguished with "honorable mention" are celebrated this way. Florica and Professor Andronic are last on this list. They look tired and haggard, and until the very end they keep working feverishly. They struggle to finish, and sometimes they are heard sighing.

At the table in front of the room, Comrade Dumitru lights a new cigarette, draws a few puffs and watches the rings of blue smoke. Then he begins speaking.

"Comrades, we will start now the second part of our celebration, namely decorating the dissection hall with the official portraits of our leaders, Comrades Lenin and Stalin, Marx and Engels. I want to remind you that it is a great privilege to handle these special portraits!" He points toward several large panels leaning against the wall and covered with banners of red canvas. He pauses briefly and then goes on. "The winners of the first and second prize, Comrade Toma, Lucia, Peter, Dan and his team are going to work with the pictures of Lenin and Stalin. However, I have decided to have Professor Andronic take Lucia's place, since this work is too hard for a woman. In exchange Comrade Lucia will be in charge of the Honor Panel, which will be started tomorrow. And now will all of you winners of the first and second prize, as well as Professor Andronic, come to the middle of the room and bring your tools so we can start our project!"

With stiff, military steps he walks toward the center of the hall, waiting for the others to join him.

"We've won, we've won! Hurrah! We are the victors!" Toma whispers, giving Peter a slap on the back. "We are victorious, and we'll have to celebrate when we've finished!"

* * *

Toma and his team walk to the middle of the room and they form a circle around Comrade Dumitru. He assigns Toma and Dan to work with the portrait of Lenin, while Peter and Professor Andronic are to work with the photo of Stalin.

The first picture they hang is the portrait of Lenin. Comrade Dumitru chooses a spot just above the black marble plaque with the names of the physicians who died in the great epidemics. Toma and Dan drive the nail into the wall and hang up the picture of Lenin. When they're finished, the large portrait completely obscures the list of the heroic doctors. But Comrade Dumitru doesn't care. He looks very pleased, and orders Peter and Professor Andronic to work with the picture of Stalin.

This is a large portrait of the leader, about four feet high, bordered by an ornate gilded frame. Stalin is shown smoking a pipe. He is wearing a military uniform and, pinned to his chest, is the highest war decoration, a gold medal with the profile of Lenin, the Order of Lenin.

Comrade Dumitru wants to hang this portrait over the black marble plaque inscribed with the Hippocratic Oath.

He turns toward the wall. "Here, we have to hang the picture right here." He points to a spot just above the plaque carrying the Oath." We'll hang the portrait of Comrade Stalin on this spot. We have no more use for these reminders of bourgeois medicine!" Indeed, suspended on this point, the portrait would completely obscure the words of the ancient physician.

The dissection hall is silent now, and everybody is watching the working men. Peter has climbed to the top of a ladder carrying his hammer and a handful of nails. He steadies himself and starts hammering one big nail into the wall. The nail bends under the blows and he has to start with another nail. Once again he swings the hammer. This time, too, the nail bends under the blows and has to be discarded. After three unsuccessful attempts it becomes clear that the spot chosen by Comrade Dumitru cannot be used, and the picture must be hung on another place. To the Comrade's disappointment, the Hippocratic Oath remains completely exposed.

Peter is happy with this outcome. As he looks at the black marble plaque, he wonders whether the ghost of the great physician is alive in the stone and has the magical power to bring about this big change.

* * *

An hour later all the portraits are up, Lenin and Stalin at the front of the room, Marx and Engels, the founders of Communism, at the other end of the hall.

The two Party officials who have supervised the work have put down their briefcases and are yawning. Their eyes are swollen and red. The students too are yawning and rubbing their eyes. The loudspeaker announces the end of the workday at the factory 'The Red Tractor.'

Comrade Dumitru walks to the front of the room and starts to speak: "Comrades, you have well served the Five Year Plan with your work here today, and your effort has produced good results. But we have to keep vigilant, we can never relax. Tomorrow we will have to be here again and finish the work. It's our first duty, we can never relent!"

He pauses and raises his left fist in the revolutionary salute. As he turns around and walks toward the door he is joined by Dan and Professor Andronic, while Florica and the Party officials follow a few steps behind.

The students too jump from their seats, and the humming of voices soon fills the air.

"Time to go!" says Lucia, gathering her pencils and papers and stuffing them into her bag. Then she slips on her coat, wraps a woolen scarf around her neck, and walks to the door.

* * *

Chapter 15

Left alone in the dissection hall, Peter sets out to tidy the room. He starts sweeping and picking up trash, but everything he touches slips out of his hands. "Damn!" he curses under his breath as he sits on the lowest rung of the ladder.

A moment later the door opens and Toma walks in.

"Are you ready? Where's your coat? This is our night to celebrate!" Toma is wearing his coat and hat and is all buttoned up.

"My coat? Why? Where are we going?" Peter stares at Toma.

"Are you dressed? Get moving! We have no time to waste!"

"Why, what's the rush?"

"I told you, it's our night to celebrate!" Toma is frowning and pulling his gloves off.

"But I have work to do. I'd rather stay in."

"Nonsense. Put on your coat, quickly...or..." There is a threatening edge in Toma's voice. He makes a step toward Peter, raising his hand. Peter steps out of his way. He keeps staring at Toma, facing him, motionless.

Toma is not his friend. He was not part of Professor Munteanu's team of young associates. As the Secretary of the Youth Organization he was always conferring with Comrade Dumitru. Peter doesn't trust him.

"I'm tired. I don't want to go."

"Really?" Toma is grinning and cocks his head. "If I were you, I would think twice. I wouldn't make fast decisions!" He slips his gloves into his pocket and drums with his fingertips on the nearest table.

Suddenly Peter remembers Toma's words in the library telling him that he had seen him taking Professor Munteanu's atlases of anatomy. It is foolish to say no! "All right," he sighs, "I'll go with you."

Toma grins. "I knew you'd come around! Get your coat! Are you ready?"

Peter walks into his lab and grabs his coat and hat.

"Very good! Let's go!" Toma touches Peter's shoulder, pushing him out the door, just as he had done early that morning.

They walk so quickly through the dark corridors of the basement and take so many turns that Peter almost loses track of where they are heading. It is only when they step out into the freezing driveway and find themselves standing near the black van without headlights that Peter realizes they are near the gates of the mortuary. The sudden cold wakes him up, making him jittery. Why are they standing near the mortuary van? Where are they heading, and why? It all seems so weird and frightening. He looks around for a way to escape. But Toma drags him along toward the car, and knocks at a window.

"Come on! Let us in! It's freezing out here!" he says, tightening his grip on Peter's arm.

He takes a step back when the car door opens, and the driver climbs out of the van. He is a tall man wearing the uniform of the Securitate, and it seems to Peter that he is facing the officer he met on Mariana's block only a few weeks ago. He looks away, trying to avoid the officer's gaze, but the man pays no attention to him. Toma offers him a cigarette and the two men start a friendly conversation. After a few minutes the officer throws his cigarette away, arranges his tunic, and climbs back into the car.

"Get in!" he says as he sits at the wheel. Peter still wonders how to get away from the van but Toma pushes him inside, then gets in behind him and shuts the door.

"Keep the black curtain closed over the window at all times!" says the Securitate officer.

It is pitch black inside the van. The car starts abruptly and they have to hold on to each other so as not to fall off the bench. Soon they are driving at full speed, and at every bump and every sharp turn they can hear the rattling and sliding noises made by the corpses which lie behind them on the floor.

At one time a head comes to rest on Peter's foot. He moves away, and as he does so, he feels the touch of a hand. It makes him think of long ago, when still a watchman at the cemetery, a gravedigger told him that sometimes the dead hung on to the living and pulled them into their graves by clinging to their legs. Peter didn't believe him, but he never forgot his words. He tries to find a safe place for his feet, but both the head and the hand of the dead seem to follow wherever he moves.

Suddenly there is a hard bump. The car swerves and the corpses slide to the other side of the van. At the same time the clasp fastening the black curtain to the windows falls to the floor. The drapery slides to one side. Peter tries to pull it back and cover the window, but Toma points to the partition between them and the officer in the front seat, indicating that the latter cannot see what is going on in the back.

"We can watch the road," he says in a low voice.

Outside it is still snowing. Large flakes brush against the window and white drifts settle on the ground. They see no cars traveling in any direction, and there are no tracks in the snow. There is only a large sign inscribed with the words "ROAD CLOSED FOR REPAIRS."

"What road is this? What repairs?" asks Peter.

"There are no repairs. It's only pretense. Official talk. This is a closed road, open only to a select few," Toma whispers.

As they drive on, a row of small, dark houses appear. They look deserted and empty, half-ruined and desolate. There are no lights in the windows and no smoke rising from their chimneys. When they come closer, Peter and Toma see that these houses are boarded up, with windows and gates all covered up. Snowdrifts are gathering along their walls and fences. The whole row of houses seems to be vanishing under the snow.

* * *

The van makes a sharp turn to the right, and suddenly the glow of a fire shines through the darkness, and there is the smell of burnt charcoal.

Peter and Toma pull back from the window, but they can still see the road. It is crowded with thin, shivering figures dressed in rags. They are shoveling snow, watched by Securitate guards who keep their rifles pointed at them.

The van comes to a halt. Not far from them stands an old man with a long beard. The man is bent over, swaying under the weight of his load. As he tries to keep his balance the snow slips off his shovel. Immediately a Securitate man leaps toward him, screaming and cursing. He hits the old man with the butt of his rifle making him lose his balance and fall to the ground.

Peter and Toma gasp in the dark.

"Who are these men?" asks Peter.

"Politicals! They must be political prisoners who are locked up in the mental hospital," says Toma. "It's not far from here, if I'm not mistaken."

"Politicals held in the mental hospital! That's it. Maybe that's where Mariana is too, wandering, lost, in the dark corridors of the musty buildings, or she might be forced to clear a path in the ice-covered yard. She could be shivering in the cold, without gloves and without boots.

The car starts again and they ride for a while in silence, ducking their heads whenever they pass close to a fire or a torch held by a Securitate officer. They see other prisoners covered with rags and shoveling snow, all guarded by special police armed with rifles and bayonets. Like the old man with the beard, they too are bent over under heavy loads.

After a while, the road makes a sharp turn and the corpses in the van slide to the left. The row of dark houses has disappeared. They are driving along the frozen Dîmboviṭa River which is covered with a thick, immaculate blanket of snow.

At the end of this stretch they cross a bridge of white stones. As soon as they reach the other side, Peter recognizes the driveway leading to the Palace of the Principesa. No prisoners are working here. Only Securitate men with big fur hats and heavy boots are clearing a path in the snow.

The bright light of two powerful reflectors reveals every detail. It looks like high noon. "Close those curtains!" whispers Toma. "Nobody should ever know that we've been watching the road!"

Peter pulls the curtain tight, and for a short while they drive in total darkness. Then the engine slows down, and they can hear the banging of a metal gate being opened and shut behind them.

"This is the palace of the Principesa, right ?" he asks, listening to the short military orders barked outside the van.

"Used to be, but not anymore," says Toma. "Now it is the Center for Medical Research of our Great Commander and of the Central Committee. Didn't you know?"

Peter doesn't answer. He is thinking of the Principesa and of the sunny afternoon with tea and cookies he spent here, a long time ago. Everything comes back to him so vividly, as if it happened yesterday. The drive to the Palace in the luxury car with the school principal and the running coach, the Principesa welcoming them on the great lawn, then sitting next to him at the table, holding her tiny Chihuahua in her lap. He can still see her white hands, her lavender eyes and smell her strong French perfume. He remembers how flustered he was when she placed her palm on his thigh. Even though she never followed through with her promise of looking after his training and education, and abandoned him to the greed of the school principal and the running coach, even though she had let him down, Peter has forgiven her and keeps a warm spot for her in his heart.

"Where is the Principesa now? What happened to her?" he asks Toma.

"She never came back from her trip abroad. They say that she joined the King, somewhere in Switzerland, after he was forced to abdicate three years ago," says Toma.

The van comes to a sudden halt and the door opens wide.

"Come on out! We've arrived!" the driver says, standing at attention near the car.

Peter and Toma crawl stiffly out of the van. In the light of the reflectors Peter recognizes the entrance gate to the park with its gilded crown of the Principesa and her coat of arms. A red banner with hammer and sickle is draped over it, partly concealing it. Two watchtowers manned by Securitate men with machine guns and rifles now flank the gate.

A few steps to the right, on the great lawn, stands the hundred-year-old chestnut tree under whose crown the lavish table had been set. It was protected by the golden umbrella, with its fringe of tiny glass bells. Peter can still hear the tinkling of the bells in the wind.

Suddenly Toma grabs him by the shoulders and pushes him aside as two Securitate men start unloading the corpses. Wearing stained lab smocks over their uniforms they rush around, place the corpses on wooden stretchers and carry them up the marble staircase into the palace. Peter is surprised that all the corpses are children or young adolescents.

"Let's follow the stretcher-bearers!" says Toma, holding his arm.

"Where to? Where are we going?" asks Peter, his eyes blinking from the blinding light.

"Surprise! Surprise! You'll see when we get there!" Toma is climbing the marble staircase two steps at a time.

Soon they reach the large entrance doors where they are stopped by a fat Securitate officer seated behind a heavy desk. He is reading the newspaper and checking identification papers. Toma pulls out his Young Communist card.

"This comrade is the research expert I was told to bring along," Toma says. "I vouch for him on my Party card." He waves the red card in front of the guard. Then, in a compassionate voice, he asks, "How are your kids? I hope they're okay. Here are some candies for them!" He slips a few chocolates into the officer's hand. The man takes the candies, sliding them inside his pocket, and waves them through without saying a word.

What a smooth operator! Peter tells himself as they step into a hall with marble floor and gilded ceiling. They walk through it quickly and enter another large, high-ceilinged hall which once served as the palace reception and ballroom. Peter recognizes it immediately from the photographs he has seen. It is brightly lit by several rows of crystal chandeliers, and the walls and ceiling are covered with frescoes. From the door Peter can see battle scenes against the Turks alternating with paintings from the Last Judgment in which the fallen enemies are burning in the flames of Hell. In the past the colors were bright and lively with gilded highlights, but now the walls are grimy, the paint is peeling, and here and there a faucet, a rubber hose or a sink has been affixed to the wall.

Near the spot where they are standing a golden angel floating on the wall seems to be spewing water through a rusty faucet, and a demon is breathing fire through the rubber hose of a Bunsen burner. A banner with the words "Marxism is the Greatest Science!" spans the whole length of the room.

"Come on! Come on! Stop staring at the walls!" says Toma "We have a lot to do tonight!" He pulls him by the sleeve.

Peter takes a few steps, then stops. His legs are heavy and his shoes seem glued to the floor. He has the same dark feeling as when he first climbed into the van.

He looks around and sees that the hall is filled with marble tables with colorful mosaic tops. In the past, when banquets were held in this room, the tables were piled high with mountains of sweets and exotic fruits. But now they are covered with corpses of children and adolescents. Peter has never seen so many bodies of children in one place. He steps in front of Toma and blocks his way.

"Why are there so many young people here? Where are they coming from?" he asks. Toma looks around to make sure they are alone.

"They come from the orphanage," he says.

"From the orphanage? Why?"

Toma hesitates. "Orders from the Great Commander and his physicians!" he whispers." In the Orphanage the children can be kept under strict nutrition and dietary control, just like experimental animals. And this is what the scientists working here are looking for."

"In other words, they're starving them to death?" asks Peter.

"I'll explain the whole thing to you later," says Toma. He cocks his head and listens.

Voices and footsteps are approaching outside. Soon two stretcher-bearers walk in carrying the body of another dead child. They place it on a table not far from Peter and sigh with relief after they put it down, even though the body is light. The little boy is still wrapped in a uniform coat from which his spidery arms and legs stick out. His face is shrunken and lined like that of an old man.

When the two stretcher-bearers turn their backs and walk to the door Peter goes to examine the new corpse. He bends down and, to his surprise, he sees that the label sewn on the coat bears the name of the orphanage in which he had been raised as a child. *My God, this could have been me, had I been younger!* He tells himself. He remembers how sick he had been at the age of eight and how close to death! Had it not been for fat Maria the cook who nursed him back to health by spoon-feeding him her thick soups every day, he may not have made it. He remembers her big breasts and round belly under her apron, and her deep lap, all softness and warmth. Later it was she who washed and ironed his white shirt the day of his visit to the Principesa, and it was she who had placed cuppings on his back and covered his chest with mustard compresses when he had pneumonia. But nothing had worked magic like the soups she had cooked just for him.

Peter stares at the small body which lies in front of him, wondering why these poor children had been marked for death. He wants to ask Toma all kinds of questions, but when he looks in his direction he sees him laughing and joking with the two stretcher-bearers who are getting ready to remove a dissected body.

Peter turns back to the corpses of the children surrounding him. All of them have been reduced to nothing more than disembodied human shells. Some have had their ribcage severed with a saw, their heart and lungs taken out. Others have been cut open below the waist, and their stomach, kidneys, liver and spleen are missing. Behind him, the skull of a boy about ten or eleven has been plied open, both eyes and the whole brain have been scooped out, making the child look like a demon with a monstrous head.

But why? Why? What is really going on here?

It is warm in the room and Peter feels a wave of nausea welling up inside him. He becomes aware of a sweet sickly smell which reminds him of the odor in Mr. Bantu's funeral home on hot summer days, when corpses were gathered there before being embalmed.

* * *

The two men leave the room and Toma walks back toward him.

"These bodies have not even been injected with formaldehyde!" Peter tells Toma." I don't understand what is going on, I don't get it at all. But I know that I don't want to be part of it!" He turns around and heads toward the door.

"Wait! Wait! You can't leave just like that!" says Toma, stepping in front of him.

Peter turns right, but as he does, his sleeve catches on the bone cutting-saw which has been used on the corpses and now rests on a table nearby. It falls to the floor, and when he puts it back on the table he discovers a full set of instruments used to work with the bones. There are hammers and chisels, pliers and saws. They all bear the label of the medical school and the seal of the Professor's lab.

Peter looks at Toma "What is this all about? Why are these instruments here?" But Toma only shrugs and says, "Sshhh! Sshhh!" pressing his index finger against his lips and turning his face toward the door. Another group of Securitate men is walking into the room.

"I will explain everything to you as soon as I can," he whispers. "Just take it easy and don't blow your top! We'll talk about this later on!"

He pulls Peter toward the wooden partition at the far end of the room. Peter follows him grudgingly, still holding the bone-cutting saw in his hand. When he looks at it, Professor Munteanu's words come to his mind: "We can never forget that every inch of a corpse represents the remains of a real person, a unique temple of nature which we have to respect even in death."

* * *

They are standing now on the other side of the wooden partition, in a small room which looks like a modern lab and is bathed in the eerie blue light of an ultraviolet lamp. The light is meant to sterilize the room, and its unearthly glow makes one think of the light of the moon.

Toma turns on the chandelier and switches off the ultraviolet lamp. Then he hitches himself on top of a mosaic table and makes Peter sit in a low armchair covered with rose velvet and decorated with the coat of arms of the Principesa. He takes off his hat and coat, folds it on his knees, and starts speaking in a low voice. "It all has to do with the Great Commander's severe illness and his mysterious pain. Nothing has been found to control it. No injections, no painkillers, no prayers or magic potions. And when the Great Commander is seized by pain, he loses control and can even become violent. In a fit of pain, like in a fit of rage he has physically hurt people around him.

This is why it was agreed to send doctors to the farthest corners of the country to look for old folk remedies. Other physicians had to scan the Western medical journals for new, modern treatments. Needless to say, they were all sworn to secrecy and couldn't tell anybody what they were looking for. But they found nothing new in the journals.

Although the physicians who went to the countryside came back loaded with barrels of oils and tinctures made from wild weeds, roots, berries and mushrooms, none of these remedies was successful.

"In the meantime the Great Commander's personal physician and best friend, a man who knows much about Russian medicine, told him about the famous 'Serum of Mogomelets.' Maybe you have heard about it? It is a concoction extracted from human tissues and organs and is supposed to heal and restore severely damaged body parts. The most effective serum was the one prepared from the tissues of people who had died of starvation during the long siege of Leningrad. At that time, a great general, who suffered from chronic, intolerable pains, was treated with a solution secretly made from the organs of children who died of starvation during the siege. Rumor had it that the general recovered so well with this treatment, that not only did he return to active duty in Leningrad, but he went to battle the German troops at Stalingrad.

It was the same physician-friend of the Great Commander who gave him the idea to use the orphanage for these experiments. It was his suggestion to transform the diet of the children in the orphanage into the starvation diet of the siege of Leningrad and thus, always have a human source for the serum on hand."

Toma finds a pack of cigarettes and a box of matches on a shelf and lights himself a cigarette while Peter becomes aware that the room is filled with the sharp and pungent smell of ammonia. Here, the sweet, sickly odor of the corpses has disappeared. The floor is wet and shiny, showing that it had been freshly mopped. A large flask of ammonia is hidden under the table. Peter had noticed the smell earlier but did not pay any attention to it.

Toma shakes the cigarette ashes into a Petri dish and goes on talking. "The trouble is that since the serum has to be prepared only from fresh organs, many corpses—meaning a lot of children—are needed all the time. The other trouble is that, since the Great Commander is so crazed by his pain, he has fits of rage almost every day, during which he behaves like a madman. Sometimes he breaks whatever stands in his way! Other times he threatens and punishes the people who are working for him. He fired the old director of the lab, had him arrested and this is how my father got his job."

Peter listens, but his gaze wanders from the refrigerator which stands near the window to the centrifuge in the corner, then to the large distilling machine and to the cabinets filled with sterilized glassware. Everything inside is wrapped in paper which has turned yellow and brittle from the dry heat of the oven in which it was baked. This makeshift lab looks so sparkling clean that even though the walls are covered with the same frescoes of battle scenes and vanquished enemies burning in hell they appear to Peter like gleaming white tiles, just like the tile-covered walls in the anatomy lab.

He watches the red light of the thermostat blinking without interruption, and listens to the low, regular humming of the other electrical instruments. All the objects in the room are familiar, he knows them well, since they all come from the anatomy department. He has handled them, washed, and cleaned them so many times in the past. These instruments too have been lifted from the anatomy lab and brought here secretly in the dead of night with the mortuary van, just like the bodies of children and the bone-cutting tools from the other room. They too are hidden booty looted from the medical school!

A deep sadness, a sense of mourning for the Professor and his lab, for the work they did together for so many years, takes hold of Peter. Maybe it is better that the Professor is not around anymore. He doesn't have to put up with the humiliation of seeing his department robbed and cannibalized! God only knows what it might have done to him!

* * *

It is quiet in the room. For a while nobody speaks. Then Toma brushes away some ashes that have dropped on his round belly and jumps to his feet.

"As you can see, it is here, in this improvised lab, that the whole operation takes place," he says, walking to the refrigerator. "It's here that all the organs—the brains, kidneys, livers, spleens and hearts—are cut into tiny pieces, then frozen and thawed several times to break up the cells. I can show you examples of each step of the operation," he adds as he opens the door of the refrigerator.

Inside every shelf is packed with neatly labeled jars filled with an unrecognizable mass of minced meat soaked in blood. Without the labels on the lids of the jars it would be impossible to recognize anything. Only the beaker filled with brain tissue stands apart and can be easily distinguished by its light gray, pasty content. It makes Peter think of raw fish gone bad.

"And here is the serum, the magical, life-giving potion!" Toma pulls out a large flask filled with a rose-colored liquid. "This is the serum, the tissue extract which now only needs to be passed through the microfilters and then mixed with a special chemical solution before being used. It has already been frozen and thawed several times and spun in the centrifuge."

Toma smiles lovingly at the flask which he raises in the air, making it sparkle in the light of the chandelier. "Look at it, you can easily mistake it for the best French Rosé d'Anjou! One should drink it slowly, in unhurried sips from long-stemmed crystal glasses, rather than spurt it from a syringe!"

Peter is watching him, his right hand still clutching the bone-cutting saw which he brought with him from the other room.

"But why did they have to take all the instruments from the medical school and leave nothing for the students and for research?" he asks. "It's bad for the students and just as bad for research."

"Oh! The students, the students! Who cares about the students today?" Toma answers with sarcasm. "I am a student and I should know. Comrade, you're naive, if I may say so!" He closes the door of the refrigerator. "To answer your questions, the equipment was brought here because it was the best available, the most modern equipment they could obtain. And, to be fair, who would have used it now anyway? Who would do any research in the Department of Anatomy today? Comrade Dumitru? Florica? Professor Andronic? You must be kidding! They're all too busy goose-stepping in Comrade Dumitru's tracks. Let's face it, since the Professor is gone, there is nobody left to do serious research in the department!"

Toma stops, takes two steps toward Peter and lowers his voice. "Speaking about Professor Munteanu and his lab," he goes on, "I must tell you that not only did they bring all his equipment over here. They even tried to find the Professor himself and bring him back. They would have liked to bring him to work here, since nobody is as experienced and as knowledgeable as he is!"

Toma examines his short, fat hands as if seeing them for the first time. He goes on in a whisper. "Unfortunately when they started looking for the Professor they couldn't find him. They couldn't remember where he was. Nobody could remember what forced labor camp he had been sent to. His papers were lost. And when they finally located him working in the deep marshes of the Danube-Black Sea Canal, he was too weak and too sick. They brought him back to the hospital and started to treat him, but he didn't last very long!"

Toma drags Peter to the window overlooking the backyard of the palace. In the bright light of a strong reflector several Securitate men are reloading the black van with the remains of the dissected bodies. They are wrapped in pieces of cloth, and look like shapeless bundles of rags. Suddenly a pack of howling dogs surrounds the car. They remind Peter of the stray dogs which roam about the medical school.

The men put their stretchers down in the snow and start pelting the dogs with rocks and pieces of bricks from a mound of rubble nearby. Then, a couple of shots are heard. The dogs run away, barking and howling. Only the black, motionless body of one dead animal is left behind, like a dark stain on the snow.

Peter stares at it absentmindedly. He has watched the whole scene from the window but it all seems to take place in another world, as if it were part of a movie with no beginning and no end. He is troubled by Toma's words, stunned by the news of the Professor's death. He imagines him, stooped down, cutting reeds, wading through the mud of the mosquito and leech-infested canals with bleeding sores on his arms and legs. Or he sees him standing in line in an endless gray queue for a bowl of watery soup.

But he cannot hold on to these thoughts. They soon become blurry and fade away, replaced by memories of the Professor active and healthy, examining slides at the microscope or giving his talk in the lecture hall. What would have happened had he returned from the camps in good health? What would he have done? Would he have agreed to work here and abandon the lab, take charge of this operation for the cure of the Great Commander? Peter shakes his head, knowing too well that the Professor would have never accepted such an offer. He didn't do it in the past and he wouldn't do it now!

Peter still remembers the summer of 1943 when the German SS, Professor Doktor Ettimger came to visit. It was so hot on that day in July that the asphalt was melting in the street. The blond German doctor, who was accompanied by a translator, walked into the Department of Anatomy, and gave the "Heil Hitler!" salute, clicking his heels and raising his right arm. Sweat was pouring down his face and neck, forcing him to take off his military cap decorated with the badge of a human skull. He placed it on top of a skeleton hanging nearby, and joked about the similarity between his badge of the "Totenkopf" and the real skull. He invited Professor Munteanu to participate in "special genetic experiments" on "certain groups of the population."

"The scientific experiments we are conducting specifically on Jews and Gypsies will, in the long run, benefit our superior Aryan race," he said, staring into Professor Munteanu's blue eyes. "You are a geneticist and these experiments will be most fascinating for you... You will meet other geneticists, like Dr. Mengele and Professor Mrugowski, and there will be advantages and rewards. You will be able to travel to Berlin as often as you want, and you may receive an academic appointment at the University of the Reich, not to mention gifts and endowments for your present department here in Bucharest."

The Professor had listened carefully to the young doctor, thanked him for everything, and politely refused his offers and invitation. He never changed his mind and never had regrets, not even when he was demoted from his position or when threatened with being dismissed from the school altogether for refusing this invitation. No, Peter thinks, if the Professor hadn't bent to the Nazi pressure he certainly would not bend today!

He looks up and sees Toma biting into a chocolate candy. His round cheeks are shiny and red, and there is a brown smudge around his mouth. "Here, one for you!" Toma says, throwing another chocolate in Peter's lap. "I was thinking about the Professor," he adds, "and I must say too bad for him, and too bad for us. But I was also wondering...you worked with the Professor hand in hand, so to speak, and helped him devise all these techniques and prepare all his publications. You must know everything about the equipment, these instruments and the chemical solutions we need to prepare..."

"What do you mean? What are you trying to say?" Peter jumps from his seat.

"Sshhh! Sshhh! Don't get excited! We really can't talk here," Toma replies, listening for voices and footsteps on the other side of the wall. "Let's go talk in a quiet place...and celebrate! We haven't even celebrated our victory in today's competition!"

He throws his coat over his shoulders, makes sure the refrigerator door is shut, then switches the ultraviolet light on and turns off the chandelier. He opens the door in the opposite wall. Peter follows him slowly, trailing behind, not knowing where they are going. He is too overwhelmed to ask. He finds himself standing in a very quiet, soft-carpeted corridor.

* * *

Chapter 16

The corridor is long and winding, with the same high ceiling and gilt chandeliers as the ballroom. They walk up one staircase and down another and open several noiseless doors. They pass through a wide gallery lined with tall, ornate mirrors, an imitation of the Gallerie des Glaces at Versailles.

More than once Peter looks back, trying to get away, but he sees that they are followed. He can hear faint footsteps on the soft carpet. When he looks in the mirrors of the gallery he sees that they are being trailed by a Securitate officer armed with a rifle and bayonet. He feels suspicious and apprehensive.

Finally, Toma opens a large door decorated with the coat of arms of the Principesa, and they enter a gold-pillared salon still filled with the scent of the Principesa's French perfume. A fire burns in a marble fireplace. In front of it a table is set for dinner. In the middle is a basket of oranges, bananas, dates and tangerines. Peter has not seen the like in many years.

"Let's celebrate! This is our night for celebration! Let's drink to our victory! Toma claps his hands and snaps his fingers as he dances over the carpet, turning round and round and trying to make Peter join in his dance. Soft music is playing and he claps his hands and snaps his fingers until a butler enters the room and takes their coats and hats.

Peter looks at the man, at his dark face which is framed by gray, thinning hair, at a purple birth mark on his cheek. He recognizes the butler who had served tea during his visit at the Principesa a long time ago. His skin is as smooth as it had been then, only his hair has turned silver. His black suit looks shiny and threadbare over the elbows and knees.

"Caviar and champagne! Bring us caviar and champagne! We have come to celebrate!" Toma says to the butler. "My father is away at a conference and the apartment is mine until he comes back," he adds, turning to Peter. "We live here, in this wing of the Palace, since my father is in charge of the project in the lab. Other scientists who are also working in this project live in different wings of the Principesa's Palace."

Toma stops by the fireplace and, holding the poker with his short hands, stirs the logs on the grate.

The butler brings a large crystal jar filled with glistening black caviar and a bottle of champagne in a silver bucket of ice. Toma opens the bottle with a pop and pours the champagne in the glasses.

"Let's drink to our victory!" he says as he raises his glass and clinks with Peter. "To our health! To the newest Heroes of Labor!" He empties his glass in one long swallow and pours himself more champagne.

As they sit down to eat, Peter suddenly becomes aware that he has carried the bone-cutting saw with him from the lab. He looks at it with embarrassment, not knowing what to do. Finally he bends down and lets it slide to the floor near the gilded foot of his chair. But Toma grabs it.

"You are ready for work! Bringing the instruments from the lab with you, even to dinner! Bravo, I admire your dedication! And a perfect decision indeed for a Hero of Labor who always lives up to his tasks!"

He shoves a spoonful of caviar into his mouth. "Congratulations and bravo again! You've made a great decision to work in this lab. I always knew that you were a true scientist at heart."

Toma has finished the caviar almost by himself and is watching the butler place a large tray filled with the crusty roast of a whole suckling pig on the table. The roast is surrounded by fluffy mountains of mashed potatoes.

Toma puts some meat and potatoes on his plate. "Listen to me," he goes on, "this lab is going to grow, to develop, while not much is going to happen at the medical school. Believe me, it's here that you can do important, meaningful work, and it's here that you will be able to meet the talented, rising stars from whom you can always learn something new. You can watch them closely or you can work with them and, if you want, you can even make friends with them."

The butler brings more trays of food from the kitchen and Toma stops talking to fill his plate with *sarmale* or stuffed vine leaves topped with sour cream, and grilled pork sausages with *mămăligă*. He then reaches out to fill Peter's plate and adds a thick, juicy pickle.

"Yes," he goes on, licking his greasy fingers, "you can learn from these comrades, and, if you make friends with them, they will be useful too! Should you need them, they can find the whereabouts of people who have mysteriously vanished!" he adds in a whisper, bending toward Peter after the butler has left the room. "They can bring these unfortunates back, even save their lives! Remember Professor Munteanu? They tried to save him, but it was too late! So, if you *ever* think about saving someone, maybe Mariana," he says without looking at Peter, "then you must act quickly, before it's too late."

Toma stops talking and grabs two glasses into which he pours steaming red wine sweetened with honey, raisins and cinnamon. Peter tries to speak but Toma interrupts him, raising his hand. "Besides, my father will be delighted to find you working for him in the lab when he comes back. He'll be happy to have somebody who understands how to mix the chemicals for the serum and how to handle the microfilters."

Toma has finished the first glass of wine and is pouring himself a second one. "If I were you," he goes on, "I wouldn't waste any time. I'd start right away, particularly if I were in possession of two anatomy atlases which belonged to Professor Munteanu and are written in French, an Imperialist language!"

He stops talking and turns to his plate, digging with gusto into the sausages and the stuffed vine leaves, and washes them down with wine. "Eat! Drink! To our victory and to your golden future!"

"See, they've slaughtered the suckling pig of the Principesa in the Christian tradition for this Communist Christmas!" he adds. He makes the sign of the cross over the roasted piglet.

"Eat! Drink! Don't be shy! Everything here is of the finest quality; everything comes from the former estate of the Principesa. You simply can't afford to miss the opportunity not to partake in this feast!"

Toma is heaping more food on Peter's plate, but he can't eat at all. His mouth feels dry, parched, and his stomach is ready to turn. The various smells in the room, the garlic, the roast meat, the wine and the cinnamon, even the old perfume of the Principesa which lingers in the air, make his head throb. The more Toma urges him to eat and drink the sicker he feels, and the more he longs for fresh air.

As the butler brings in a golden, newly baked Christmas cake, decorated with raisins, almonds, walnuts and poppy seeds, Peter suddenly springs up, almost toppling the chair behind him. "I have to get out...I'm sick!" He hangs on to the table to keep from falling.

Toma is startled. "Don't tell me that you want to leave before the dessert! It can't be true!"

"I have to go! I'm sick!"

Toma stares at him. Finally he shrugs and says, "Well, that's too bad! Just don't forget that you must come to a decision and you have no time to waste." He turns to the butler who is standing near the table, holding the tray. "Get his coat and hat, and give me that cake!"

The butler puts the tray on the table and Toma cuts a large slice, wraps it in a clean linen napkin and gives it to Peter. "Here, take this for the road!" He stuffs it into Peter's coat pocket, and they walk toward the door. Nobody speaks and after a few steps Toma goes to the fruit basket and picks out a banana and two oranges. "For later tonight or breakfast tomorrow...with your hot chocolate!" he says, winking.

Finally Toma opens the door and stops, listening. They hear muffled footsteps on the soft carpeting and then they see a tall Securitate officer coming down the corridor toward them.

"Comrade officer, please take this comrade and see him out!" Toma says, gently pushing Peter toward the man.

* * *

The officer gives Peter a bored, unfriendly glance. He looks tired and doesn't seem thrilled by the idea of stepping out into the cold night. He walks slowly down the corridor followed by Peter. He stops in front of one of the tall mirrors and straightens his cap. "We'll leave shortly, but not before fixing a small grooming detail. You cannot walk out of here as you are. You have to put on these special sunglasses." He makes Peter wear a pair of opaque spectacles made of tin and covered with black paint, like a small curtain of iron. The sharp edge of the tin cuts into his flesh. The elastic band squeezes the back of his head like a vice. Without thinking, he raises his hand to loosen the band.

"Don't touch the spectacles or I'll put you in handcuffs! And keep your head down!" orders the officer. Peter lowers his hands and stops walking, unable to take another step. He feels frightened and powerless. His throat is dry.

The militiaman grabs his elbow and pulls him along the carpeted corridor. Peter tries to keep up, but when he reaches the top of the staircase and his outstretched foot encounters only thin air, he steps back in a panic. He thinks they are forcing him to jump into the void and he freezes.

"Don't stop! Move! Don't drag your feet!"

Peter feels dizzy. With every step he fears that he will fall into a void.

When they reach the landing he is exhausted, convinced that he is a prisoner, but not a simple captive: he is condemned to death. Only prisoners sentenced to death are marched off blindfolded. They are not allowed to meet the eyes of their executioners, nor are they allowed to see where they are taken. In the past it was the executioners and hangmen who were not supposed to meet the eyes of their victims, and needed protection against them. This was an old custom; it came from the belief in the evil eye. For it was believed that the condemned man could put a hex on the executioner, making him die unexpectedly. Or he could lure him into the netherworld in some mysterious way. It was also believed that if the face of the executioner was caught in the eye of the victim his features and his deeds would be engraved forever and transcribed into the Book of Divine Justice.

"Turn right! Turn left! Keep moving!" orders the officer.

He drags Peter along the corridor, making him take sharp turns, and then leading him down another steep flight of stairs. This blind descent fills him with horror. He imagines that there really are hidden execution rooms in this basement, under the palace, execution rooms of the kind Mustafa told him existed throughout the city in secret houses. Blindfolded prisoners were herded and pushed into these low, windowless cubicles, with walls and ceilings smeared with the dried blood of other victims. They were then gunned down by militiamen they could not see.

He too must be on his way to an execution chamber where he will be shot. Then the Securitate officer who is leading him will be decorated for Service to the Party and to the Great Commander and will be distinguished as Special Hero of Socialist Labor, while Peter's body will be taken to the dissection hall and his fresh organs will be turned into healing serum for the Great Commander. He can see his dead body lying on a stone table in the high-ceilinged ballroom, surrounded by the corpses of many adolescents. Even though he is no longer a teenager, his organs are still young enough to be used for the serum. These thoughts frighten him, and he feels his shirt dripping with perspiration.

"Turn left! Go straight! Turn right" shouts the officer, digging his fingernails into Peter's arm. He tries to follow the man as fast as he can, but the heel of his shoe gets tangled in the tassels of the rug. He loses his balance and falls, pulling the man down with him.

"Damn! Son of a bitch! Watch where you go!" he cries, scrambling to his feet. "Let's go and keep walking!"

"Where to?"

"Shut up and keep moving, or you'll break your neck on the next staircase!"

* * *

They descend another flight of stairs. Now the carpet has ended and they walk on bare cement. They have entered a basement filled with the odors of latrines, disinfectant, unwashed clothes, stale sweat and rancid cooking oil. It is hot, and Peter can hear the roaring of the furnace behind him.

Loud voices shout commands. Curses and fits of hoarse laughter compete with the hammering of marching boots. Heavy doors screech open, and Peter thinks that he hears muffled moans behind them. He imagines himself standing in a long corridor with a vaulted ceiling, bordered by many cells. There is a prison here, after all, with numerous low and narrow chambers.

Soon he is going to be pushed into one and locked inside. His heart races and his hands are cold. He feels lost and helpless. He is ashamed of this helplessness. If only he had stayed home in his lab! If only he had said, "No!" to Toma early on and pretended to be sick!

"Stay here and don't move!" says the officer, suddenly letting go of Peter's arm. He walks away, his footsteps growing fainter in the distance. Peter is so surprised that he doesn't budge, but he raises his hand to remove the spectacles. "Don't!" a voice roars close by. "Don't touch the spectacles!" A new Securitate officer grabs Peter's shoulder and stands so close that Peter can smell the tobacco on his breath. He struggles to free himself.

"Let's go!" says the man, tightening his grip. He pulls Peter to the end of the corridor and then, puffing and wheezing, up another steep flight of stairs. At the top he opens a door. Freezing air comes rushing in.

"Out of here! Get out!" orders the officer, pulling Peter along. But he stops in the doorway, and refuses to go on. The cold air makes him shiver and brings with it the image of the dead dog sprawled in the snow. He shudders and steps back.

"Let's go! What are you waiting for? We're not standing in line for sugar!" The officer is angry. He gives Peter a sudden push. He is propelled forward, then stopped by the hard, cold surface of a car. The door opens and he is pulled into the back seat.

It is quiet inside, and the air is filled with cigarette smoke. Peter starts to cough. The militiaman climbs into the seat next to him and the car takes off. Peter hears the iron gate of the park shut. Then everything is silent.

They drive on noiselessly. Even the engine is quiet. And at every sharp turn the butt of the officer's gun pokes Peter in the ribs.

Where are they going? Nobody says anything. Will he remain forever blindfolded and imprisoned in this moving tomb? He longs for a small sign a life, the barking of a dog, the call of a bird, but nothing happens, nobody breaks the deep silence of the night.

Then suddenly the car stops. The tin spectacles are ripped from Peter's face and a strong light shines in his eyes, blinding him. He winces with pain.

"Sign here!" says the officer, holding a sheet of paper in one hand and a flashlight in the other. "Sign here at once!"

In the light of the lamp Peter can see the officer's small, glinting eyes and his blotchy, unshaven face. He is pressing a pen into Peter's hand and is bending toward him. Once again Peter smells the cigarettes on his breath.

"Sign and be done with it!" says the man, pushing the paper under Peter's nose. "This is your declaration that you will never tell anybody where you have been tonight! Nobody! Understand? Or else!"

Peter takes the pen and signs his name at the bottom of the page.

"All right, now get out…and…not a word! Not a single word to anyone!"

He crawls out of the car. When he looks around he sees that he is standing at the back of the medical school, near the basement entrance to the anatomy lab.

* * *

Chapter 17

Back in his room Peter throws his clothes on a chair and gets into bed. He has waited for this moment for so long. He is so tired that his eyes close right away. He is drifting to sleep, sinking deeper and deeper, but just when he is ready to let go and slide into nothingness, he perks up, suddenly startled and fully awake. Has somebody called him? Whispered his name? Is somebody watching him?

Peter sits up and listens. Everything is silent except for the tolling of the grandfather clock above his room in Comrade Dumitru's office. He lies down, closes his eyes, and drifts to sleep again. But then he feels it again. Is somebody there in the lab with him? He sits up. But nothing, nobody seems to be there.

He stretches out, but once again he is startled out of his slumber. Still he doesn't hear anything. Lying on his couch with his eyes closed he can clearly feel that somebody is watching him. He opens one eye just a bit, and through the window which forms the upper part of the door he sees two eyes watching him. They are large and they stare at him fixedly and sternly. Whose eyes are they? Who can it be? In his drowsy state it takes him time to recognize the eyes of Stalin's portrait. He had forgotten that the official picture in the dissection room was hanging on the wall opposite his door. The large and penetrating eyes are staring at him through the transom window.

In the light of the street lamp the eyes are glowing with a ghostly radiance. They are hypnotizing him. Peter remembers a story about a museum portrait of Stalin whose eyes had an unusual, otherworldly glow. A strange light shone in them, as if from the eyes of a living god or a miraculous being. People came from near and far to see it and worship. Old women fell to their knees and crossed themselves as if in front of a heavenly apparition. Peasants brought icons and candles to be blessed by "Father Stalin."

But after some time, everybody who had touched the portrait with their hands fell sick and died. The first one to die was the painter who created it, followed by the framer who had framed it, and then by the museum guard who kept watch in that room, and even the cleaning lady who dusted the picture day after day. They all got sick and died because, by a strange mistake, the eyes of the portrait had been painted with a special paint which was radioactive. That gave them the unnatural glow!

Peter tries to bury his head under the pillow but he feels suffocated. He jumps out of bed, turns on the light, and starts searching for something he can hang over the upper part of the door. The first thing he sees is the print of Anubis, the jackal-headed god who is testing the purity of a dead man's heart with the Great Scale. The print is fastened over his bed. He peels it off the wall and pastes it on the transom. Now Stalin's portrait is hidden from view. The room is peaceful and quiet. He goes back to bed and falls into a deep, restful sleep.

* * *

When he wakes in the morning the loudspeaker is blaring in the dissection hall and Comrade Dumitru is shouting military commands.

Half asleep Peter jumps out of bed and throws cold water on his face. Then, as he puts on his clothes, he finds the piece of cake, the banana and the orange Toma had given him. He hasn't tasted a banana or an orange in nearly ten years, since before the war. As he peels the banana, the events of the day before come back to his mind. The ride in the van with Toma and the corpses, the dissected bodies of children spread out in the gilded ballroom, the chopped organs stacked in the refrigerator, the flask of rose-colored human serum. Everything is whirling in his mind, like a giant merry-go-round. Toma's question looms above all: has he made up his mind about working with him and his father in the new lab? When would he start?

Peter dreads confrontations. He knows Toma is not going to take NO for an answer and will look for other ways to convince him. He hates walking into the dissection hall and meeting him face to face. All he wants to do is slip back into bed and pull the blanket over his head. But this is not possible so he will try to avoid Toma, stay out of his way, no matter what.

He finally puts on his smock, finishes eating a slice of cake and a piece of banana. Then he opens the door and steps into the dissection hall.

* * *

As soon as he walks in, he sees Comrade Dumitru standing in the front of the room, under the portrait of Stalin, talking to the Party officials. He is frowning and nervously scratching his left ear with his long fingernail. Then he turns toward Peter and puts a heavy hand on his shoulder.

"Quick, go help Professor Andronic carry his Honor Panel! It must be ready for transportation at..." The rest of the sentence is lost in a burst of static from the loudspeaker.

Peter walks toward the Professor. Without a word they pick up the large plywood panel and carry it to the door. Professor Andronic avoids Peter's eyes. He keeps turning his face away. There is anger and envy; Peter can feel it.

No, the Professor did not forget the humiliations he suffered yesterday in front of Comrade Dumitru, the Party officials, and the students! He will not forgive Toma's sarcastic remarks. He won't accept the victory of Toma and Peter's team over his own. Somehow he must take his revenge. And, if Toma is not around, why not aim his anger at Peter? Why not take it out on him?

Peter watches his face. It makes him think of a cunning snake, with unblinking eyes.

They walk very slowly as Professor Andronic is limping from the hip, dragging his left leg behind him. His gait makes him sway out of balance. The heavy panel swings side to side, and when they get close to Peter's lab the panel sways so heavily to the left that it bangs into the door. It opens immediately, bringing into view the old Egyptian print of Anubis with the Great Scale which is pasted on the other side of the door.

Nobody should see this picture! Least of all Comrade Dumitru and Professor Andronic! Peter wishes he could run and lock the door or post himself in front of it and cover the print with his body. But he can't move away. He is forced to stay where he is, holding onto Professor Andronic's Honor Panel.

The Professor turns toward the picture to study it. "Put down the panel and prop it against the wall!" he orders. After they place the Honor Panel on the ground, he limps to the picture and examines it closely. He puts on his glasses to see better, then he turns toward Peter. "So you've become religious! A mystical experience? You belong to a movement? A cult? And practicing here, in the medical school?" he asks in an official tone which he tries to keep casual. "You're not only plain religious, but mystical too! You've joined the forces of superstition, of darkness, the forces of our enemies—the archenemies of the Party, the world of organized underground cults! Haven't you learned that religion is the opium of the masses, the dangerous poison against the Socialist Revolution? But it seems that you have already joined these enemies!"

A broad grin appears on the Professor's face. "Now I understand everything. It's all very clear to me!" He nods as if he has made a great discovery. "Very interesting indeed. Something worth looking into and following up!" He takes off his glasses and starts cleaning them with a white handkerchief. The grin is still on his face. "We'll see...This certainly needs further investigation!" he says as he comes back to the panel and picks it up.

* * *

The following night Peter has a dream. He dreams about snakes, hundreds of them, each one with the face of Professor Andronic. In his dream he and Mariana are working at the microscope in the lab and the snakes are crawling toward them from all directions. They come out from under the cot and from under the worktable, they spill out of crates full of bones and out of the skulls on the shelves, squeezing through the empty eye sockets, the missing noses, and the toothless jaws. Small and thin in the beginning, they grow quickly, some becoming as thick as logs and writhing on the ground, then knocking loudly against the floor and the walls.

A large and hissing snake comes very close to Mariana's leg. Peter grabs a long bone from the worktable and starts hitting the snake. Its body shatters in tens of separate pieces and each piece grows a head with the face of Professor Andronic. They hiss and crawl toward Mariana, ready to slide up her leg, while Peter keeps hitting them with the femur.

But to no avail! They continue to advance through the room, crawling up the walls, dropping from the ceiling with loud thumping sounds and growing new heads whenever they break. One of them, a long, black snake with a slimy body, is hanging from a light bulb, balancing in the air, just above Peter's head. Then suddenly it drops on his back, winding its body around his shoulders and arms. Peter tries to free himself from this choking embrace but the thick coils only grow tighter and tighter. He turns his head, searching for an escape, but finds instead the snake's pointed fangs and its forked tongue flush with his face. The room is filled with hammering sounds.

I am lost! This monster will strangle me or poison me with its venom! I have to act fast! He tries once more to push the snake's head away with the bone. But it is too late. The touch of the snake has paralyzed him, his arms grow numb, the hand with the femur goes limp, and the snake's open mouth grows suddenly very large and swallows him completely. Inside its stomach it is cold and pitch dark, while the knocking sound grows louder and louder. This is the end he thinks as he falls into an abyss.

Finally he stops as he hits the bottom of the pit. Peter opens his eyes. He is lying alone on his cot, and the snakes have disappeared. But the hammering is still there. The nightmare has ended. He is not quite awake. Someone is pounding at the door.

At first Peter is stunned and can't move. A few seconds later he gets up and opens the door just a crack. Professor Andronic is standing there, drenched by the rain. Water is dripping from his fur hat which looks like a wet rat; it is trickling down his thinning hair, his myopic spectacles, his waterlogged overcoat. It gathers in a puddle under his feet. Peter is surprised to see the Professor so early in the morning, since it is Saturday and the first day of winter recess. Is he still dreaming? Is Professor Andronic going to change into a snake and attack him?

Peter takes a step backward. The Professor is pushing the door open without walking into the room. He blows his nose, then takes off his glasses and wipes them with the same handkerchief. He glances at Peter with a frown on his face. Then he clears his throat, as if preparing for a speech. "We need rubber tubing to embalm the new corpses for the students," he says as he puts on his glasses. "You must go immediately to the tire factory 'Victoria Poporului' and bring twenty meters of rubber hose. Why are you standing here with your jaw hanging? Hurry up and get dressed, you know how long it takes to go there and get back!"

The Professor avoids Peter's eyes. He keeps looking away as he speaks. Peter listens and wonders if the Professor came just for rubber tubing or for something else? It is unusual for him to be there so early on Saturday! He looks at the man carefully. He does, indeed, resemble a snake with his pockmarked skin, his bulging eyes and narrow shoulders! He thinks of his dream, of the large, venomous serpent which had strangled and paralyzed him and pushed him down into the freezing pit. But that was just a dream, a nightmare which has come and gone. The serpents have vanished, and he is alive! No reason to fear anything! Maybe something good lies ahead.

A new beginning: Professor Andronic asking him to do "real work" with the students...His time of banishment from the mortuary ending soon...Maybe a sign of change...Even Mariana perhaps coming back!

* * *

Chapter 18

L ess than ten minutes later Peter is out on the street, trudging through slush and melting snow, rushing toward the tram station. On Saturday the factory closes earlier than other days, and the streetcars and buses don't run very often. But he has to be there in time, no matter what!

It is raining heavily now. A strong wind is blowing and icy water is gathering on the streets which are covered with melting snow. It is dark and the street lamps have not yet been switched off.

Peter hurries past a bakery which is still closed. In front of it a long line of people in shabby clothes huddle under broken umbrellas. He runs past the grocery store which has only pea soup and cabbages for sale. He hurries toward the tram station, hoping to be there before the onslaught of the rush hour. But he finds himself surrounded by a crowd of farmers who have reached the city at the crack of dawn. They charge into the streetcar with such force that Peter is lifted and carried up the stairs, but he's unable to get inside the car. He is forced to hang on the stairs, clasping the metal bar in the freezing rain. But he doesn't care. All he wants is to reach the factory in time.

After a while he gets inside and finds a seat near a broken window. He wonders what time it is and begins looking for his watch. It is an old-fashioned pocket watch with a long silver chain, a present from Professor Munteanu. He always feels protected when he has the watch with him, and he usually carries it in his pocket. He starts searching through his pockets, removing everything, but he can't find the watch. "Damn! I must have left it at home!"

He is immediately filled with apprehension. Not having the watch is a bad omen. Also, knowing the time is particularly important today when he is in a hurry to get to the factory. He goes through his pockets a second time. When he has no success, he gives up. He leans back and closes his eyes.

Things are going to work out in the end! He tries to tell himself. This will be a good opportunity to work with the students again, an opportunity he can't miss. If he can only bring back the rubber tubing in time everything will be all right. Maybe Mariana too will be coming back! They will work together and one day they will escape together.

The monotonous sound of the wheels and the rocking of the car make him drowsy. Behind closed eyes he imagines himself with Mariana in a small boat on the Black Sea, sailing away. It is the dead of night and there has been a storm with strong winds, thunder and lightning and waves as tall as a house. The storm has stopped the Coast Guard from chasing them. He and Mariana nearly drowned. Their boat almost capsized. They had to lie down for hours in the bottom of the cabin to avoid being flung overboard. But now the storm has ended, the wind has died down, and the sky is covered with millions of stars. In the east, the horizon is turning red. The elegant shape of a minaret suggests that they are in Turkey. The air is clear and cool after the rain, and a lone seagull is circling their boat.

A sudden jolt. The screeching of brakes makes Peter open his eyes. The tram has stopped and new passengers climb into the car. A fat woman with a flowery skirt under her heavy shawl takes the seat facing him. She carries a large straw basket which she holds on her knees. An old man with a threadbare army coat and a pointed fur hat sits next to her.

As soon as they are settled the tram starts moving again. It climbs very slowly uphill and Peter wishes it would go faster. He thinks that they are going backward, not forward, and that time is moving faster and faster. He would get off the streetcar and push it forward if it would help.

They have long passed the center of town with its tree-lined boulevards, its statues, theaters and movie houses. They have reached the outskirts of the city and they are now riding past narrow streets bordered by low huts that are covered with melting snow. People are wading through ankle-deep floods in which all kinds of refuse is floating: old newspapers, pieces of cardboard, potato peels, dirty rags, even pieces of broken furniture.

The wooden fences between courtyards are gone and old trees have been cut. "They've used everything for firewood!" the fat woman says to the man next to her. "But winter has just started. What are they going to burn in a month or two?" The man shrugs. He has padded his army coat with old newspapers. Peter can hear the rustling of paper when he moves. He doesn't speak. He only keeps shrugging and spits on the floor.

Peter looks out the window and sees a stuffed toy, a rabbit or a teddy bear float by, followed by the bloated body of a drowned kitten.

"It looks like a dead rat!" says the woman. "They're selling dog and cat meat on the black market. It tastes sweet and nauseating, people say. Anything goes these days. My neighbor told me that she went to buy a chicken, but when she came home and put the bird in the pot, she saw that it was an old crow. It had black feet and a large, black beak! Devil's work!" the woman adds, crossing herself three times. The old man doesn't say anything; he only shakes his head, while the newspapers rustle under his tunic as he moves.

The tram turns right and a small butcher shop comes into view. The line of people in front of it curls around the block and disappears around the corner. They have brought stools and crates on which to climb so they don't have to stand in the water. Peter looks without really seeing them. He keeps searching for a clock to time his progress.

There are many clocks in the city, some standing in open piazzas, others perched on church towers, and others adorning the entrances to public buildings. But there are none in the outskirts of the town.

He closes his eyes and keeps very still. His thoughts rush toward Mariana.

* * *

Here they are, on their little boat. It is morning now. The sun has risen and they pull ashore. They step on land and follow a narrow path between grasses and bushes of pomegranates. A church bell tolls at the end of the path and they follow its sound. They arrive at a small shrine hollowed into the rock. They climb down into a round chapel lit by candles. It has painted walls and a gilt ceiling. The air smells of incense and beeswax. A tall man with a white beard stands in the middle of the shrine. He waves at them to come closer, and when they are near, he takes two gold rings from a silver box and slips them on their fingers. Then he says a short prayer in a language they don't understand, and makes the sign of the cross over them.

Peter looks away from the old man and, when he turns back, the man is changed into Professor Munteanu. Now they are standing inside a lab and the altar has been replaced with the round face of a large clock. Peter tries to read the time, but the figures are written in a mysterious script he doesn't know. The hands are turning with dizzying speed.

* * *

Suddenly there is another jolt. The screeching of brakes. Peter opens his eyes and looks at the woman in front of him. As the tram comes to a halt the straw basket rolls down from her knees. A young piglet jumps out of it. It grunts loudly, runs to the open door, and dives head first into the icy water that fills the gutters. The woman runs after the pig, screaming and cursing, ready to jump off the tram and wade into the water. But a young man wearing a worker's cap catches the pig by the tail and brings it back. "Here's your treasure! Be careful, don't let it catch cold!" he says.

Everybody laughs. The woman takes the pig in her arms, and wraps it in a dirty towel which she pulls out of the basket.

"*Porcul dracului! Stai linistit ca te tai*" (Damned pig! Stay still or I slaughter you!), she curses as it tries to wiggle out of her lap. Then she slips it back in the straw basket and pushes it under the seat.

Peter watches the woman in silence, drumming with his fingertips on the windowpane. His patience is wearing thin. Time is running out. It will get dark and night will set in. He is convinced that this is his only chance to work with the students again without the help of Toma or Comrade Dumitru. He doesn't want to miss it. If I don't do it now it will never happen again! he tells himself.

Then he changes his mind. Bad thoughts attract bad luck! It is no help spinning bad thoughts, particularly now, when the tram has started to move again and is slowly climbing uphill.

It runs for a short time but then stops altogether. He looks out the window and sees that they are surrounded by a herd of cows being led to the slaughterhouse. They are slowly wading through water and slush. Next to his window an old cow with a broken horn and dirt-covered sores stumbles out of line and slips on the ice. A young man hits the cow with a whip. Blood gushes out of its wounds. The animal makes a plaintive sound that resembles a human moan. The cow sways on its thin legs ready to fall. But the man whips and kicks it back in its place.

Peter feels the blood rushing to his head. The beating of the cow makes him very angry. He wants to jump out of the streetcar and strike the man with the whip. But the doors are locked and he can't get off. He clenches his fists and sits motionless, his muscles tight, ready to snap.

They are riding along the brick wall of the slaughterhouse and the stench of rotting meat is everywhere. The tram stops at the entrance gate which is decorated with a large portrait of Stalin. Underneath is an inscription: "It is a Communist duty to love and care for the animals!"

Is this a joke? A dark, funereal Communist joke? It makes Peter want to laugh and cry at the same time.

* * *

The next stop is the crematorium. Peter remembers that it is a very modern building with a large round clock over the main entrance. He watches the road impatiently, eager to catch sight of the clock. But when they reach the building, he sees that the clock is hidden behind a red billboard with the inscription, "Full speed ahead for the Early Fulfillment of the Five Year Plan!" Yes indeed, full speed ahead! Peter muses. Maybe they're going to burn people while they're still alive! Maybe they'll even enlist volunteers! The more the merrier! That will be a great victory for the plan! But, be this as it may, no sense searching for a clock anymore! He leans back and looks out the window. At least they are moving ahead. And it seems to him that, as long as the tram is moving, time is slowing down.

* * *

"End of the line! Everybody out!" yells the conductor. The tram stops and starts haltingly a few times before coming to a full stop. Peter gets off and takes cover under a broken shelter where passengers have to wait for the bus to take them further. Across the street, on top of a hill, stands the onion-shaped church tower of an old Byzantine monastery which has been converted into a jail for political prisoners. At the bottom of the hill is a gate and a garret guarded by a young militia officer with a gun topped by a bayonet.

While Peter and the other passengers huddle under the leaky roof of the station, the fat woman with the pig crosses the street and walks straight to the officer in the garret. She stops, pulls the pig out of the basket and dangles it in front of the officer, while talking to him. The man shakes his head and waves her away. But the woman stays put; she keeps dangling the pig in front of him. She even tries to squeeze through the gate. The officer shakes his head and pushes her away. Finally when she doesn't leave, he grabs the piglet, throws it up in the air, and lets it drop in the ditch filled with icy water.

The woman shrieks, jumps after the pig, and grabs hold of its ears. But three large dogs appear from behind the garret and move very fast. Even though she holds onto the pig's ears they sink their teeth in its belly and tear it apart. The woman keeps screaming and her wails get mixed with the shrieks of the pig and the barking of the dogs. She holds the empty basket in one hand while the other hand hangs limp and bloodstained at her side.

"She must have a loved one inside the prison if she brings the warden such a fine Christmas gift!" says the man with the worker's cap.

Peter sighs. He wonders whether they are on the way to inferno rather than to the rubber factory! Did the conductor make a wrong turn? Did he, Peter take the wrong streetcar?

He takes a deep breath and paces back and forth under the leaky roof. Finally, with loud rattling and honking, a red bus stops at the station. Peter climbs in and sits in the last row. He leans his head against the wall and stretches his frozen legs. It feels good to be out of the cold. He takes off his mittens and squeezes the rain out of them. He is feeling at peace.

But not for long! After a while they must get out of the bus. They are climbing a steep hill and because of the ice, the bus is sliding back. Everybody has to get out and push. Peter joins the others and steadies his back and shoulders against the bus. But the ground is so slippery that he loses his balance and almost falls down. Fortunately he catches the door handle and pulls himself up. Finally the engine starts again and everybody climbs back in the bus.

He looks out the window and sees that they have reached the top of the hill. In the distant valley the tire factory with its tin roof and its smoking chimneys awaits. The fog has lifted, but the rain is still pounding the road. How late is it? Faint lights start blinking here and there in windows. And in the dim, bluish glow of the afternoon, he sees that all the roads to the factory are filled with long lines of gray army trucks. They are barely moving. They are all headed toward the tire plant, where more trucks are lined up in front of the entrance and parked inside the courtyard.

How is he going to reach the gate of the factory? When will he step inside to get the rubber hose?

It all looks very disheartening with the army trucks bumper to bumper like a chain with no end. The bus can't advance between them. And by foot it is very far. Peter finds no solution. He looks around and sees that inside the bus most passengers have closed their eyes and have fallen asleep. Only the woman with the pig is not on the bus. She has stayed behind, staring at them when they left.

* * *

They advance very slowly. The rubber factory comes into view again and Peter starts hoping anew.

They are getting closer. They only have to cross the railway tracks and keep driving downhill. He will get the rubber tubing at last.

A very large army truck roars by, rattling and honking, followed by another huge, gray army truck and another. The bus is now wedged between two heavy trucks, and they are all driving at full speed. Then the lorry in front of them slows down, halts, and starts again. The brakes screech, it stops. Nothing moves. Peter waits and waits.

He stares fixedly at the back of the bus driver's head. He wants to get up, open the doors and get off. But they have stopped between stations and the driver is sitting patiently, reading the Communist daily, *Scinteia*. Then he takes off his cap, folds the newspaper and puts it in his briefcase. He crosses his arms over the steering wheel and rests his head on his arms.

Peter stares at him, even though he knows it is useless. After a while the man raises his head and yawns. Then he shifts on his seat and rubs his eyes. He gets up and pushes the button to open the doors. "Fresh air! A bit of fresh air will be good!" he announces as a stream of cold air mixed with a strong smell of sulfur and gasoline pours into the bus.

Peter leaps from his seat, runs to the door and jumps off the bus. He hurts his ankle, but he pays no attention. He starts running.

"Comrade, where are you going? You're in the middle of nowhere! You'll be hit by a truck!" yells the bus driver, waving his arms. But Peter doesn't look back. He runs quickly, stretching his long legs as if he were in a race. He moves along the column of motionless cars stretching far into the distance. The heavy trucks take up so much space that he has to run along the edge of the road on a narrow path by the ditch.

Suddenly the cars start moving, and soon they gain full speed. They're splashing him with mud as they roar by, drenching him to the bone. But he doesn't care. Down in the valley he can see the chimneys of the factory spewing dark smoke mixed with glittering sparks, like a gay firework. And when the wind blows uphill it brings a pervasive stench of sulfur and gasoline. It means that the factory is still working full blast. He will get there on his own, without anyone's help.

He turns a corner, wading through puddles, and keeps staring in front of him. Not too far ahead are the glistening railway tracks. He is going to make it! He will leap over the tracks as he did in his childhood! One more step and he will be there.

But just as he reaches the red and white crossing barrier the wooden pole is lowered, forcing him to stop. He can hear the train whistle and see the steam engine getting closer.

Peter leans against the crossing barrier and waits. Should he sneak under it and venture across the rails? The train lumbers forward and the black locomotive stops right where he stands. It is a huge engine with a wide smokestack and tall, shiny wheels. The bulging body is covered with thousands of droplets of water, like sweat. A large reflector is burning at the front of the locomotive. It has a greenish-yellow glow, like the eyes of the snakes in his dream. The train looks like an unending snake crawling along the tracks. As he stands near the barrier, Peter is engulfed in a cloud of moist heat. He hears the loud hissing of the engine letting out steam. He barely manages to jump aside to avoid being scalded.

* * *

As he keeps waiting, he suddenly feels very tired and cold. His feet are wet and his clothing is drenched. He is exhausted and full of doubt. What has he accomplished by jumping off the bus, wading through puddles and slush, leaping in front of army trucks? He could have been killed. The bus driver was right. He is still in the middle of nowhere. And he didn't find any shortcut to the factory either.

Peter turns and looks at the road, searching for the bus. But he doesn't see it. The bus is far behind. Even if he wanted to, he couldn't go back. All he sees is a huge military truck and behind it another, and another. If they start moving again they may very well run him over.

He stares at the nearest truck, its powerful, rumbling engine, its dirty windshield all splashed with mud. Suddenly he hears honking. He looks around. He is alone on the road. Nobody else is standing nearby. He keeps staring at the cab of the truck. It seems to him that somebody is waving inside. A hand is moving; a head is nodding. He rubs his eyes in astonishment and, to his surprise, the door of the cab opens and a man in military uniform leaps down from the truck. He walks toward Peter waving his arms. He is wearing a greatcoat and a green army cap. His young face looks familiar, with sallow skin and big black eyes half hidden under his cap.

"Peter," the man yells as he comes closer "It's me, Ali. What in hell are you doing here?"

Peter stares at the apparition. He can't believe that he is talking to Mustafa's son who he had last seen in the devastated restaurant. "Trying to get to the rubber factory!" he says.

"What a coincidence! I am also headed to the factory! Let me give you a lift, you'll never make it on foot!" He shakes Peter's hand and slaps his back.

"The factory closes at 3:30 on Saturdays and we'll just be in time. How great that we'll drive down together!"

As they climb into the truck's cab and sit on the bench covered with a woolen army blanket there is a loud whistle from the train engine, followed by the sound of brakes loosening up. The train starts to roll. The crossing barrier is slowly lifted.

* * *

"We're lucky!" says Ali. "We're going to make it!" It's a bad day today, too many people, too many trucks, and all that rain...It's hard to advance."

They have crossed the railway tracks and are driving along the left side of the train. "I can't believe that I ran into you, old chap!" says Ali. He keeps slapping his thigh with his hand. "How have you been? You know, so much has happened since I last saw you! What do you need the rubber hose for?"

"For embalming the corpses in the Anatomy Department!" Peter is still staring at Ali. "But...how come you are in the army? ...and driving a truck?" he blurts out.

Ali gives him a sharp look. "I'll tell you everything after we're finished at the factory. How much rubber hose do you need?"

"At least 15 meters, 2 centimeters thick. That's what they use in the department."

They are silent for a while as they drive. Ali starts rummaging under his seat with one hand. He brings up two china cups and an army canteen. He hands the cups to Peter. Then he props the canteen on the seat next to him and removes its cap with his free hand.

"Hold the cups straight so I can pour!" he says, and soon the fruity smell of *tsuică* fills the cabin. "To our encounter!" Ali raises his cup and clinks with Peter.

"Yes, to our meeting!"

Peter can't believe that he is sitting in this army truck with Ali. He rubs his forehead with his free hand, trying to remember something. His last memory of Ali is the winter night in Mustafa's restaurant. There were fragments of smashed crockery and broken glass all around them. And the fish, the giant sturgeon, ripped from the wall and shattered to pieces on the floor. Mustafa had just been arrested and Ali's mother was sobbing in the kitchen.

Peter looks at the cup in his hand. He has seen it before. It is made of dark blue porcelain with a golden rim and a golden fish, a sturgeon, frolicking in deep waters. The words *"La Nisetrul de Aur"* (at the Golden Sturgeon), the name of Mustafa's restaurant, are inscribed in shiny letters inside the cup.

"I tell you how we're going to do this. When we reach the factory I'll go in and you stay in the truck. I will get the tires and your rubber hose because you see, my friend, today only the military are getting service. Everybody else will be sent home empty-handed," says Ali. "As a matter of fact, civilians are not allowed in the courtyard today! But..."

Peter nods. He can't say a word. They are passing through a gray cornfield and its vista is interrupted here and there by tall scarecrows hitched to a pole. Black crows are perched on top of each pole. On the right, the train runs along the highway, also headed toward the rubber factory.

Soon they reach a busy crossroad. An armed militiaman stops all the buses and cars that don't belong to the army and turns them back to the city. All the civilian cars are stopped, there is no exception. Peter sees a bus being forced to turn right and then back to the city. Maybe it is the bus in which he had traveled.

He keeps watching it and cannot believe his luck. He cannot believe that he met Ali and will get the rubber hose on a day none is available to regular citizens.

* * *

They park the truck at the foot of a brick wall, at the furthest corner of the courtyard. A few cars are leaving the factory when they arrive, and they find a spot between a pile of discarded tires and a puddle of ill-smelling, sulfurous acid. A street lamp with a stained bulb is burning nearby.

Ali stops the engine and opens the door. "I'll go in, get the tires and the rubber hose while you, old chap stay here quietly. I won't be long!" He gets out of the car, takes a few steps and comes running back.

"Get down on the floor and let me hide you under the blanket! There are Securitate men patrolling the courtyard, and you're not allowed to be here!" He is frowning and the dimple on his cheek has disappeared.

"*Bine! Bine!* All right!"

Peter slides to the floor and pulls his knees to his chin. Ali drapes the woolen blanket over him. Then he locks the door and walks toward the building.

* * *

It is getting dark and is very quiet. Peter's eyes close, he is almost dozing. His head is swimming after the glass of *tsuicā*. Mariana's face smiles at him from the shadows. She is winking and calling him. Peter smiles with his eyes closed. But soon his legs feel cramped in the narrow space and he turns, trying to make himself more at ease. As he moves his elbow hits a hard object with an irregular surface. He tries to push it out of the way and as he does, the knapsack, for it is a large knapsack, falls over and opens. Its contents spill on the floor.

Peter is quite surprised: there are rings, bracelets and brooches, knives, forks and spoons, their handles engraved with the shape of a sturgeon. He sits up and plunges his hands inside the knapsack, sifting the objects between his fingers. Clumps of earth have also found their way inside the sac, and the smooth surface of some of the objects is encrusted with soil, as if everything had been buried under the earth.

Peter sinks his hands deep into the sac, until he reaches the bottom. Here he finds a silver cigarette lighter and next to it a large object, a curved sword in its sheath, a short Turkish "Yatagan." It is wrapped in a towel and it takes some effort to pull it out. He unwraps the towel and sees that there are clumps of earth in the folds, just like in the rest of the sac. The sheath of the yatagan is studded with precious stones which glow in the light of the street lamp. The curved steel blade is adorned with gold letters. It looks like an Eastern, Arabic inscription, which he is not able to read. He touches the knife with the tips of his fingers and remembers that Ali had once spoken about an old "magic" sword. It was a family heirloom which had come down from father to son for many generations, when they still lived in Istanbul. The blade was decorated with a golden inscription of the Koranic verses which told of Victory in the Holy War and the magical powers of the Sultan Suleyman the Magnificent. Ali had told him that this yatagan had vanquished enemy armies by beheading the soldiers in their sleep. This is how it gained great victories for Suleyman the Magnificent, for Baiazid and other great sultans, and this was how it may even have conquered the City of Constantinople for Mehmet the Great.

Ali had never shown him the sword. He had only once spoken about it to Peter, and even then only in whispers as if he were afraid to wake it up from its slumber. How it had ended up in Ali's army truck Peter can't understand.

He is still examining the yatagan when he hears people outside. There are voices and footsteps approaching and he has just time to hide under the blanket before a flashlight shines through the window. He slips everything under the cover and doesn't move.

The steps and voices come closer until he hears dogs barking and scratching at the door.

"I've never seen the dogs so excited!" says one of the men. "They act as if there is someone inside!"

The flashlight shines through the window again and the men try to open the door. Peter still doesn't move. He is clenching his fists and holding his breath. What now?

The Securitate men rattle the door and the dogs bark and scratch. He is choking under the dusty blanket and his throat is burning from the acid fumes of the sulfurous puddle. He is afraid he will burst into a coughing fit. He takes a deep breath and then stops breathing. One...two...three...he keeps counting in his head. But how long can he last? How long can he hold his breath? Maybe he should raise the ancient yatagan from its sleep and order it into action. Then he would be as victorious as the sultans of old! He is sure that the blade with the golden inscription will obey his command. But how about Ali, how can he protect him? In his hand the yatagan will certainly bring forth a devastating blood bath!

Peter cannot decide. He is at the end of his wits. His clothes are drenched in cold sweat. He opens his mouth without making a sound. And just as he is ready to speak he hears quick steps approaching and Ali talking rapidly with the men.

"What's up? Why are you standing here?"

"We've never seen the dogs so excited, barking and jumping like this at the door! They act as if someone is hiding inside!"

"What a thought! They got wild from the smell of the meat and the sausages I carried yesterday to the army barracks!" says Ali. "I swear that smell drives them crazy! But today I have nothing, and there is nobody inside the truck! But better than standing here and wasting time, give me a hand with the tires so I can put them in the back of the truck."

"I don't know! I don't know...this is quite strange!" Some of the men are insisting. Peter can hear them conferring with each other in low voices. Then somebody comes closer and rattles the door again while the flashlight cuts through the darkness.

"Come on! Give me a hand with the tires. You're wasting your time. My word, there is nobody here!" says Ali.

"I don't quite believe you! We should have a look inside the cab!" comes the reply.

"Oh! Stop it. It's getting late, time to go home," say the others. "Besides, he's with the army; we can trust him!"

Finally they follow Ali to the back of the truck. Peter can hear them swearing and cursing under the weight of the tires and he feels the jolt of the big rubber hoops hitting the bed of the truck. The dogs are still barking at the side of the cab.

* * *

"Pfew! Finished, thank God! They're gone and here, my friend, is your rubber hose!" Ali says after he climbs into the truck and closes the door.

Peter has scrambled up from the floor and is sitting on the bench, holding the rubber hose in one hand. He is still holding the cigarette lighter in the other. Ali starts the engine, steps on the gas, and the truck turns right, slowly rolling through the tall entrance gate. At the same moment the factory siren sounds the end of the workday.

"Good timing! You know, we just got out of the plant before being drowned by the crowd of workers going home!"

* * *

They are on the highway driving back to the city along the gray cornfield dotted by scarecrows. Ali pulls out a cigarette and Peter lights it with the silver lighter.

"What are you doing? How did you get this?" Ali asks when he sees the lighter.

"How did you get this? And why are you dragging this stuff around in your truck?" Peter pulls the yatagan from under the blanket and shows it to Ali. "What does this have to do with you and the army? There are clumps of earth all over the place...Where does it come from?"

Ali is silent. He stares at the road and draws on his cigarette. "All right," he says finally without turning his head. He shifts in his seat, trying to find a more comfortable position. "Remember the night you came to our home? Remember how we stood in the smashed up dining room after they took my father away? You know, that same night, soon after you left, they came back and arrested my mother and me, because we were 'homeless' now. See, we had been ordered to leave the house the next morning and the city as well, but we had no place to go. We could not give them any street address, so we were arrested as 'dangerous vagrants' and 'parasites,' *elemente parazite*, that's what they called us. They took us and pushed me into one car and my mother into another. I don't know how many people there were because they blindfolded me and did not speak at all. The radio was playing loudly all through the trip. We drove for a long time and when we finally stopped they also turned off the music. I could hear a metal gate being opened and locked behind us. Finally they let me out and made me climb a long flight of stairs. Then they led me through a narrow corridor and down several steep staircases. In the end they pushed me into a small cell in the basement and locked the iron door. Later I learned that I was held in the old Palace of the Principesa. I don't know how long they kept me there because, you see, my cell had no windows and only a dim light that burned night and day. There was music again. They played the same tune over and over without interruption. It was so loud that I thought it was going to break my eardrums, and sometimes it was very faint and suddenly loud again. I swear it was really deafening! You could never tell, but it kept me awake all the time, and in fear.

"Much later they unlocked my cell and took me to a large room where a Securitate officer asked me to sign a declaration volunteering to join the army. I refused. I was very angry.

"They took me back to my cell, and that night and the next day they gave me nothing to eat and nothing to drink. But when they called me again and asked me to sign up for the army, you know, I still refused. They took me to another room where a fat officer sat behind a desk and ate creamy petit fours out of a cardboard box. He said, 'Okay, I am very patient. I have all the patience in the world, but you will be sorry, young man.'

"Again they blindfolded me and took me back to my cell, and, what do you think? This time they gave me plenty of food and drink, even hot chocolate and black caviar, which I hadn't tasted in a very long time. It was a great feast, and, my word, I slept very well after all that food.

"In the morning they blindfolded me again and led me through endless corridors, and up and down many staircases. When they finally removed the bandana, I was standing in a dark, windowless cell, peering through a glass door into a lighted room. There were iron bars in front of the door. Loud music was blaring, it sounded like a military band. And there, my friend, in the large room was my mother, slumped to the floor, her arms tied to a hot radiator. She was squirming to get away from it. I could see her face all distorted with pain, and her arms blistered and red, even turning dark.

"The music was playing so loud that it drowned all other noises. But when it suddenly stopped I could hear my mother screaming and howling at the top of her voice. I wanted to run to her and cut the leather thongs that tied her to the radiator, but I was locked in that cell. The door was locked. I screamed, I kicked and pounded the door and the iron bars with my feet and my fists, but nobody came. Only much later when I had run out of steam and was totally exhausted did they unlock my cell and let me out. They promised to untie my mother as soon as I signed their declaration."

Ali is silent. He keeps puffing at his cigarette making it glow in the dark. They are nearing the crossing barrier where Peter and Ali met. The barrier is lifted now, there is no train in sight, and they drive over the railway tracks without any trouble.

Peter is watching the road and thinking of Ali, his mother, and his stay in prison. It isn't long since he himself had been led, blindfolded, through the long corridors and up and down many staircases! The foul-smelling, airless basement of the old Palace of the Principesa is still fresh in his mind. He remembers how sick with fright he had been.

"It is hard to forget!" Peter says.

"Hard to forget? I don't even think about it anymore!"

Ali throws his cigarette on the floor and crushes it with his boot. He raises his arm and wipes a stain off the windshield with the cuff of his sleeve.

"But let me go on, old chap. After I signed the declaration they gave me my clothes, my coat, hat and boots, and took me to the Army Command. I was sent to Battalion 5, in Ploești, not too far from the city, for military training. As soon as I arrived the Commandant asked if I knew how to drive. He had just lost his chauffeur who had broken his legs in a drunken fight with the cook. That's how I got the job. Remember, my father taught me to drive the restaurant truck!"

* * *

They pass the crematorium and the slaughterhouse and are nearing the old jail for political prisoners. Peter remembers the fat woman with the piglet, and wonders what happened to her? Then he turns back to Ali and points to the knapsack. "How about all these objects, how about this?" he asks, lifting the yatagan from his lap. "Why are you dragging it around in your truck?"

Ali shifts in his seat and sighs, "These...these...most of these objects, you know, are my father's most precious possessions. I must tell you, he cherished them more than anything in the world. Two years ago he was tipped off by a man connected with the Securitate that they were planning to close all private businesses and confiscate whatever they found on the premises and in the owners' houses. So my father immediately gathered his heirlooms and other possessions, wrapped them in towels and buried them under an old willow, that very night. They stayed there, buried under the tree, all this time, even after the restaurant was closed and we were all arrested.

"But now when the Commandant sent me back to the city with the army truck I sneaked back to the garden one night and dug up the treasure and took it with me. You know I was afraid to leave it there. They might cut down the willow or demolish the house and dig up the garden. And whoever found these objects would take them and make them their own. My father could never stand that, it would break his heart!"

"By the way, you speak about your father. How about him? Is he OK?"

Ali doesn't answer right away. Peter can feel him stiffening, then clearing his throat. Finally he lights another cigarette.

"My father... I have no real news, only rumors, you know! He was sent to the Canal, the Danube-Black Sea Canal to cut reeds. He had to stand in the water, or on the ice. In the winter they're sometimes ordered to break the ice to get to the reeds. It is very dangerous, I was told. It is not uncommon for a prisoner to slip and fall through the cracks, under the ice, and then drown. I heard that this is what happened to my father, that he slipped and fell through the hole and drowned under the ice. They couldn't rescue him, they couldn't pull him out. It was too slippery. Other men, while trying to rescue him, could have slipped through the hole and drowned."

Ali's voice is faint. He stops talking. His breathing is shallow and fast as if he was climbing a mountain. He coughs a few times, then goes on. "And I heard that before he drowned he slept in a new hut, you know those barracks for a hundred men which had been built right now in the winter. People told me that the pillars which propped up the roof, the sustaining columns, were made of stacks of frozen bodies which could not be buried in the hard, icy ground. This is what they said."

His voice fades away, and he stops talking for a short while. He then clears his throat and starts again. "But my mother, I have news about her."

As they keep driving, he doesn't move his head to look at the forbidding structure of the old monastery turned prison, and pays no attention to the pack of dogs which run after the truck. "My mother, I was even able to speak to my mother," he goes on. "She was treated in the prison-hospital until her wounds healed. She was very lucky; she got no infection. And after she recovered they kept her on as a nurse's aide. You know she had worked in a field hospital, when she was young in World War I! Anyway, it was here, in the prison ward that she saw Mariana!"

Peter feels his heart skip a beat. His breathing stops. He covers his eyes with his hand. Ali's voice is very loud.

"They brought her in one night and my mother found her in the morning." Ali goes on. "Mother sat with her, moistened her lips with a wet handkerchief and held her hands. One evening when Mariana could only talk in whisper she asked mother to take her earrings, the gold earrings with the small blue lotus flower, from Egypt and give them to her grandmother. Mother said she was very weak. She couldn't eat. She couldn't open her eyes. The next morning she died.

"My mother took the earrings and gave them to me...but I don't know what happened to her, to her body. Mother told me that she was as small and thin as a child."

Peter's chest feels very tight. He can barely breathe. He sticks his fist in his mouth and bites hard on his knuckles. He wants to scream and howl like a dog, but he cannot, with Ali next to him. He presses one hand over his eyes. The image of the thin bodies of the children laid out on the mosaic tables in the Palace dissection room comes back to his mind.

He breaks out in a cold sweat. Did Mariana have the same fate? Did they carry her upstairs to the Grand Ballroom and lay her body on one of the mosaic tabletops?

Peter keeps pressing his hand over his closed eyes. He tries to push the image away. It fills him with pain. He cannot bear the thought of her death.

* * *

"Here are the earrings, my friend, says Ali. He pulls them out of his coat pocket. They are wrapped in a coarse handkerchief and tied in a bundle. "Maybe you can give them to Mariana's grandmother. I tried to find her, I went to her house, but it was all deserted and locked up. The street was closed and guarded by the militia. You know, they did not let me into the street with the truck, even though it belongs to the army. I tell you, I had to park at the corner across the boulevard. Maybe you can find the old lady! And if you cannot, then keep the earrings yourself. They shouldn't fall into the wrong hands!"

Peter takes the handkerchief with trembling hands. A wave of lassitude sweeps over him. He feels numb, like an empty shell. It is like standing alone in a deserted world. He feels like the last man on earth.

* * *

When his strength comes back and he looks out the window he sees that they are driving along narrow, waterlogged alleyways bordered by dark houses. The street lamps have been turned on but all the lights are dim and blue, for the blackout bulbs from the time of the war are still in place. The blue street lamps are reflected in puddles that fill the streets. They make Peter think that he is traveling through the dark, underground tunnels of the Land of Duat, depicted in the Book of the Dead. In the canals of the Land of Duat rows upon rows of flesh-eating monsters that have swallowed the sun are swinging these blue lanterns in the eternal night.

Peter unties the handkerchief with the earrings. He strokes the flowers with the tip of his fingers. This blue water lily with its pointed petals and its delicate perfume was the most sacred of all the lotuses, Professor Munteanu had said. It represented rebirth and immortality, and its perfume symbolized the breath of divine life.

Peter thinks that, if Mariana was wearing the blue earrings during her hospitalization they should have protected her and not let her die. Maybe the news of her death is not true. Sometimes people in jail or in labor camps, who were believed to be dead or whose death had been even officially announced, came home after memorial services for them had already been held. It was a trick the Securitate loved to play, spreading frightening rumors about people locked up in prisons or camps, saying that they died in a fire, drowned in the sea, went blind or lost their limbs or their mind.

Maybe the information Ali had given him was not true! After all, how much could he really trust Ali? In the end he too had signed a pact with the devil for the sake of his mother!

Peter feels relieved by this thought. Yes, it was the Securitate providing and spreading misinformation. Maybe Ali too had been forced to lie and play the game!

He slips the handkerchief with the earrings back into his pocket. Let the power of the enchanted lotus bud work its full magic and protect Mariana from death! He makes the sign of the cross three times, very quickly. Let heaven add its holy strength to that of the ageless, mysterious stone!

* * *

After they cross the bridge over the swollen Dîmboviţa River they turn left and drive by Mustafa's restaurant. The old sign of the restaurant, the sign with the golden sturgeon which hung over the entrance, has been removed. A black van of the Internal Police is now parked in front of the door.

"Look at this, they have placed a guard in front of the building, and a red banner with a hammer and sickle over the entrance!" says Peter.

"That was quick. Three days ago everything still looked the same, even though there was a big padlock on the door," says Ali. "I should have known that they were going to confiscate the restaurant for some official use! You know, with its large kitchen and dining room it can serve many needs! I wonder whether they've found my tracks in the garden, in the snow, when I dug up my father's treasure. Maybe they thought that thieves or saboteurs were trying to rob the place, now that it belongs to the State. I guess that's why they put a guard at the door!" Ali turns in his seat to have another look. "But, my word, it's really none of my business anymore," he says and shrugs.

* * *

Chapter 19

T hey rumble past once stately mansions on the edge of the oldest part of the city where two hundred years ago wealthy aristocrats, "*boieri*," built their elegant townhouses. They had red tile rooftops, ornate doorways and windows, and steep turrets guarded by stone gargoyles, winged dragons, and knights in shining armor. The mansions were surrounded by gardens and their walls covered with ivy. But now all these buildings belong to the State. The wealthy aristocrats are gone, and the buildings are falling in ruin. The turrets are crumbling, windows are broken or missing and have been replaced with paper or cardboard, the gargoyles, dragons and knights in armor have fallen to the ground. Some are still balancing precariously from cornices and balconies. Drainpipes are also missing, and the rainwater rushes down from the roofs like a tropical waterfall. In the middle of the block one old mansion is leaning dangerously to one side and is propped up by a rotting scaffold. Further down, stand the massive columns of the medical school, an ambitious imitation of the lofty Parthenon. Above them, the library tower is shrouded in mist. And beyond the turrets and roofs lurch the dreamy poplars of the Botanical Garden with their rustling leaves.

* * *

Peter is clutching the rubber hose in his hand and is thinking of the anatomy lab. Surely he is going to be asked to work with the students now. He is bringing a rubber hose of superior quality which can be used for a long time to come.

Then his thoughts wander to Professor Munteanu and to Mariana, and sadness takes hold of him once again. It is no use trying to stop this onslaught of darkness. His thoughts and feelings are like the wind and the clouds. He cannot control them.

The truck slows down and then stops altogether. They have reached the main entrance to the medical school.

"Here we are!" says Ali. "Good meeting you! Hope to see you again before you need a new rubber hose!" He smiles, and in the light of the street lamp Peter can see the dimples in his childish face. No, no, he thinks. Ali is too honest to get involved in dirty business with the Securitate and spread false rumors about Mariana.

"Goodbye!" he says. "Take good care of yourself and of the Yatagan! Many thanks for everything!"

They hug and shake hands. Then Peter jumps down. He stands at the gate and watches the truck until it is out of sight. He is going to miss Ali now that he has met him again. He can't tell when he will see him again.

He walks by the main entrance of the building. The giant red banner is fluttering between the thick columns. He then steps inside, through the small back door he always uses. He runs down the winding stairs to the basement and follows the narrow corridor toward the Department of Anatomy. He doesn't switch on the lights. He can follow this corridor blindfolded. He knows exactly how many steps it takes from the entrance to the door of his lab.

Everything here is the same! The air is saturated with a mixture of fumes: formaldehyde, the smell of burning fuel in the old furnace, and the lingering odor of cheap *Marasesti* cigarettes. He can hear the hissing of radiators and the sound of his own steps on the cement floor.

He walks quickly because he suddenly feels hungry and cold. He hasn't had any food since this morning and his clothes are still wet. He can't wait to get to his room, take off his shoes, and make himself a pot of hot soup.

He runs toward the dissection hall, and as soon as he turns right he sees a glimmer of light under the door. Professor Andronic has probably forgotten to switch off the light, he tells himself. Nobody is ever around on Saturday night.

Nevertheless an uneasy feeling takes hold of him. He opens the door to the dissection hall, enters the room, and sees that the light comes from the lab. The door of the dissection hall locks behind him, and when he steps into the lab he is blinded by bright light. He keeps blinking, and when he finally looks around he can't believe his eyes.

The small room is full of people. Comrade Dumitru is sitting on a high stool near the workbench, while Professor Andronic and the two Party officials are sitting on crates. The whole room looks as if it had been hit by a hurricane. Peter's few clothes are strewn over the floor, the cot is overturned, and so are the large crates. The bones are scattered all through the room. The skulls have been knocked off the shelves, and some of them have bad chips and breaks.

His two knives and forks, a cup and saucer, his cooking pot and breadbox are lying on the floor among the bones and skulls. A broken glass jar with formaldehyde and pieces of a small human fetus has rolled near Professor Andronic's left foot and are mixed with the carrots from Peter's soup. The chicken feet, with their claws, the only meat in the soup, are on the floor near the fetus.

Peter is dumbfounded. He can only think of Mustafa's smashed dining room and the shattered sturgeon on the night of the arrest.

* * *

When he sees Peter, Comrade Dumitru gets up and steps forward. "Sit down! Right here!" He points to a crate which stands in the middle of the lab. Peter's old trousers and a pair of brown socks lie on the floor all crumpled up. He picks them up, throws them in a corner and sits down. A shiver passes over him. He feels like a prisoner in a court of law. He looks at the others, but everybody turns away. He notices that the Egyptian print of Anubis and the Great Scale has been peeled off the door of the lab and is now lying on the table behind Comrade Dumitru. Next to it are the two French anatomy atlases which he had brought from Professor Munteanu's office.

Comrade Dumitru sits down, looks sharply around, and starts to speak. "Comrades, *Tovarasi*, let me tell you that we are all gathered here on account of a most serious situation. I am speaking about Comrade Peter and his devious behavior, his hostile attitude to the construction of Socialism!" He pounds the workbench with his clenched fist, making the white mice jump out of their hiding place in the skull and run across the table. Everyone starts and moves away. Comrade Dumitru turns toward Peter.

"Even though you have been given plenty of opportunities to work constructively for our common cause, the Victory of Socialism, you have chosen to turn your back on this goal and engage in counterrevolutionary activity. Fortunately there are highly devoted Comrades among us. I must tell you that it was Professor Andronic's vigilance that made him blow the whistle and make us aware that we are hiding a snake in our midst."

Comrade Dumitru lifts the print of Anubis from the table and holds it up for all to see. "It was this print and the propagation of these mystical, anti-Communist ideas which raised the suspicion of the Comrade Professor and made him request a thorough, exhaustive search of this room. It was good that we listened to him, since our efforts were greatly rewarded. We found these two French anatomy atlases," Comrade Dumitru goes on, lifting the two books from the table and holding them up. He raises his voice and speaks passionately. "These two books are interdicted now because they are the products of a bourgeois culture which poisons our young science with its imperialist philosophy. Not only have they belonged to Professor Munteanu, a reactionary geneticist, a known enemy of our new Socialist biology created by the great Professor Lysenko! But these books were stolen by you from the Professor's lab, since they bear his name and his signature. And you took them for yourself in your persistent effort to sabotage our progress and victory."

Comrade Dumitru stops talking and takes a deep breath. Then he gets up and takes a step toward Peter. "In conclusion, we think that you are not only a thief, but also an ideological enemy. You are a mixture of both, a mixture too dangerous for this institution of higher learning which practices strong Communist policies. I am convinced that your crime is of such magnitude that you deserve to be thrown in jail and locked up for many years."

Peter can barely make sense of what Comrade Dumitru is saying. He sees his lips moving, but he doesn't hear any sound. Then suddenly the words boom loudly, as if they came from a loudspeaker. Everything is swimming in front of his eyes. When he looks around he can barely distinguish the features of Professor Andronic who is gently rocking on his crate. Peter stares at him, and only after a while does he see the vengeful grin on his face and the yellow glint in his eyes. Just like a snake! Peter thinks. He remembers the nightmare in which he was attacked by an enormous serpent. Is he still dreaming? Was Comrade Dumitru really speaking to him? Maybe all this has nothing to do with him!

There is a moment of silence in the room. Outside, a large piece of ice falls from a balcony, splashing the windows. Everybody starts. The two Party officials pick up their briefcases, ready to run. Comrade Dumitru goes on with his speech.

"As I said before, I am convinced that you should be thrown in jail and kept there for the rest of your life. But the Party, in its compassionate wisdom, has decreed otherwise. It will be lenient with you. It will give you a chance to reform yourself through work, through real work with your hands, and thus turn you into a useful participant in the creation of Socialism in our country. You will be transferred to a construction site, to the Danube-Black Sea Canal, the new project which will greatly shorten the trips of the boats to the sea. You will have the privilege of working at this magnificent construction, the greatest accomplishment of our Socialist revolution!"

As soon as they hear these words the two Party officials put down their briefcases and start clapping. Professor Andronic is glancing at them and then joins in the applause. Comrade Dumitru waits two minutes, then signals them to stop. He continues his talk.

"You will be enrolled in a special program of Reform and Reeducation that will transform you into a new man. This program will reform your thoughts. It will make you recognize your crimes against Socialism, crimes which you have yet to confess. You will become vigilant and eager to unmask all those who sabotage our work through their words, their beliefs and attitudes, or through their actions!"

Comrade Dumitru's face is flushed and he is pounding the air with his hands. He stops talking and in the silence Peter hears heavy steps in the corridor. The steps come closer; the door opens, and in walks the tall Securitate officer he had met some time before.

I must be dreaming! Peter thinks. The officer is wearing a new fur hat with a shiny red star, and his collar and epaulets are decorated with gold stars and stripes. He looks very important. It is clear that he has been promoted! His coat is wet from the rain and his left boot is still stained with the blood of the dog he kicked in the mouth on the day they met.

"*Tovarăşe Ofiţer,* you came just in time!"

Comrade Dumitru walks toward him and shakes hands. "We were just having a meeting regarding the individual you will take with you!" he says, pointing at Peter. "The search of the room has been completed under qualified supervision." Comrade Dumitru nods toward the Party officials. They stand up and bow deeply in front of the militiaman.

"Here are the counterrevolutionary materials I mentioned to you!" Comrade Dumitru pushes the two atlases and the Egyptian print toward the officer. "That's all. You can take them with you if you want."

The officer puts his hat on the workbench, unbuttons his coat, and sits at the table. His coat smells of sweat, cheap cigarettes, car fuel and wet cloth.

"Books, foreign imperialist books which belonged to an enemy of the people already arrested, you say?" The officer keeps looking at the atlases and examining Professor Munteanu's name and signature.

"Yes," says Comrade Dumitru. "A known enemy of our great new science!"

"And here an occult, mystical, counterrevolutionary picture!" The Securitate man is looking at the print of Anubis with much interest.

"Hm! Never seen such wild scribble before! Looks weird to me, like the work of the devil!" He shakes his head and starts to make the sign of the cross, but catches himself, stands up and says with authority "Yes, Comrades! I can see the handiwork of the enemy. Congratulations on your vigilance! This individual certainly deserves punishment. He needs to take responsibility for his crimes, and he must be prevented from propagating his dangerous and destructive ideas. He must be taken into custody at once!"

The officer stops short and turns toward Comrade Dumitru. "Can I talk with you?"

Comrade Dumitru looks surprised, but joins the Securitate man at the workbench. They turn their backs to the others while they confer in low voices. Nevertheless Peter can hear their words.

"I can do the arrest procedure right away, but I can't take him with me tonight," says the officer. "We'll have to wait until Monday! There's no more space at our new safe-house, The Golden Sturgeon down the road, at Mustafa's old restaurant. You know, we just moved in a few days ago. The place is so overcrowded they're sleeping on top of each other on the floor, and we don't yet have any bunks. The toilet is stopped and overflowing. A pipe has burst because of the cold. We have no water, no heat, and we don't have enough bread. The truck got stuck in the mud near the factory! I'm afraid the men will get sick and faint! And if they are ill and lose consciousness we can't put them on the train and send them to work at the Canal. We'll be stuck with them for God knows how long! And it will look bad to our superiors!"

The officer scratches his head and kicks the breadbox with the tip of his boot. He points to the faucet at the end of the room and goes on. "But here, if we keep him here over the weekend, we have all we need. We can lock the doors and take all his keys. The locks work just fine. And there are iron bars at the windows. I can have a van drive around the building and watch all the doors! He has running water and plenty of bread, like a hotel, a luxury hotel, I tell you! I know that these are not regular proceedings, but even Comrade Stalin has said that sometimes we have to bend the rules for the good of the Party."

"We'll do as you say!" Comrade Dumitru stands up and thanks everybody for giving their time on a Saturday afternoon. "Go home, Comrades, and enjoy your weekend after work well done!"

He puts on his coat and his fur hat and walks out with the others, leaving only Peter and the Securitate officer behind. As they file out nobody looks at Peter. It is as if he had vanished in thin air.

* * *

Shortly after they leave a young militiaman walks into the room. He is tall and thin, with very long arms and a thin neck. The blue uniform is too large for him. It hangs and flutters around his body as if he were a stick figure wrapped in cloth. The sleeves of his coat and his pants are too short for his long limbs. Is he a real man or is he a shadow without a body? Peter once read a story about a shadow who had cut himself off from his master and went about wearing the master's elegant clothes. He must have looked like this officer.

The young man carries a pistol in his belt and a bulky briefcase in his right hand. He greets the officer with a military salute and hands him the briefcase.

"Go sit by the door. I'll take care of the arrest procedures." The officer pushes the young man toward a crate near the wall. Then he sits on the tall stool by the workbench, opens the briefcase and pulls out a stack of papers. His gun rests next to him at the edge of the table.

He turns toward Peter. "Come here immediately!"

Peter sits facing him.

"Your name? First name? Last name?"

The officer is completing the forms lying in front of him.

"Date of birth?"

"Quickly, father's name?"

Peter doesn't know his father's name. "I have no family. I was raised in an orphanage."

The officer frowns and goes on with his questions. "Distinguishing marks? Scars? Birthmarks? Burns? Tattoos?"

Peter shakes his head. The officer glances at him and writes down the color of Peter's hair and eyes. Then he pulls out of a briefcase a special pad soaked in ink, puts it on the table and takes Peter's fingerprints by rolling each finger on the black, oozing surface. When he is finished he carefully wipes his hands on a piece of cloth, sets the pad and the forms with the fingerprints on one side of the table, and pulls another stack of papers out of the briefcase.

"Do you or your family own any factories?

"Land?

"Farms and animals?

"Stores?

"Houses? Apartment buildings?

"Offices with paid employees?

After each question Peter shakes his head and says "No." The officer stops and looks at him sharply.

"Do you have any relatives living abroad, in Western countries? Any gold or money in foreign banks?"

Peter shrugs his shoulders. "No, I don't know!"

The officer narrows his eyes.

"Parents, grandparents or any relatives in prison or labor camps?"

Peter again shrugs. "I don't know. I don't have any family!"

"Lying and hiding the truth is not going to help you!" the man says, shaking his finger. He makes a careful note on a pad he has pulled from his pocket. When he is finished he pulls a few blank sheets from his briefcase and pushes them under Peter's nose. "Sign here!" He hands Peter the pen and points to the bottom of the page.

"I'm not signing a blank sheet." Peter shakes his head and pushes the papers back to the officer.

"You must sign! It's an order!" The man is raising his voice and clenching his fists. "You must!" His face is turning red and his eyes are full of anger.

But Peter keeps pushing the papers away. They stare at each other in silence and after a while it is the officer who shrugs and says, "Very good. *Treaba ta*! It's your choice. But you'll be sorry for this. They'll make you sign in the end!" He makes another note on his pad.

Then he gathers all the papers in one pile and slips them into his briefcase.

"Stand up now! Your keys!"

Peter fumbles in his pockets and brings out the keys.

"Identification papers!"

He gives the officer his official identification paper, *Buletinul Populatiei*, his union card, and his bus and tramway cards.

"Weapons!"

Peter blinks. "I have no weapons!"

The officer makes another note on his pad.

"Money! Your wallet!"

Peter searches his pants pockets and comes up with an old leather wallet which contains a few bills and small change.

"Empty the pockets of your jacket!"

Peter buries his hands in his pockets and gathers a pack of *Marasesti* cigarettes, a half-empty box of matches, a black pencil and an eraser.

"Your pants pockets!"

Peter plunges his hands in his pockets and comes up with a few loose coins and a used handkerchief. But as he searches inside his pockets he feels with the tips of his fingers Mariana's gold earrings with the blue stones. He cannot hand them to the officer! So he pushes them all the way down, tearing at the seams and the fabric until he makes a hole in the pocket and lets them slide into the lining of his pants.

"Your belt!"

Peter unbuckles his belt and gives it to the officer. He now has to hold his pants with one hand.

"Your tie!"

Peter struggles to open his tie with his left hand.

"Shoelaces!"

He bends down and strains to pull out his shoelaces with one hand while holding his pants with the other.

"Your jacket!"

He takes off his jacket and gives it to the officer. The man grabs it with both hands, shakes it a few times, then lays it flat on the workbench. He runs his palms over it, pressing down and examining it, feeling it with much attention. Then he slashes the lining with a razor blade, picks up the jacket and shakes it again. But nothing falls out of the lining.

* * *

Meanwhile the young militiaman has gathered Peter's clothing from the floor. Now all his belongings are displayed on the workbench. The Securitate man is busy arranging them in an orderly manner.

At the end of the table, within Peter's reach, is the officer's gun. Peter stares at it, mesmerized. He could easily grab it while the officer is concentrating on organizing his booty and his young helper is crouching on the floor, his back turned toward them. He is watching the white mice who have taken refuge behind a crate.

Peter stretches out his hand and touches the gun with the tips of his fingers. He tries to clasp it with his one free hand. But the officer turns around, half facing him. Peter has just enough time to pull his hand back and hide it in his pocket. The man eyes him sharply, full of suspicion. He takes the gun and places it on the other end of the table. Then he gets up and walks toward Peter.

"Turn around! Face the wall! Don't move!" Peter turns to the wall and the officer calls his adjutant. "Come here and watch him!" The young man comes running and stops right behind Peter. He can hear him cocking his pistol.

"Keep an eye on him! Don't let him move! I don't want any trouble!"

Peter feels the cold muzzle of the pistol on the back of his neck. He thinks that he has turned into a worm or insect, a zoological specimen pinned down in a collector's case. He imagines the sharp needles fastening him to the wall, his hands and feet first, then his chest, his neck and his head. He holds his breath, waiting for the pistol to fire. But the shot never comes.

* * *

The Securitate officer walks to the end of the room and begins rummaging noisily through the open medicine cabinet, metal clinking against metal and metal scraping against glass. After a while the officer returns to the workbench and Peter watches his reflection in the shiny tiles of the walls. The man has taken all the scalpels and scissors from the medicine cabinet and put them on the table. He has gathered all the sharp objects he could find in the room. Peter's razor with all his razor blades, his nail clipper and an old pocket knife are resting there, side by side.

"Leave your gun on the table and come give me a hand!" he orders the adjutant. The young man joins the officer and they divide the objects into two separate piles. On the left are Professor Munteanu's French anatomy atlases and the print of Anubis, a workbook with Peter's lab notes, his jacket, the clothes that had been scattered around the room, and the scalpels and scissors. To the right in a much smaller heap are Peter's more personal belongings, his ID cards, his keys, tie, belt, and shoelaces. The young man pulls a big potato sack out of his briefcase and fills it with the first pile after wrapping the scalpels and scissors in Peter's jacket. Then the officer stuffs the smaller pile into a brown paper bag and slips it inside the briefcase.

"Finished?"

"Yes." The young man ties the sack with a rope.

"All right, then let's go!"

The officer orders Peter, "Turn around! No more need to stare at the wall!"

Peter turns around very slowly. He can barely move. He still feels like an insect with needles pinned through his limbs. He watches the men put on their hats, button their greatcoats and shoulder their guns.

"Monday, we'll see you Monday at dawn, on your way to the Black Sea Canal!" says the officer. Then they walk out the door and turn the key twice in the lock.

* * *

One hour has passed since the militiamen left and Peter is still sitting on his stool. He has put on dry socks and a pair of old slippers which were hidden behind the crates. He has tied a piece of wire around his waist in place of a belt. He bends down and takes hold of the seam of his pants. He opens the lining, pulls out Mariana's earrings still wrapped in the handkerchief, and slips them into the left pocket which is not ripped.

The words of the Securitate officer and of Comrade Dumitru keep ringing in his ears and he knows that he is caught in a trap. Comrade Dumitru and particularly Professor Andronic have their revenge. All the doors are closing on him. In the beginning when Comrade Dumitru spoke, it seemed to him that he was talking about a stranger, about somebody else. But after the Securitate officer had taken away his identification papers and all his belongings he couldn't fool himself any longer. As he sits staring in front of him all the rumors he has heard about the Black Sea Canal come to his mind.

He can imagine himself blindfolded, his wrists chained to other prisoners, being loaded into an overcrowded cattle train heading toward the Canal. The train moves slowly, the trip can last several days, and no bread, no food and no water is given to the prisoners. There are rumors that sometimes the older and weaker men die on these trains. Upon arrival their naked bodies are thrown into a common grave at the site of the Canal while their clothing is kept for the next convoy of prisoners. Clothing is scarce, and every bit has to be saved!

Or the scene changes and Peter sees himself faint with exhaustion, or sick and half dead from typhus, dysentery or malaria like Professor Munteanu. Or he could be drowning in the deep marshes among the reeds like Mustafa.

Winter frostbites are another killer, they say. They progress slowly but surely, leading to the spontaneous amputation of toes, fingers and ears, and sometimes to the loss of a hand or a foot. And starvation is easy to reach for those who are too weak or too sick to fulfill the work quota which is allotted to them. As punishment they are not given their ration of food.

While the "Court" poets and writers and the Party officials celebrate the Danube-Black Sea Canal as a magnificent accomplishment and speak about "Reeducation," "Rehabilitation," and the "Birth of a New Man," it is no secret that people who are sent there to die must first do some work, such as cut reeds, drain the marshes, and move large mounds of earth in the process. Few prisoners have come back alive from this site. The people have named it the "Canal of Death."

Peter remembers the image of the cattle driven to the slaughterhouse. No, he thinks. He can't sit here helplessly, waiting to be marched to the killing ramp.

But death and the danger of death are not everything. Even if he survives his stint at the Canal, what is his future? Years, even decades of servitude and humiliation in which he will be reduced to a brainless automaton. He knows that he will never be allowed to return to a city of learning, let alone to a university! He will never be able to work with students again, never step into a lab, and make his own, even small contributions to the study of anatomy! His life will lose its purpose; his days will be empty, without joy or hope. His mind will go to waste, his hands will become scarred and stiff from the stalks of the reeds, and his fingers will lose their agility and nimbleness.

Worst of all is having no control over his life. No! He will not go. But neither will he sit here with his hands in his lap waiting to see what will happen. This is the worst, the most humiliating, sitting here without any hope and purpose. It is already changing him into an object, a helpless victim. He has to take action, look for an escape, even if it is full of danger. He has to do something before it is too late and the trap closes over him. That way he will still be himself and stay in charge of his life!

The old, underground tunnels come to his mind. He remembers the stories about the subterranean passageways which run under the medical school and lead out of the city. He has to find them tonight, at any price!

He looks up, and through the window he sees the black van of the Securitate driving by slowly, keeping watch from the street. Peter gets up and turns off the lights. Then he pulls down the heavy black-out curtains which have been here from the time of the war. His watchman will think that he went to sleep and will not grow suspicious!

Peter walks to the far end of the room and steps into a small closet which is half hidden behind a medicine cabinet. He has to reach the cellar which is beyond the lab and the dissection hall. Comrade Dumitru and his militiamen were so rushed with their search that they never inspected this closet.

He takes a rusty key from one of the shelves and a partly burned candle as well as a box of matches from behind an anatomical jar. Then he unlocks a narrow door hidden in a corner behind the shelves, lights the candle and steps into the cellar. The basement is dark and has only a tiny window near the ceiling on the opposite wall.

It is from here that Peter had taken the anatomical preparations to show to the students, and it is here that he wants to search for a trapdoor or another secret opening to the tunnels. He tried to find them before, hoping that these subterranean galleries that crisscross the town and the countryside would lead him to the sea and to the boat of his dreams! He is haunted by the hope of escape to the sea!

As he walks into the drafty cellar, the light of the candle flickers and almost goes out. He brushes the cobwebs from his face and feels his way with the tips of his toes. He climbs over a pile of old, broken lab furniture, and crates filled with pieces of old skeletons. The air is stale, moldy, and mixed with pungent fumes of formaldehyde.

He is seized by a coughing fit and has to put down the candle. When he stops coughing he crouches on the ground and starts tapping the floor gently with the tips of his fingers, listening carefully for the hollow sound of a trapdoor or a loose slab or stone. He crawls slowly through the room, pushing the heavy crates out of his way, sometimes having to lift and carry them from one place to another.

It is cold and damp in the cellar. The work is slow and painstaking and after a while he gets very tired. He sits on the floor wondering whether he will find an escape and whether it is worth going on. But immediately the image of the cattle led to the slaughterhouse comes to mind and he resumes tapping the floor.

A small pebble falls from somewhere and startles him. Then, far above him in the Dean's office the grandfather clock tolls ten. "It's getting late! I must work faster. I should be well on my way in the tunnel when they come looking for me."

He has finished checking the floor and gets up to examine the walls. He goes to the right and starts tapping, up and down, from floor to ceiling, listening carefully. But he hears nothing, no hollow ring, and no sign of loose bricks. His hands and fingers are swollen and hurting, and his legs are getting stiff from bending and getting up. The grandfather clock tolls eleven.

He has finished exploring the walls he can reach. Only the wall hidden behind the tall cabinet with the anatomical preparations remains unexamined. To get behind the cabinet he has to move it. He raises the candle to check the height of the cupboard. From the top shelf a round eye stares at him with cold disapproval. It is the glass eye of the dissected head preparation which he himself placed on that shelf some time ago. Peter shudders. He turns away. He props himself against the cabinet and pushes with all his strength, but it doesn't budge. He stops to catch his breath and tries a second time. Again nothing happens.

The third time he braces himself against the wall and uses his feet. The cabinet moves very slowly, inch by inch, and every time it slides a little it makes a strange noise, like a moan. Its top part is swaying, ready to topple and smash everything underneath.

Finally when the clock strikes twelve in the Dean's office, the cabinet is far enough from the wall to allow Peter to slide behind it and have a look. Holding the candle with unsteady hands he crawls into the newly-opened space. At first he doesn't see anything, but after he takes a second step he finds a recess in the wall which houses a narrow door. He pushes the handle and the door opens with a loud groan.

Peter ducks and crawls through it. He finds himself in a dark and narrow corridor with a low ceiling. Advancing on all fours he starts tapping the walls and the floor. But he doesn't hear any hollow sounds.

It is moldy and wet here, with water dripping from the walls and the ceiling, like a cave. The floor is littered with pieces of brick, sacks of cement, and old buckets of paint. A rat scurries over his feet and he hears other rats moving inside the walls. The corridor is very drafty and the light trembles in his hands.

He follows the gallery as it takes a sharp turn, and soon he comes to another low and narrow wooden door. He pulls the handle several times, and when it finally opens he finds himself standing in front of a doorway which was closed up with bricks.

Even though his fingers are sore and swollen from tapping and knocking he tries to pull some bricks from the wall. But they are closely fitted together and don't move. He stops in front of a bulwark which puts an end to his search. All his hopes, his dreams, have turned to ashes.

As he stares at the walled doorway he sees a small mouse sliding between the bricks and vanishing into the dark. Suddenly he feels envious of the small creature, and he wishes that he too could change into a tiny animal able to crawl through these openings and reach the outside world! He wishes to change into a mouse, even better, into a bird, a bug or a mosquito, and fly out through the chimney. Or, even turn into a roach which could squeeze through the narrowest cracks.

Suddenly there is a strong blast of wind from nowhere. It blows out the candle in his hand. The door to the cellar slams shut.

Peter shivers. He is drenched in cold sweat. Will he be locked in here forever, in these forgotten catacombs? He remembers the story of the ancient Egyptian tomb robbers who were trapped inside the grave they were looting by a rock slide. Their skeletons were found much later, together with those of the royal mummies they had come to rob. Will he have a similar fate?

He crawls back in a hurry, slipping on the wet floor, tripping over piles of loose bricks, afraid that the door has been locked. To his relief it opens as soon as he gives it a push, and he crawls back into the cellar. He takes a step in total darkness and suddenly he sees a bright star shining in front of him. He is taken aback, but then he realizes that he is standing near the broken mirror, the "magic" mirror with many cracks which was thrown into the cellar. He had seen this mirror before. And he remembers the popular belief that demons live in those cracks, through which they pass back and forth to the underworld. As he raises his eyes and looks out the small window above the mirror he sees that the clouds have vanished and that a lone star has appeared. It shines as brightly in the sky as the star of the Annunciation. Peter looks back at the mirror and sees how the cracks act like a kaleidoscope, reflecting the star so many times that it turns into a whole galaxy. Somehow, the stars make him think of Mariana. Is she smiling and waving at him from far away?

Now he knows what he has to do. He is going to join her, up there in the Milky Way! He remembers the clear summer nights when he lay in the grass behind the medical school breathing in the perfume of roses and watching the stars. He has always thought that they were the pure souls of the departed wrapped in vestments of light. And he remembers Mr. Bantu telling him that in the Book of the Dead it is written that every "just" soul that survived and escaped the attacks of the flesh-eating monsters who dwell in the eternal darkness, is reborn in the splendid light of a star!

Without thinking Peter slips his hand into his pocket and touches the small earrings with the blue lotus buds. He strokes them gently with the tips of his fingers, and as he does so he has no more doubts about what he is going to do. He will make a final decision, and he is going to make it of his own free will. He will determine his own destiny!

He is not going to let himself be blindfolded, chained to other prisoners and pushed into freight cars heading to the Canal! As he thinks about this and about life out there, everything slips further and further away and becomes smaller, until there are only tiny black spots lost in the distance. Now he knows that he doesn't have to scurry any longer through underground tunnels like an animal trapped by a poacher, or crawl through small trapdoors or narrow rat holes.

He doesn't want to live an empty life, a life without purpose and meaning. Such a life would cancel him out as a person and turn to naught his whole past and his future. He would be forced to live as if he never existed. He still has a last shred of freedom, the right to make decisions, some power over his own life. This, and only this, will save the essence of his existence.

He feels strong and free now, like a bird soaring toward the sky. He is calm, with a feeling of stillness for which he had waited a very long time. He takes a deep breath, filling his lungs with the musty air of the cellar. He imagines he's standing on a mountaintop above a pine forest, breathing in the pure air of the heights.

* * *

Peter walks out of the cellar, crosses the lab, and stops in the dissection hall. He looks up at the ceiling, searching for something. The blackout curtains have been lowered over the windows so he doesn't worry about being seen from the street.

He stops in front of a skeleton which hangs from a hook in the ceiling. He has found what he was looking for. He climbs on a stool and checks the hook. Yes, it is solid.

He unfastens the skeleton. He looks at it thoughtfully and shakes his head. He feels like apologizing for taking him down, moving him. He finds himself talking to him, as if he was alive. "You must be very old! Did you live a long time ago? I found you hanging here, when I first arrived. And I cared for you for so many years! Washing and dusting you with a soft piece of cloth, fixing your bones with bits of shiny wire when they came loose. I don't want to disturb you and move you, but I have no choice. Where shall I put you? Maybe here, on this empty table?"

Peter lifts him gently and lays him to rest on the nearest dissection table. Then he goes to the clothes locker in the lab and rummages on the top shelf. He finds a long cylinder wrapped in purple silk. It contains the ancient Egyptian pictures from Mr. Bantu's funeral parlor which Peter had rolled up and wrapped in a piece of silk. He has carried them with him wherever he went. He is happy to find them. He wonders how they have escaped Comrade Dumitru's "thorough" investigation, as they were lying in the same closet where the forbidden textbooks were found! "They" must have stopped searching as soon as they found the "Imperialist" anatomy atlases, the "hard evidence," Peter thinks.

He pulls the old pictures out of their silk wrapping, lays them flat on the workbench and smoothes them out carefully. The paper has turned yellow and become brittle in so many years, but none of the pictures are torn. The colors too are still vivid and have faded very little.

Each picture has a small, round hole in the center where Comrade Dumitru's bullet hit long ago. Peter remembers that day in front of Mr. Bantu's funeral home when the young, green-shirted fascists and their bushy-haired leader stormed the door of the building and fired shots at the pictures.

He takes the prints to the dissection hall and pastes them over the official portraits of the Communist leaders: the mummy of King Tut over the picture of Lenin, the pyramids of Gizah over the photo of Marx, and the picture of the jackal god Anubis, the Lord of the "Righteous Dead" over the portrait of Stalin.

He takes a few steps, looks at the prints from a distance, and nods. He likes what he sees. He then walks into his lab, takes the bedsheet from his cot, rips it and twists it into a rope. He remembers the night when he ran away from the orphanage, many years ago. Then, too, he used a bed sheet twisted into a rope to climb down the wall from his window.

It had been a clear, starry night. As he ran through the orchards in bloom he heard the song of a nightingale. And then, when he reached the outskirts of the city, the dogs started to bark, scaring the nightingale away.

But it didn't matter. He felt light as a feather and free, as he was running toward town.

Now too, a dog barks across the street. In the Dean's office the grandfather clock tolls three. Soon it will be day, soon the stars will vanish. He has to hurry, his time is running out.

Peter walks back into the dissection hall, climbs on a stool and ties one end of his rope to the hook, while he fashions the other into a noose which he slips around his neck. He stares into the large eyes of Anubis, the jackal god of the Righteous Dead. He kicks the stool from under his feet, letting his body swing in midair.

At first there is only darkness, but it is followed by a dazzling burst of light which surrounds him and slowly penetrates his being.

THE END